CHRISTOPHER BUSH
THE CASE OF THE RUNNING MOUSE

CHRISTOPHER BUSH was born Charlie Christmas Bush in Norfolk in 1885. His father was a farm labourer and his mother a milliner. In the early years of his childhood he lived with his aunt and uncle in London before returning to Norfolk aged seven, later winning a scholarship to Thetford Grammar School.

As an adult, Bush worked as a schoolmaster for 27 years, pausing only to fight in World War One, until retiring aged 46 in 1931 to be a full-time novelist. His first novel featuring the eccentric Ludovic Travers was published in 1926, and was followed by 62 additional Travers mysteries. These are all to be republished by Dean Street Press.

Christopher Bush fought again in World War Two, and was elected a member of the prestigious Detection Club. He died in 1973.

CHRISTOPHER BUSH

THE CASE OF THE RUNNING MOUSE

With an introduction
by Curtis Evans

DEAN STREET PRESS

TO

JOHN BUDE

MAY HIS STATURE, AND HIS
CIRCULATION INCREASE

INTRODUCTION

Winding down the War and Taking a New Turn

Christopher Bush's Ludovic Travers Mysteries, 1943 to 1946

HAVING SENT his series sleuth Ludovic "Ludo" Travers, in the third and fourth years of the Second World War, around England to meet murder at a variety of newly-created army installations—a prisoner-of-war camp (*The Case of the Murdered Major*, 1941), a guard base (*The Case of the Kidnapped Colonel*, 1942) and an instructor school (*The Case of the Fighting Soldier*, 1942)--Christopher Bush finally released Travers from military engagements in *The Case of the Magic Mirror* (1943), a unique retrospective affair which takes place before the outbreak of the Second World War. In the remaining four Travers wartime mysteries--*The Case of the Running Mouse* (1944), *The Case of the Platinum Blonde* (1944), *The Case of the Corporal's Leave* (1945) and *The Case of the Missing Men* (1946)--Bush frees his sleuth to investigate private criminal problems. Although the war is mentioned in these novels, it plays far less of a role in events, doubtlessly giving contemporary readers a sense that the world conflagration which at one point had threatened to consume the British Empire was winding down for good. Yet even without the "novelty" of the war as a major plot element, these Christopher Bush mysteries offer readers some of the most intriguing conundrums in the Ludo Travers detection canon.

The Case of the Running Mouse (1944)

Dedicated to British mystery writer John Bude (Ernest Carpenter Elmore), with the wish that "his stature, and his circulation increase" (a wish that has certainly come true in the last few years as John Bude's mysteries have been reprinted by the British Library, ironically causing Bude's name to eclipse, for the moment, that of many once much better-known mystery writers from his own day), *The Case of the Running Mouse* finds Christopher Bush's series sleuth Ludovic "Ludo" Travers again confronting, as he did in *The Case of the Magic Mirror*, ill deeds done by dissolute London elites, something in the manner of a more genteel and gentlemanly Philip Marlowe, the LA PI created by renowned Anglo-American crime writer Raymond Chandler, whose readership, it appears, included Christopher Bush (see my introduction to *The Case of the Magic Mirror*). In *Mouse* Ludo enters a blacked-out world of illicit sex and drugs and high stakes gaming, where the men are bad and the women worse, and the war is but a dim backdrop to the heedless pleasure seeking of wealthy hedonists. Down posh streets a man must go, and that man is Ludo Travers.

The Case of the Running Mouse opens in February 1943, a month that in real life saw the war turn decisively in favor of the Allied cause, with the resounding defeats of Japan at Guadalcanal and Germany at Stalingrad. On fourteen-day leave from his post in Derbyshire, Ludo Travers heads to London, his "spiritual home," which he has not seen in five months. Ludo and his wife Bernice, who is serving with the Red Cross in northern England, have relinquished their "far too commodious" flat in St. Martin's Chambers and pensioned off Ludo's manservant, Palmer, a longtime welcome presence in the series; yet the couple maintains a small furnished place at Norfolk Mansions in east Kensington, with three ample rooms and service meals included, along with the attentions of an agreeable *Telegraph*-reading hall porter named Frank. On Ludo's first morning home at this *pied-à-terre*, a maid at the breakfast table hands him a private communication, pregnant with strange meaning, from one "P. Worrack."

Seemingly under the impression that Ludo Travers is a professional private detective, this P. Worrack expresses the desire to consult Ludo "on a matter of particular secrecy." Ludo is immediately dazzled with the prospect of being "almost implored to undertake some case or other entirely off my own bat," having for so many years been a "colleague and often very much a subordinate of George Wharton" of the Yard. Ludo admits to doubts, however:

> In our day-dreams we see ourselves performing the heroic and incredible with a craft and aplomb that years of futility have kept in repression. Maybe you have been yourself in some giant bomber, roaring across Germany at roof height, manoeuvering over Berchtesgaden and dropping an eight-thousand-pounder plumb on Hitler, and then shooting down a dozen or so Focke-Wolfs on the way home. We will omit the resultant Victoria Cross and the world acclaim, and pause to wonder in cold blood just how we should feel if a Lancaster were suddenly to materialise and we were hoisted into it. That was how I felt at suddenly undertaking the role of a first-class private sleuth.

Despite these misgivings borne of an innate modesty which is rather at odds with the hard-boiled ethos, Ludo can never resist the lure of detection, and he soon finds himself in a private consultation with his first client, Percival "call me Peter" Worrack. Having lost a leg in the fighting at Dunkirk, Peter Worrack on behalf of wealthy and attractive young widow Georgina Morbent now manages a London nightclub—or, as Worrack to be "perfectly frank" puts it, "what the papers call a gambling den." To Worrack's evident consternation, Georgina Morbent has seemingly vanished, having departed at Euston station for Ireland, allegedly to see William O'Clauty, the Dublin trainer of her two racehorses, and apparently never arrived there. Besides Peter Worrack and William O'Clauty, those individuals in some way or another concerned in Georgina's disappearance are Mrs. Barbara Grays, Georgina's younger widowed sister ("her husband was killed in France just before Dunkirk"); Barbara's friend Tommy Hamson ("used to be in the Indian police . . . a pretty fast mover, like all of our particular crowd, and he seems to have plenty of money"); gambling den habitués the Hon. Harold Lewton-Molde and Miss Scylla Payton ("the grandson of a peer" and a "weak-chinned specimen, but she's tough"); Lulu Mawne ("a kind of secretary, spare croupier, and general receptionist" at the club); ersatz French barman Jean; and a prankster naval commander, just back from six months at sea, nicknamed "Tubby," naturally enough.

To help him investigate the challenging case, filled to the brim with questionable characters, Ludo employs his own private detective, Bill Ellice, a bright chap who will figure importantly in later Travers mysteries. The mysterious Morbent affair soon takes a darkly sinister turn, however, when one of the people in the case dies from poisoning after imbibing brandy at Georgina's nightclub, right in the presence of Ludo himself (not to mention the novel's titular "running mouse.") Ludo finds himself in the position of holding back certain information from Inspector Brontway, whom the Yard has sent to investigate the suspicious death (though George Wharton will soon horn his way into the goings-on as well). Indeed, for much of the novel Ludo daringly plays a lone hand, hoping that a deck direly loaded with death cards--the mystery woman's gloved hand; the pawned emerald ring; the withdrawn 250 pounds in one-pound notes; the altered will; the dismissed maid who listens at keyholes; the beautiful blonde dubbed Goldilocks; the radio comic's stale joke about the egg-laying hen; and, last but certainly not least, the horrifically severed head--does not get the better of him and put him underground!

Curtis Evans

PART ONE
THE RELUCTANT AMATEUR

CHAPTER I
FIND THE LADY

IT WAS ON A February morning, in 1943, that I had what I shall always regard as one of the most gratifying surprises of my life. I doubt, too, if I can find anything commensurate in general experience to convey to you how great the surprise was. That it was a mistake did not matter in the least, for it was a mistake by which I could legitimately profit. Perhaps the thrill I got was the kind that comes to a naval lieutenant when he is given command of a ship and a roving commission at that. Or a humble servant of Intelligence perhaps, who, after years of decoding, is suddenly told he is to be dumped down in Germany as a master spy. However, perhaps I had better explain.

In the previous autumn I had missed seven days' leave, and when later I had the chance to take it I preferred to wait till the next leave was due, and have one glorious burst of fourteen days. The one snag turned out to be that my own leave did not happen to coincide with the short leave that was due to my wife, who had been transferred to a hospital up north. But I had no fear of time lying heavy on my hands. London is my spiritual home and as I had not seen it for five months I was anticipating a crowded fortnight.

Our flat in St. Martin's Chambers had long since been given up as far too commodious for war-time, and we had taken a little furnished affair on the east side of Kensington. Its three rooms were ample, and service meals were available; and as the different in rent was considerably in our favour and some sort of pied-à-terre seemed essential, we saw no reason to regret the expense. I arrived there rather late that February afternoon, and after a bath and a change into mufti, treated myself to one of the service teas. Then I rang up Scotland Yard.

George Wharton was away, I was told, but expected back in a day or so, when he would be given my message. I was rather disappointed at that, for I had looked forward to taking George out to lunch and hearing about his latest activities. Before the war, George—Superintendent Wharton to you—and I had worked together on a score or so of cases. A bit presumptuous perhaps, my talking of working together, though George would always have it that way. I had begun by being called in on a certain case as the financial expert I was supposed to be, and what I was able to contribute turned out to be of considerable use. It so happened, too, that my flibbertigibbet, crossword kind of brain took George's fancy, and when his next case materialised he felt lonely with nobody around as an amiable mascot. Besides, we had grown uncommonly fond of each other, and, to cut a long story short, whenever anything in the nature of a tricky case turned up from then on, he either contrived to bring me somewhere near the spot or else had me flagrantly called in as a consultative expert. And now, perhaps, you have spotted why I rang up the Yard about George. What I had fondly hoped to hear was that he was engaged on some case that might not be without interest, in which event I should have spent some of my fortnight on a busman's holiday. That confession also gives you a good inkling of the distance I have travelled from grace since I first worked with George. Then I had a horror of duplicity. Now, thanks to ten years of his influence and three in the Army, I am not only an accomplished and unblushing liar, but have up my sleeve tricks that would make a quartermaster mute with jealous rage.

I went to a show that first night of my leave, and in the morning took my time about getting up. When the service breakfast appeared, the maid brought with it a letter she had found on the mat. And that, I knew at once, was curious, for the letter was a private one. Everyone likely to send me a private letter knew my military address, and this letter, moreover, had not been forwarded from St. Martin's Chambers. Perhaps it was a begging letter of sorts, I thought as I opened it, but even then I was rather puzzled for my address at Norfolk Mansions was not in the telephone book. Then, when I began the letter, I was more puzzled still.

Flat 34,
Dromore
Knightsbridge.
Feb. — 1943

Dear Mr. Travers . . .

That was the immediate surprise. Not Major Travers, but Mr. Travers, and I trust you will believe me when I say that in the surprise was no suspicion of snobbery. It was just that for two years I had seen myself as Major Travers, and that abrupt return to the incredible days of pre-war was just a bit of a jolt. So I turned the letter over to see the name of the writer.

Yours truly,
P. WORRACK

was what I read, and the name conveyed nothing on earth, so I turned the letter over again and began to read it.

Dear Mr. Travers,

I want to consult your firm on a matter of particular secrecy, and shall be glad if you will either make an appointment at your office or call and see me. I rang your old address at St. Martin's Chambers and was given your new one but they didn't appear to know where your office was.

The reason I rang you was that I remembered seeing your name in connection with Scotland Yard, which gave me, if you will pardon my saying so, a guarantee of the kind of firm yours is, for in the circumstances in which I now find myself, I should hesitate to employ a detective agency that was not of the highest class.

I am not a wealthy man but I shall be prepared to pay any retaining or other fees that are usual. I know also that it is a lot to ask but I should be glad if you could attend to me as I am not disposed to put the matter in the hands of any subordinate, however trustworthy. Needless to say I am prepared to pay accordingly.

Yours truly,

P. WORRACK

The Travers Detective Agency,
(At) *Norfolk Mansions,*
E. Kensington.

I read that letter a second time, and my first reaction was a feeble smile. Then I was really interested, and, strangely enough as it may seem to you, just the least bit nervous. It was not that the letter didn't seem genuine enough, for there was no doubt in my mind about that. My name had appeared often enough at coroners' inquests and in courts of law. Moreover, the hall porter at St. Martin's Chambers was a new man, and when asked for a Mr. Travers would naturally have said merely that Mr. Travers was now at such-and-such an address.

What intrigued me was that I should have been taken for the head of a private detective agency, and as such should be about to be consulted on a matter of delicacy and importance. There was I, in fact, for years a colleague and often very much a subordinate of George Wharton, being asked and almost implored to undertake some case or other entirely off my own bat. And this had happened with fourteen days' leave in front of me. On a gold salver there was being offered me the kind of job I had longed for all my life. Why then, you may ask, the uneasiness?

Well, you know how things are. In our day-dreams we see ourselves performing the heroic and incredible with a craft and aplomb that years of futility have kept in repression. Maybe you have been yourself in some giant bomber, roaring across Germany at roof height, manoeuvring over Berchtesgaden and dropping an eight-thousand-pounder plumb on Hitler, and then shooting down a dozen or so of Focke-Wolfs on the way home. We will omit the resultant Victoria Cross and the world acclaim, and pause to wonder in cold blood just how we should feel if a Lancaster were suddenly to materialise and we were hoisted into it. That was how I felt at suddenly undertaking the role of a first-class private sleuth.

For one thing, I look about as like a detective as the Archbishop of Canterbury. Before the war I might, perhaps, have been regarded, if with some amusement, as a kind of neophyte or apprentice, for my clean-shaven face was then somewhat pallid, and my horn-rims gave me the look of an earnest intellectual who was groping for his real *metier*. My six foot three, a leanness of frame, and a genteel stoop, might have helped the illusion, but now my glasses are less obvious, my face tanned, my back is straight and my tooth-brush moustache looks almost aggressive. My vocabulary, too, is far from intellectual, and has become garnished with slang and expletives that are my wife's dismay and despair.

But I knew from the very first that it was only a question of time before I should be getting in touch with the unknown Worrack. What worried me was just how I was to convince my client, and then, in a matter of moments, that uneasiness disappeared. After all, I should not be committed to undertaking whatever commission it was that he had in mind for me, for I could listen to all he had to say and then back out, and I knew at least a couple of reputable firms whom I could recommend as more in his line. Nor had I any doubt of my powers of duplicity and conviction. Three years of Army conferences, and inspections, and extemporisings are quite good training for nimbleness of manoeuvre. In fact, it was when I realised my own adequacy that I suddenly found myself dialling the Knightsbridge number on Worrack's letter.

"Hallo?" a voice said. A man's voice, and what I might call the voice of a man of the world.

"Mr. Worrack?" I asked.

"Speaking."

I gave a Whartonian grunt and cleared my voice.

"This is Ludovic Travers, Mr. Worrack," I said. "I've just received your letter. I shall be glad to see you." He was cutting in but I went hastily on. "I'm very much of a free-lance these days.

Loss of staff, and office, and all that, but you know how things are. Would your flat suit you?"

"Splendidly," he said. "When can you come? At once?"

"In an hour?" I said, and glanced at my watch. "Ten o'clock precisely, that will be."

"I'll be here. And I'm much obliged to you."

"Not at all," I said lamely, and then almost added something about business being business. But there was a click as he rang off, and that was that. The receiver was still in my hand when I knew the extent to which I had committed myself, and when I had replaced it, I think I was smiling rather fatuously and then feeling for my glasses, which is an old trick of mine when at a mental loss or on the edge of discovery. Another minute, and I was setting about my breakfast and deciding on a certain brown suit which was neat and far from gaudy.

Dromore Place was a quarter of an hour's walk, and as the morning was sunny I made the mile journey on foot. I had three minutes to spare when I reached the block of flats, and a highly select block it seemed. Flat 34 was on the second floor, and as I tapped at the door my watch showed ten o'clock to the second. Nothing like punctuality to impress a client, I told myself complacently, and then composed my face to something of austerity as the door opened.

Worrack was a man of about forty, so my first glance at him told me. A second later I thought he was rather older than that, perhaps, because, as he turned towards me, the light from the side window showed the wrinkles round his eyes. But it was a most attractive face, and his voice was as pleasant a baritone as it had sounded over the 'phone.

"You're Mr. Travers?" he said, and smiled.

"And you're Mr. Worrack?"

Already he had been ushering me in. Five foot ten was his height and his build rather slim. As he drew back to close the door I noticed he was slightly lame.

"Shall we sit here?" he said, and waved a hand at the couple of easy chairs by the electric fire. I took a quick look round the room, which was large and airy, for it was a corner one and had two large windows. A door, slightly ajar, was to my right, and a closed door to the left. In the air were two faint scents. The stronger was the kind one sniffs in a club smoking-room, and underneath it was a rather tantalising smell of some attractive perfume.

"Do let me take your hat," he said as I was placing it on the carpet beside my chair.

"No, no," I said. "I'm not expecting to be here all that long, Mr. Worrack."

"You think not?" he said, and gave me a quick look.

I smiled. "Well, it's a good opening in any case. Part of the bedside manner. First reassure your client, and all that."

He gave me another look. If it had not been at variance with my role I think I should have asked him, with just a touch of the quizzical, what he thought of me. So it came as something of a shock when he put his question.

"Reassure the client," he said. "Well, it's a good idea. And what do you think of this particular client?"

My fingers went to my glasses as I wondered if I should treat the question seriously.

"You think it a curious question?" he said, and either it was some trick of the light or there was something cynical in his dry smile.

"Perhaps no," I said. "An awkward one, yes. If I give the wrong answers you'll think you're employing a fool. If I give the right ones—"

He laughed. "Then the boot will be on the other foot." His lace straightened. "But have a shot at it. Take it that I've got special reasons for asking."

I had brought a new notebook with me, and it was lying ready on my lap. Perhaps it was because there was something so really likeable about him that I discarded somewhat the role of a staid professional man. As I made my first notes I spoke the written words aloud.

"'To attempting general description of client—one guinea. Name of client—P. Worrack.' The P. stands for?"

"Percival," he said, and perfectly seriously. "But I've changed it unofficially to Peter. Rather a convincing name, Peter, don't you think?"

I put the pencil between the pages and closed the book. "It depends on whom you want to convince. As I think you're married, the change was probably an idea of your wife's."

"Why should you think I'm married?" His eyes had narrowed curiously, and in a moment the face had lost all its attractiveness. The lips clamped together and the cold directness of his look gave the face a hardness. Then it suddenly went and he was smiling again. "I'm really afraid you're wrong. This isn't a divorce case, Mr. Travers."

"If I had thought it was I shouldn't have been here," I told him. "Divorce evidence is not in my line. But where did you lose your leg? The Middle East?"

"Good Lord!" he said. "How'd you guess that?"

"The way you walked and the way you sat with it stretched out," I said. "You can always tell an artificial leg. There's something about the odd shoe and sock."

"As a matter of fact I lost it at Dunkirk," he said. "Anything else you have noticed?"

"I don't know that there is," I told him. "Except, perhaps, that you spend pretty late nights, and very few days in the country. Your first meal is probably a whisky and soda. And you're vain of your appearance. Either that, or you're concerned to make a good impression. Also, at this moment you're decidedly nervous, and that's something I shouldn't always associate with you. In fact, it intrigues me. Which is why I'm anxious to know just why you thought of employing me."

"And suppose I'm not nervous?" He shrugged his shoulders.

"Suppose it's because . . . well, you were uncommonly shrewd in some of the things you said, and also . . . well, you were hardly the kind I was expecting to see." He smiled rather lamely. "That sounds a bit rude but perhaps you know what I mean. You're not the detective type. You're more like a lawyer with a sense of humour."

"Good," I said, and opened the notebook again. "And now what about getting down to brass tacks. Just what do you want me to do for you, Mr. Worrack?"

He leaned back in his chair. In the intervals of talking he would nervously smooth his moustache with the back of a finger.

"It's a longish story," he said, and then gave me another of those quick challenging glances. "I take it everything's in strict confidence?"

"Otherwise I shouldn't be here," I told him portentously. "You can trust me as you would your doctor or your lawyer. But, before you begin. Just why did you decide to employ me? What I mean is that your letter was either not too true to fact or else you have a good memory. My name hasn't appeared in the Press in connection with a case for at least three years."

He gave me another quick look.

"I admit it," he said. "It was really a man at my club who mentioned your name. He didn't want his own name mentioned." Then he was going on just a bit too quickly. "But about what I was going to say. It concerns a Mrs. Morbent—Georgina Morbent. You've heard the name?"

I shook my head. "I'm afraid I've been out of things recently. A special government job these last three years."

"Her husband was killed in the Blitz, in February of '41." he went on, "and he left her a packet. Over half a million, when duties were paid. I've known her since she was a kid, and I knew him too. Very good chap he was. Kept a horse or two in training, and Georgina's still got a jumper or two over in Ireland. Her father was a Colonel Amber, also something of a racing man, and she has a sister, a Mrs. Grays—Barbara Grays. Her husband was killed in France just before Dunkirk."

He waited till I looked up to show that I had the details down.

"Georgie's about twenty-eight," he said. "A fine-looking girl, and a damn good sort. The sporting type and a simply wonderful head of red hair. What they call a man's woman. Barbara's about six years older. She has just about enough money to jog along with, by the way, and Georgie used to insist on making her an allowance. And where I come in is this way. We were always old friends, the three of us, and when I got my packet at Dunkirk, Georgie insisted on doing something for me. I don't mind telling you I hadn't any prospects except my pension. I've always been a pretty fast mover—as you judged—and luck hasn't been any too good. Even so, I couldn't let anyone—even like Georgie —make me an allowance or anything like that. What she decided was that she'd set me up in business. Perhaps we hit on the idea together; at any rate she put up the cash." He hesitated for a moment or two while the knuckle moved backwards and forwards over the moustache. "What she invested in was a kind of night club. To be perfectly frank, what the papers call a gambling den."

His smile had something cynical about it as he caught the quick lift of my eyebrows.

"I thought you'd be surprised. But this is a different show from the usual sort. As a matter of fact, it was meant to be so from the word 'go.' I don't claim to be a philanthropist but I do run everything on the square. All sorts of people—officers on leave if you like—do feel the need of a gamble and I cater for it. No terrific stakes and no excessive drinking. Numbers strictly limited and the company carefully scrutinised. The atmosphere's that of a private party, if you know what I mean."

"Any bribing of the police?"

He shrugged his shoulders. "Not so that you'd notice it. Something occasionally in the right quarters. Not that we have anything to fear, except, of course, the letter of the law. I take it you understand what I mean?"

"And how's the investment prospered?"

"We clear about two hundred a week," he said. "Doesn't sound much, but it's safe. We've dodged all trouble except once, and then nothing came out. Just a change of quarters, that's all. And we have an excellent clientele. The right sort of people and just enough of them."

He waited while I made a note or two, and from the nervous stroking of that cavalry moustache I guessed he was near the main point. I put the question to help him along.

"And now something's gone wrong?"

"Yes," he said. "Georgina's disappeared. That's what we think, I mean—that's what I wanted to see you about." This was his story. Three weeks previously, Georgina suddenly announced her intention of going over to Ireland to see the trainer in charge of her couple of jumpers, and she obtained the necessary permit. Worrack saw her off at Euston by the 1.30 p.m. train, and she seemed her usual self, though, as he now remembered, just a bit chatty and rather too bright, as if she was concealing some nervousness. With her she had only one trunk, and no maid. But the following morning Worrack received a package which had been posted in London the previous morning. It was the deeds of the club premises legally conveyed to him, certain IOU's he had insisted on signing, and a brief letter.

> *Dear Peter,*
>
> *I know you'll think me an awful fool but these are tricky times—submarines and bombings and all sorts of unexpected things. So these are yours, with my love, just in case we shouldn't meet again. Bless you, darling, and don't rag me too much when I really bob up again.*
>
> *Georgie*

"It was only by luck that I didn't put these IOU's on the fire," Worrack said. "You'll think I'm a bit of a swine, taking a present like that, but you don't know what she was like. The contents of this envelope mean about twenty thousand quid to me, and that was nothing to her. All the time I had to be holding her back. I could have had it all long ago if I'd been that kind, but I just didn't happen to be. I insisted on a strict business basis."

"Just a moment," I said. "What I'd like to do is analyse your feelings when you got the letter. Am I right in saying you were grateful in . . . well, what I'd call a warm, amused kind of way? You thought she'd got her own way in her own way?"

"That's it exactly," he said. "I was damn fond of Georgina, and she was of me. You won't mind my telling you this, but one day not so long ago she said to me, 'You'd like to ask me to marry you, and you would do it if it weren't for my money.' That wasn't quite what she said, but that's the hang of it. Then, before I could get a word in, she said she wasn't marrying a second time. Kids and a home and all that sort of thing weren't in her line." He shook his head. "And they weren't."

"To get back to the letter," I said. "You believed in that nervousness about submarines and bombing?"

"Good God, no!" he told me bluntly. "There never was a woman less nervous. She was in London during most of the blitz and never turned a hair. And about submarines, there's never been an attack reported in the Irish Sea. But there's something more, and this time it's the real mystery. It was a Wednesday when she left Euston. That same Wednesday night two people whose word I can trust said they saw her at Euston Station, just getting into a taxi, and a porter with that trunk of hers. It was just before blackout time, but they hadn't a shadow of doubt but what it was Georgie. They knew her as well as I did, and what with that hair of hers and other things they couldn't have made a mistake."

"What did you do about it?"

"Acted like a fool," he said. "I thought they *had* made a mistake. Wouldn't you have thought the same thing? Then, a day or two went by and she hadn't written or wired. That didn't worry me too much, because she was very erratic about correspondence, and she wasn't the demonstrative sort. Then a week went by and we—I mean Barbara Grays and I—got in touch with Ireland and found she'd never made the crossing. She'd written that she was coming but she just hadn't turned up. After that we waited a bit longer, then something had to be done."

"You've applied to the police?"

He gave a queer sort of smile. "That's just what I didn't want to do. You see, there'd have been all sorts of awkward questions. I didn't mind a damn about myself but they'd have found out about the place I run and her connection with it, and I wasn't standing for having her name in the headlines like that. Also we kept hoping something would turn up. She might have lost her memory temporarily. All sorts of things happen these days."

"And yet she wasn't the kind of woman to be subject to an attack like that," I said. "She showed so little nervousness at Euston that it was only afterwards that you remembered it."

"I know," he said. "The whole thing's beyond me. The last day or two it's driven me nearly crazy. Not that I feel that way now—I mean, now you're here, and we're going to do something."

I shook my head. "Everything you've told me, tells me it's a case for the police," I said. "They've unlimited powers and resources, so to speak. They can press a button and do in half a day what'd take a private firm a month or two, even if they could do it at all. And about your private affairs," I went on. "The police don't act in the way you think. They're not interested in scandal. I don't say they won't be pretty strict about that club of yours, and if you apply to them, I'd advise you to close it down straight away. But Mrs. Morbent's name will be protected, you can be sure of that."

"I haven't got only myself to think of," he said. "Mrs. Grays thinks my way too, and she's her sister. And we're prepared to pay, as I told you. All we want you to do is to find her. If you like, we'll say this. Get to work at once and if nothing happens in a week or so, then we'll really apply to the police."

"It's not so simple as all that," I told him. "The trail's cold and it'd be sheer blind blazing luck if I picked up a thing in the course of the next few days. Also, when you do apply to the police, I don't see how my name can be kept out of things. And, frankly, I don't care for the police to know that I've taken on something that ought to be referred to them at once. The police—Scotland Yard, if you like—and myself have worked together and we have the same standards. The injury to my reputation would be too great. And I still consider that it's to the police you should apply."

I put the notebook in my pocket, reached down for my hat and got reluctantly to my feet. Worrack sat on and his face had a deep dejection. Then as he looked up at me as if he only then realised I was refusing to handle the case, I all at once said something, and before I was really aware I was speaking at all.

"Perhaps there *are* one or two things we might talk over," I said and sat down again. And this is why.

It was true I was loath to leave the case, for there were features that were definitely intriguing, and some of the reasons I had given to explain my lack of co-operation were far less genuine than I had tried to make out. But why I had sat down was this. Facing me across the room, as I rose, was a large rococo mirror in gesso and gilt, and in it, as if framed, I saw the door that had been on my right—the door that had been ajar.

In that mirror I suddenly saw gloved fingers at the edge of the door, drawing it slightly more open. Behind that door then, a woman had been listening to our conversation. Most of that conversation had been of a fairly dangerous nature as far as Worrack was concerned, and yet, as I suddenly realised, he must have been aware that the door was ajar. Not only was that door in the line of his eye from the seat he had himself chosen, but when one is about to speak of confidential matters the least precaution one can take is to see that doors are closed. That was why it came to me with a queer instinctive intuition that the woman who had designedly listened to our conversation was that very Georgina Morbent who was supposed to have disappeared!

CHAPTER II
A FEW IDEAS

"What was the exact date when Mrs. Morbent left Euston?" I asked.

"The thirteenth of January. A Wednesday."

"You're sure?"

"Absolutely," he said. "For one thing, she made a very peculiar remark. At least, I think now that it was peculiar. About the day being the thirteenth and unlucky."

"That seems to fix it," I said, and noted the date down. "Was she superstitious generally?"

"Not more than most," he said, and shrugged his shoulders.

"Pardon my being so persistent," I said, "but let me put the question another way. Did the remark strike you as being out of character?"

He frowned for a moment. "At that moment—no," he said. "When I look back at it now, I think it was."

"And who were the people who saw her at Euston later?"

"I'd rather not give their names," he said. "It's just a bit tricky. I don't mind telling you that they met her at that club of mine, so there might be complications if there was any official interference."

I'm afraid I rather stared at that.

"But there isn't going to be any official interference."

"There might be later," he pointed out. "Didn't we agree on that?"

"We're talking in circles," I told him. "If I make any enquiries they're between you and me. They're confidential as hell, if you like it put that way. Whatever I discover will never be communicated to the police."

I pretended then that I wanted something from my trouser pocket and got to my feet. A quick glance in the mirror showed the door about as much ajar as it had been when I last saw it. Then I hauled out my handkerchief and sat down again.

"For instance," I went on. "If I discovered that you'd murdered the lady, I should simply abandon the case. My duty to you would bar any revelation of that by hint or otherwise to the police. That's the basis of all confidential professional work."

He nodded to himself at that but otherwise didn't turn a hair.

"Right-ho then," he said. "The two people are the Hon. Harold Lewton-Molde and a Miss Scylla Payton. He's a weak-chinned specimen, but she's a tough. He owes me a goodish bit of money, by the way: about the only one who does."

"But you've no reason to doubt his word?"

"In that? No. I'm sure now they actually did see her. By the way, one reason why they might resent questioning is that I rather fancy they'd been away on a very long weekend. You're a man of the world, and so you gather what I mean."

"And their addresses?"

"You could always see them at the club," he said. "I don't think it'd be square of me to reveal addresses. That sort of rumour getting around wouldn't do me any good."

"And the Irish trainer," I said. "What about him? Is it only his word you have that she never arrived in Ireland?"

"It *is* only his word," he said, and then was frowning to himself again. "Do you know, I never thought of that."

"You mean you don't trust him?"

"I wouldn't go as far as that," he said. "I mean, in anything like what we're talking about now. In other things I wouldn't trust him as far as I can throw a tank. But Georgie wouldn't hear a word against him. She loved all the blarney, even when it hit her pocket afterwards."

"His name?"

"William O'Clauty, of Gilland Lodge, County Dublin."

"And now will you be more explicit," I said when I'd jotted that down. "Why did you yourself mistrust him?"

"I knew he was a twister," he said. "I like a flutter myself when the information's good, and coming from O'Clauty, through Georgie, the information ought to have been good. But it never was, except at the wrong times. The annoying thing was that we used to pass tips on to pals, and that didn't do us a lot of good. When the goddam horses won, the prices were too short. When one popped up at a long price, we didn't know about it. And the excuses O'Clauty used to produce were pretty feeble, so I thought. The trouble was that she didn't think so."

"Getting down to brass tacks again," I said. "Any reason why he should have murdered her?"

He stared at that.

"No use mincing words," I said. "It's one of the things we've got to consider."

"Yes," he said slowly. "I suppose it is."

Then he was shaking his head.

"There is a reason, though I doubt if it's a good one. He's always hard up; I do know that. All those little trainers live from coup to coup. But one of those two colts of Georgie's is a damn fine animal. The other's won a few times, but this other animal—

Amber King's his name—is something out of the ordinary. She turned down an offer of a couple of thousand for him, and that's good money for a lepper these days. After this is all over he'll be nearing his prime, and he's a cert National winner if nothing goes wrong with him. That'll put him in the ten thousand class. And if anything happens to Georgie, O'Clauty takes the horses. It's in her will. I told her it was scandalously generous of her, but there you are."

It was my turn to frown and nod. "An Irishman's said to consider his soul a pretty poor exchange for a damn good horse," I said darkly. "If he trained a National winner he'd be made for life. If he owned one, then he wouldn't swop Gilland Lodge for heaven. But about that will you mentioned. Who gets the bulk of her money? The sister?"

"That's right," he said. "I get ten thousand, tax free, and what I've had already. I mean those things you saw in that envelope."

He was giving me a definitely challenging look.

"If you ask me how I know, then I can refer you to Barbara— Mrs. Grays," he went on. "Georgie never made any secret of what she intended to do with her money. We didn't worry, because we didn't want the damn money, at least not enough to think of her as dead. By all the rules, she should outlive both of us."

I liked the way he put that, and in spite of the believe-it- or-not tone of his statement, I believed him readily enough. In fact, I had a considerable respect for him. His class and those he made his money from were not mine, and usually I avoided them like the devil, but there was no denying the fact that al- ready I had more than a sneaking liking for Worrack.

"No other bequests?" I asked.

"None of any consequence."

"Well, so much for that," I said. "And now can you give me a photograph of her?"

He must have anticipated the request for he had a couple ready. They were too large even for my breast pocket, and while he was cutting off the mounts I had a leg stretcher. The door was now definitely more ajar than when I saw it last.

"What do you think of her?" he asked, and there was something I would go so far as to call pathetic about the way he said it and the look on his face.

"A fine-looking woman," I said. "I like her face. I like the whole look of her. If you'll forgive my saying so, she looks a damn good sort. One you could trust to the last inch."

"You're dead right," he said, and shook his head again as he dropped into the chair. "Her sister's a good sort too. One of the best, but rather different from Georgie. I mean, even she would say that. She just worshipped Georgie. We all did."

It took me a moment or two to find my next question after that.

"I could meet the sister?"

"I'd like you to," he said. "What about lunch to-day? I could fix it up."

I said it would suit me very well, and we fixed the rendezvous for Moroni's, which is just off Coventry Street, at one sharp. Worrack would be there and I was supposed to drop in casually and hail him as a friend, and then would follow the introduction.

"And suppose I say I knew Georgie?" I suggested. "Would that help?"

"Wait a minute," he said. "I think you've got something there. Just let me think a moment and I'll see how it'll work out."

I made a note or two in my book but I'd finished before he had his scheme ready. It was a bit complicated at first, and then the introduction of a new name didn't help matters.

"Our talk this morning is off my own bat," he began. "Barbara Grays mustn't know a word about it. She's worried, naturally, but she's still hoping Georgie will turn up. I've got beyond that, which is why I wrote to you. But what I want to do is to invite another man to lunch with us. He's quite a good sort, and a pal of Barbara's. A chap named Hamson, who used to be in the Indian police. He's a pretty fast mover, like all of our particular crowd, and he seems to have plenty of money."

He had been hesitating a bit and when he came to that stop, things as far as I was concerned were very incomplete.

"And where's he to fit in?" I asked.

"I hardly like suggesting it," he said, "but you said something over the 'phone about being understaffed so I thought Hamson, as an old policeman, might lend you a hand. If you mentioned Georgie at lunch, then you might make Hamson prick his ears. He's been asking where Georgie is. So have other people, and you can't keep on saying she's in Ireland. You can't say it with enough conviction—at least I can't."

It seemed a cock-eyed scheme to me, and he must have seen the reluctance on my face.

"I'd like you to do things that way," he said. "I know you ought to have a free hand, but I've got a hunch that Hamson might be a bit of a help."

Then he was frowning in a rather peculiar way and rubbing that moustache of his.

"I'll try anything once," I told him. "Give me some more of the low-down on Georgie so that I can make my yarn convincing."

Well, we concocted a set of circumstances that looked as if it might meet the case, and we had a five-minute rehearsal. Perhaps I was not too enthusiastic; at any rate something made him open up, and in a perfectly staggering way.

"It's damn good of you, Travers, doing all this," he said. "Perhaps there's something I ought to tell you." His voice lowered, and he gave a quick glance round like a man who instinctively wonders if he can possibly be overheard.

"Half a million's a hell of a lot of money, even when death duties come off it," he said, and then drew back. "Do you get me?"

"You mean—the sister?"

He shrugged his shoulders suggestively. "That's for you to find out. And it's where Hamson might help. He's in her confidence. I know he's asked her to marry him, but at the moment she can't make up her mind."

"I get you," I said, though in fact everything was far from as clear as it sounded. "But about my name. I mustn't be Travers. Blunt's as good a name as any. After all, I've been pretty blunt with you."

Ludovic Blunt then, I was to be. I thought it best to keep to the Christian name in case at any time I should be hailed by an unexpected friend. Then I rose to go, and another glance in the mirror showed that the door was pushed tightly to.

"I suppose it's silly to ask if you've any ideas already?" he was asking me anxiously, as we moved towards the outer door.

"I have one or two," I said, "but they're pretty nebulous at the moment. Oh, and by the way, did she have any jewellery with her that afternoon?"

"I don't think so," he said. "I mean, I don't think she had what you might call the regalia."

"She had a lot?"

"A few thousand pounds' worth. Nothing gaudy, but everything good, if you know what I mean. You see," he told me, and as if he was anxious for me to believe it, "she wasn't the gaudy sort. Whatever she did was always natural."

I nodded. "But about that particular day? What was she actually wearing?"

He thought for a moment or two. "I know she was wearing that square-cut emerald ring. Brooch—no. Oh, and a wrist-watch. A quiet-looking platinum one, but probably worth well over a hundred these days. And she had her platinum ciga-rette-case."

"And the ring? What was that worth?"

"Don't know," he said. "Five hundred probably."

Then he was giving me that challenging look again.

"It's all right," I said. "Just routine questions. I don't think she was murdered for her jewellery."

He gripped my arm and the look he gave was even more challenging.

"But you do think . . ."

"You've got to think of everything," I said, and shook my head. "At the moment I don't actually feel sure she's dead. She might have gone off with a man."

I saw him stiffen at that. Then he smiled quietly as he shook his head. "If you're counting on that you're wasting your time. There wasn't any man she'd have looked at twice."

"Except you."

He gave me a look, then turned his head away.

"Yes," he said slowly. "Except me. Just as I wouldn't look twice at any other woman."

"And yet she didn't trust you sufficiently to let you know about all that was probably going to happen."

He swivelled round on me where he stood. I can see him now; his hand on the back of the chair, and in his eyes that deadly cold look that took the charm from his face and made it something ugly and dangerously threatening.

"Just what do you mean by that?"

"Just this," I said, and shrugged my shoulders. "You asked me if I had any ideas. Here's one that stands out as big as the Albert Memorial and about as blatantly. Mrs. Morbent knew perfectly well she was never going to Ireland, whatever she told you and her sister. She was nervous at Euston because she was playing a part; deceiving you, if you like. What she did know was that she was going somewhere to see someone about whom nobody had to be told—not even you or her sister. She expected that trip and that meeting to involve danger to herself, and that's why she remembered the day was the thirteenth, and that's why, *before* she left, she sent you that package. Also she left everything open, so that you'd merely rag her if she came safely out of wherever it was that she was going."

His hand lifted and fell again, and I could see it was shaking.

"Yes," he said slowly. "I should have seen all that."

Then the challenge was in his voice again. "Who should she be going to see? And why should it be dangerous?"

I could only shrug my shoulders. "That," I said quietly, "is what we have to find out. At the moment I can think of only one thing. The one she was seeing was a blackmailer."

His eyes narrowed again as they met mine. Then the lip curled.

"How could she be blackmailed? Her whole life was as open as—as open as day."

"So you might have thought," I said. "You can take a jolt?"

The eyes narrowed again. "Why not? I've taken plenty in my time."

"You said she refused to marry you," I pointed out to him. "Maybe she wanted to marry you, but she couldn't. Maybe she'd married again already. This is war-time. All women do queer things that are done in a moment's excitement and then take a lifetime of living down."

His head had turned away and he was doing some hard thinking. I was just about to ask him who her bankers were, and if her payments could be checked; and then he spoke first, and I knew there'd be plenty of time for my question when I'd got a better idea of things.

"There may have been blackmail, but not for that," he said, and nodded to himself. Then as if to put the whole problem aside he was reminding me that we hadn't discussed my terms.

"Blunt's my name, and blunt I'll be," I told him. "I'm still undecided about taking your case. What I'll do is work on it for two or three days and then let you know finally according to how things turn out. If I decide to go on, then we'll discuss terms. If not, then twenty pounds will probably cover everything."

"Two or three days isn't very long," he told me dubiously.

"Lots of things can happen in a shorter time than that," I said. "I'd like to give you a decision now, but I can't. Inside me, at the moment, I've got nothing but gobbets of undigested information. Also I haven't met half the people I ought to meet."

He agreed with me there, and I agreed with him that his natural anxiety couldn't help wishing for quick results, and with that we parted. I said I knew my way out, but at the head of the stairs he said that if anything went wrong over that lunch at Moroni's he'd ring me up by a quarter-past twelve at the latest, but otherwise everything would be all right.

I made my way down, at least as far as the half-way landing. There I halted for a moment and cocked my ear upwards. Then I went up again, and with no need to worry about footsteps for the pile of the stair and corridor carpet seemed inches thick. A quick glance each way and I had my ear at the crack of the door. Voices were certainly there but there was never the remotest chance of hearing what they were saying. But I did recognise Worrack's voice, and then, as another voice was slightly raised,

I was surprised to recognise that for a man's voice too. Then as I was pressing my ear a bit tighter there was the sound of people coming up the stairs, and I moved away like a streak.

It was twenty minutes to twelve when I reached my own flat again, and the first thing I did was to ring "Enquiries', at Euston. While I was waiting for the call and in the intervals of subsequent conversation, I was looking through a *Who's Who* of 1938. There was nothing about anyone of the name of Grays, but Morbent was there, though what I gathered about the missing Georgina Morbent was little more than I already knew. Henry Morbent, so it said, was a South African magnate who married, in 1937, Georgina, second daughter of Colonel Amber of So-and-so. It said also that he was a director of various companies, and that he owned racehorses. As he was thirty years older than his wife, I gathered that she had married him for his money.

A woman's voice was speaking from Euston and a very efficient voice it sounded. The 1.30, she said, did not connect with the Belfast boat from Liverpool, but many people preferred taking it and completing the journey before black-out time. The first stop of the train in question had been Rugby, at 3.20.

"Suppose I got out of the train because I knew I had to get back to London for something urgent I'd forgotten," I asked her. "At what time would there have been such a train?"

She said she'd find out, so I tried *Who's Who* for Worrack and Hamson and the Hon. Harold Lewton-Molde. Not one was mentioned, and just as I had decided to damn all double-barrelled names and was thinking of calling one gentleman simply Molde, the Euston lady was speaking again.

"About your train, sir. There'd have been a quarter of an hour's wait only. Leave Rugby 3.40; arrive London 5.35."

"Thank you," I said, "for some very efficient service."

As I had an old *Debrett* I looked up Molde, and there he was. Second son of Lord Hasbury of Medham, and at that I raised my eyebrows. Hasbury, one of a moderately recent creation, was a custodian of the old Nonconformist conscience; a situation that recalled the plaintive question of Moody and Sankey—"Where is my wandering boy to-night?" The age of the Hon. Harold, as I worked it out, was thirty-seven.

Then, just by luck, I tried Worrack, and found that he also was the grandson of a peer, but one of the sporting kind. Worrack's father was the Hon. Claude Worrack, though the name conveyed nothing to me. But it told me a good deal about my possible employer, and confirmed a bit more. It also set me thinking about the extraordinary collection of people with whom I was likely to come into contact. How was it that they all seemed to be dodging war duties, for instance; and quite logically, if they were never a damn of use to the country, then why in hell should I worry even my brains over their probably self-created troubles. I, and they, as the Pharisee in me said, would get along none too well. A queer crowd, I told myself, but a crowd that would always be with us: plenty of pals in the best places and still living like fighting-cocks, and scrounging petrol for the races, and finding the wherewithal to patronise places like Worrack's.

It was still only just after twelve, so I sat down to wait, in case Worrack should call. But I didn't begin to theorise, which was rather strange for me. Things, as I had told Worrack, were far too nebulous generally, and the situation in which I was placed was far too unusual. At any other time I could probably have found a theory to explain everything that Worrack had told me, if only because I have that particular kind of brain which pops theoretically off at the slightest pressure on the trigger. George Wharton has been heavily sarcastic about that propensity of mine, though I prefer to call it a gift. And why should he grumble? Even if only one theory in three is right, that's no bad average as far as criminal investigation is concerned. The trouble with George is that he forgets the happy one and limits his elephantine cavortings to the unluckier two.

As I took my notebook out I felt those two photographs of Georgina Morbent, and I had another good look at them. You couldn't call her handsome, and yet the face had something extraordinarily attractive. I had not exaggerated when I gave Worrack my opinion, for except a devastating beauty she had everything that any man might want. There was a touch of both amusement and challenge in the mouth, as if she enjoyed life, had a confidence in herself, and didn't give two hoots for the opinion of others. The eyes looked out clear and direct, and in them too was a touch of something like amusement, but what they gave most of all was that sense of trustworthiness, for which I had found no better word when I had commented on them to Worrack. There, in fact, was a woman I should have liked to meet, and with that I was wondering if I ever *should* meet her. Then, before I knew it, I was theorising at full speed. Had that yarn of Worrack's been a concealment of something far more important than even her alleged disappearance? Would that explain his very definite nervousness? Whose was that gloved hand that had moved round the door? A woman's most certainly, and there had been also that faint perfume. Yet it had been a man who had been also listening to our talk, for it was a man's voice I had heard when I had listened at the door. A peculiar voice too; low-pitched and rather strident, and with a quality for which I could find no better description than that it was strangely clear.

The telephone went, and the sound brought a disappointment which I had no time to analyse.

"That you, Travers?" came Worrack's voice.

"Blunt speaking," I said.

"Sorry. Thought I'd tell you, after all, that everything's all right. Don't do any dollying up, by the way. And I may be waiting for you."

"I'll be there on time," I said. "And just one other thing. I've been looking at those two photographs and I think I can tell you that I'm rather more interested."

"Good," he said and I didn't ring off because I had the idea he would make some other comment. It came.

"She's everything you said she was and then more. The kind you like to be seen out with. Makes you feel on top of the world, and every man as jealous as hell."

"I know," I said. "But I ought to have asked you for a few more personal details. What was her height, for instance?"

"Five nine," he said. "Rather tall, that, for a woman, but she had a superb figure. One of the things she was most proud of."

"Good enough," I said. "That, and the hair, ought to be enough for any identification." Then, as he was saying nothing: "Right-ho, then. I'll see you at one o'clock prompt."

But there was no hurry for I could be sure of a taxi a few yards away, and so, after I had washed behind my ears, I did a bit more ruminating. Perhaps because I could still hear Worrack's voice, I was aware of a few more home truths about myself. Who was I, for instance, to adopt an attitude superior or puritanical because he chose to get a living in his own way and meet, in what he considered a square way, a definite demand? He at least had given plenty to his country; a damn sight more, in fact, than myself. And wasn't I also fond of an occasional gamble? Hadn't I adroitly skirted King's Regulations by having more than one game of poker, and pretty long and hectic sessions at that? And who was I, in any case, to make myself a custodian of war-time or any other morals? And, even more to the point, just because I had chosen to masquerade as a private detective, what right did that give me to be hypocritical about my patrons?

The clock said half-past, so I took a last squint at myself in the glass. Then I thought I'd check the clock and my watch by wireless time, so I switched on my set. Apparently the clock was slow, for a programme had begun which I recognised as *Workers' Playtime*. That clock must have been more than five minutes slow, for the usual playing on two pianos was finishing, though that small amount of lateness was no worry, and a quarter of an hour would be ample time to get me to Moroni's. Then, as I put my watch on five minutes, there came the fruity voice of a comedian.

Pardon a digression which may seem to you to be utterly irrelevant. I thought so at the time, and I was not to know that in the half-minute that followed I might have had the solution of a case that as yet had hardly begun. This is the apparent digression.

I don't know your opinion of the comedians—the comics, as they so optimistically call themselves—of the B.B.C. Most of them—I except Mr. Gillie Potter among others—are the objects of my envy, for few can earn a living more easily. Jokes that were hoary in my youth are still their stock-in-trade, and some have not changed their patter for years. Maybe they are overworked and there are not enough of them to go round. So when my fruity-voiced comedian began to speak, I wondered ironically if by the rarest chance he would have a brand new gag. Then at his first words I couldn't help but wince.

The scarcity of eggs, that was his immediate theme.

"And do you know, girls, why they're scarce? I listened to my hens the other day and do you know what I heard them singing?"

I had heard that same gag a dozen times on the mess radio, and not only did I know it but I knew the next gag that would assuredly follow it. James Agate has said—and I don't know if the *mot* is his own—that the greatest achievement of modern science is the knob that turns off the radio. At any rate I hastened to turn off mine.

And there I was wrong. If I'd borne with that comedian for only one more minute I might have had a whole heap of ideas. If you know what I missed, and if you're a radio fan you certainly do, then you'll know what I mean.

CHAPTER III
MEET THE FOLKS

IN THE TAXI I did most of my thinking about Worrack, whom I was going to meet. Percival Halsey St. John Worrack was how he appeared in Debrett, and he had been born in 1895, which made him forty-eight. It was no great feat of deduction to imagine his career. Public school, Sandhurst and then his regiment; the Guards probably or the Cavalry. Family probably impecunious, or without too much money to spare. Service in the last war and then boredom, retirement and the life of a man about town. Private means probably eked out by commissions, racing and gambling coups, and possibly tips on the Stock Exchange. Called up at the beginning of the war, and the rest as stated.

I said I liked him, and I did, and principally because I respected his honesty. He wasn't a Pharisee, and he had his own ideas about a square deal. That, paradoxically, was why I didn't wholly trust him. I couldn't help remembering, for instance, how he was shot through, as you might say, with that passion for a square deal and never letting a client down, and yet he had been guilty of what seemed to me an extraordinary treachery. First he had spoken of Georgina Morbent's sister, Mrs. Grays, as a good sort and had hinted at a certain indebtedness. Later he had made that highly confidential suggestion that half a million was the devil of a lot of money, that Barbara Grays would find it uncommonly useful, and that I might reasonably begin my enquiries in that quarter. To put it bluntly, in fact, there was the very strong hint that Barbara Grays might have made away with her sister for the sake of the money. Melodramatic, perhaps, but such things have been. And then almost in the same breath, he had said that Barbara worshipped her sister, though I admit that he had immediately modified the statement by adding that everybody did.

Then there was that matter of the man Hamson whom I had not seen. Far too blatantly, it had been suggested that Hamson should assist me in any enquiries, particularly those concerning Barbara Grays. Apparently Hamson might be engaged to her at any minute, and yet it was expected—indeed it seemed to have been privately arranged—that Hamson should be the stool pigeon where Barbara Grays was concerned. And suppose this man Hamson was the one who had been listening at the door and whom I had later heard talking with Worrack. Suppose the woman who had been listening too was Barbara Grays, and there was some kind of conspiracy between the three.

Melodramatic again, you may say. But consider. Hadn't Worrack fairly pitchforked me into that luncheon to which the taxi was taking me? And weren't the three to be there? And if Worrack was getting ten thousand, Barbara most of the rest, and Hamson was going to marry Barbara—well, what do you make of that? And add one other thing. In that application to me by Worrack was something remarkably fishy. It was the police to whom he should have applied, and if he really was scared about their uncovering that night club of his, then the application could have been made by the sister. Indeed she was the one who should have made it.

There was something else; something that seemed partly to upset all that I have just written, and yet showing clearly that again there was something fishy as well as contradictory. Worrack had undoubtedly been deeply in love with Georgina Morbent. He had not said so in so many words, but when you have examined as many witnesses as I have in my time, or listened to the cross-examinations of George Wharton, not to mention prosecuting and other counsel, then you learn to spot what is true in the story of even the shiftiest witness. That she had been, and was at the time of her disappearance, Worrack's mistress seemed to me an unquestionable fact, and that he would have married her if she had been the marrying kind, and if he had not had his own ideas about marrying a woman with all the money. You see again that queer mixture of the square deal and the dubiously honest.

I had that notebook in my breast pocket and while we waited at some traffic lights I made a jotting or two.

> *(a) Why didn't B. see G. off at Euston?*
> *(b) Where does G. live? Has the flat (?) been examined?*
> *(c)Who are G.'s bankers?*
> *(d) W. mentioned "no maid." Then she had a maid but didn't take her to Ireland.*

That seemed to be all at the moment, and then, as we neared Piccadilly Circus, I began wondering again if I should take over the case or not, and when I was frank with myself I knew I had no real intention of proceeding much further. Intriguing though it had sounded at first, if only because it was of so unexpected a nature, there was now some deep and urgent caution telling me that the sooner I disengaged myself, the better. My own part, as cold reason told me, had been imprudent from the very first, and only a ridiculous vanity and an incurable curiosity had kept me from telling Worrack on the 'phone that he had made a mistake and that I wasn't and never had been an enquiry agent. On the other hand, I could tell myself, if the case had been something routine and simple, I might have gone through with it. If it had involved a theft, for example, or even some perfectly straightforward disappearance; but possible murder was a hellish dangerous thing to be mixed up in, and particularly for me, and that night club background and the crowd with whom I should have to work were about as attractive as the other end of the social scale, which for the want of a better comparison we might do worse than call Petticoat Lane.

When I paid off the taxi I saw I had two minutes to spare. In the vestibule, all red plush and mirrors, Worrack was waiting.

"Glad you're on time," he said. "The others are there but I haven't been in yet. Thought I'd better say I'd met you on the way."

We left our things in the cloakroom and as we were about to enter the main room an elderly waiter came up to us.

"O.K., Pierre," Worrack said. "Mrs. Grays' table. Four of us, not three."

His hand fell on my arm and he drew me back for a moment. What he wanted to tell me didn't seem too important, but perhaps, as I thought afterwards, he wanted Pierre to set the extra place at the table and announce our arrival.

"A very useful place, this," was what he said. "Do you know it at all?"

I shook my head.

"They always do you well," he went on. "And they're the people who supply my place with sandwiches and stuff. You'll see all that for yourself to-night. Which reminds me. It's quite possible I mayn't be able to see you again after lunch, so you might drop in at the club. Any time after nine. Here's the address. Quite easy to get at."

I slipped the folded sheet of paper into my breast pocket. Easy is the road to perdition. Curiosity, or lack of moral courage, stopped me getting myself still further involved, though it had been on the tip of my tongue to blurt out that I'd decided not to take the case after all. And he was taking my arm again and moving me through the red plush curtains.

The room was fairly full and it was towards one of the alcoves that he was steering me, and I could feel the swing of his body as he pivoted on his game leg. A woman and a man were seated at one of the tables, and I spotted it from a good few yards away, for Pierre was just leaving it. It was the man at whom I had a good look as we neared, though what I tell you of my first impressions includes what I saw of him and gathered while we spent that hour over our meal.

When he got to his feet at our approach I saw that he was about six feet in height, and that he had a thick moustache cropped short, in line with the upper lip. He was fairly heavy in build, and his age was probably the late forties. In manner he was quiet, and he had a quiet likeable smile. Though he was not good-looking, like Worrack, for instance, his face had a re-liability, and there was something of the soldier about him. My mind, always too keen on analysis and apt to imagine as well as theorise, found only two contradictions. Hamson had been a policeman in India, as Worrack had told me, but whereas Worrack looked the professional soldier to the life, Hamson was to my eye the civilian who has been a soldier and still wishes to be regarded as one. There was also that contradiction in his manners; easy though they were apparently, and perfect public school, there were times when they were just a bit hesitating. But did I like him? I think that I rather took to him from the first. And as soon as he spoke I knew his wasn't the voice I had heard in Worrack's room.

"This is Blunt," Worrack was saying. "An old Army pal of mine. We ran into each other just now. He was looking for somewhere to lunch so I brought him along."

"How do you do," Barbara Grays was saying casually, and: "Pierre told us you were bringing a friend."

She looked her thirty-five, which after all is a good age in a woman. She was tallish, like her sister, but plump, and as she sat with her fur coat drawn back carelessly over her shoulders, and elbows on the table, and fingers languidly holding a cigarette, the first impression I had was one of dowdiness. But it was only a studied or a natural boredom, I wasn't sure which, for when I had a close if surreptitious look at her, I saw she was not only quite good-looking, but reticently made up and really exquisitely dressed. Her voice, of the dry soprano type, had a definite petulance.

"Well, what are we eating?" Worrack asked briskly.

Barbara Grays shrugged her shoulders, then frowned. "Blast that Pierre! Why hasn't he brought that ash-tray?"

"What's the matter with you this morning, darling?" Worrack asked her amusedly. "Headache or just little tempers?"

Then Pierre appeared with the ash-tray and the menu, Hamson began talking to me and left the selection to the others.

"All food's alike to me," he told me. "In any case they always do you well here. What was your regiment Mr. Blunt?"

I inwardly damned Worrack for not consulting me about the manner of my introduction. Then I thought I'd tell him the truth, and I did—more or less.

"You're lucky," he said regretfully. "They turned me down with a wonky heart. All the same, you'd have thought they might have found some sort of a job for an old policeman."

"Policeman?" I said. "You make me shudder."

He laughed. "Not what you fear. Just the Indian police, that's all."

"Darling, must you tell everybody your life history?" Barbara asked with a drawling impertinence, but Hamson only laughed. Then Worrack was asking us if we agreed on a general menu or if we'd like variations, and Pierre stood by expectantly. I said what was good enough for him was good enough for me, especially as he was paying. Hamson chuckled and said that went for him too.

It was a good meal. I tell you that to get it over. A capital thing it may be—to do a bit of philosophising—for all of us to be rationed in essentials, but we had few essentials except perhaps a speck of toast. After all, money still counts, and it buys Scotch salmon, and game, and poultry, and even *foie gras* and caviare, if it comes to that. I was hungry and I ate accordingly, and Hamson had a good appetite too. Worrack seemed the pernickety kind of feeder, and Barbara Grays left half her food on her plate. And she had that pernicious habit of smoking throughout the meal. An American habit, I believe, but whoever invented it ought to have been made to anticipate his meals with three solid hours on a treadmill.

It was just after the soup that I put my question.

"How's your sister these days, Mrs. Grays? I haven't seen her for quite a time."

"Blunt knows Georgie pretty well," Worrack cut in.

"I wouldn't say that," I added deprecatingly.

Barbara laid her fork carefully on her plate and reached as carefully for the cigarette.

"I think she's pretty fit," she told me unconcernedly. "Over in Ireland at the moment. Call that damn waiter, Peter, will you? This blasted soda's perfectly tepid."

Worrack had ordered for her a double whisky, and we others were drinking lager.

Worrack shrugged his shoulders and looked round for Pierre. Hamson leaned forward and patted her hand.

"What's the matter, darling? Not feeling too fit?"

"Damn you, Tommy, will you leave me alone!" she told him pettishly. Then she caught my eye, and it was when she smiled that I seemed to see her face for the first time, and I knew I had seen her somewhere before.

"Are you married, Mr. Blunt?"

"Not too much," I said.

"I can't stand being pestered," she told me. "And you are a pest sometimes, Tommy, and a damned annoying one." There was no point in dragging Georgina's name in again and the meal went on its languid way. We talked about the theatre, which Barbara said was putrid, and about the blitzes which she described as vulgar and noisy. Then it leaked out, through Hamson, that she'd driven an ambulance, so there again was a person who was a queer contradiction. As spoilt as hell, bored beyond tears, and as selfish as they make them, and regarding the driving of an ambulance through the worst of the blitz as something of which to be disgustingly ashamed.

With coffee she and Worrack had liqueurs. Hamson had a glass of iced water and I merely smoked.

Worrack settled the bill for the four of us. Hamson expostulated but Barbara seemed to take it for granted.

"Sorry I've got to push off," Worrack announced. "Blunt's coming along to Arcadia to-night, by the way." Arcadia was the code word for that club of his.

Barbara's lip curled. "If he takes my advice he'll stay at home and play double patience with his wife."

"Damnation, Barbara," Worrack told her with mock exasperation. "Now you've lost me a perfectly good client." He got to his feet. "See you later then, old chap. You'll look after Barbara, Tommy."

It was then that the contretemps occurred and an awkward one it was. We had all got up and Mrs. Grays had said something about going to powder her nose, and Hamson had rushed to help her into the fur coat. I happened to glance round and there, almost full on me, was Deaker, one of the Assistant Commissioners at the Yard. My face flared to the colour of a tomato.

"Hallo, Travers," he said, and his voice had a heartiness for which I could have murdered him. "What on earth are you doing here?"

"Just taking on fuel," I said. "What are you doing?"

"Nothing in particular. You still at the same place?"

"Still there," I said, and wished to hell he'd go.

"Perhaps I'll be seeing you again," he told me and glanced across at the lady who appeared to be waiting for him. He hesitated, gave a look at the three who were with me, and then said he'd have to be going.

"Ring me up some time," I said, and he grinned and nodded as he made off.

The first face I saw was Worrack's, and it looked as sheepish as my own. Then he saved the situation, as I thought, manfully.

"A damn silly name, Travers," he said. "Do you ever get ragged about it still?"

"Travers Blunt sounds rather euphonious to me," I said.

I glanced at Hamson, but he had a queer wary look on his face.

"A perfectly ghastly combination," Barbara Grays remarked languidly. "Your parents should have been prosecuted for cruelty to children."

"Well, I'll be going," Worrack cut in. Barbara Grays moved off too and Hamson and I made our way to the washroom. Then we waited in the red plush vestibule. Barbara was always the devil of a time, he said, and I took that for a hint that he wouldn't be glad of any more of my company, and I said I thought I'd be on the move.

"Doing anything in particular this afternoon?" he asked me.

"Yes and no," I said. "Why?"

He hesitated. "Well, there's something I'd rather like to talk over with you. Sorry I can't be more explicit. What about dropping in at my place at about four?"

"Right-ho," I said. "Provided you don't want to see me to sell me a gold mine, and your place isn't too far from Kensington."

"Warfield's Hotel in Marybrook Street," he said. "Not two minutes from Harrods. And I only wish I had a gold mine to sell you."

I said I'd look in. And would he make my excuses to Mrs. Grays, whom I hoped to see again some time. He said that if I was going to Worrack's place that night I'd see her there.

As soon as I was back at my flat I rang up Worrack, though I didn't expect to find him in.

"Congratulations on getting me out of that mess," I said. "But you've landed me in another. As you called me an old army pal, and Hamson was rather persistent, I told him I was back in the Service."

"That goes for me," he said. "What sort of a job? We'd better stick to the same yarn."

"An administrative job in a camp in the Midlands. Rank of Major."

He repeated that as if to make sure he'd got it.

"One other thing," I said, and told him about Hamson's invitation. I heard him give a low whistle.

"If he gets too persistent again," I said, "what am I to tell him? That chap who spoke to me had policeman written all over him, and somehow I don't think Hamson swallowed your tale."

"He's a cute bird," he said. "But tell him anything you damn-please, provided you let me know. I'll be here between six and seven o'clock, so you might ring me up."

I said I'd rather slip along and see him if I might. Then I put a last question.

"Suppose Hamson guesses that that lunch appearance of mine was a put-up affair. Suppose he jumps even farther ahead and guesses you're doing something about a missing somebody, and I'm in it too? What then?"

There was a moment or two of silence and I could almost hear him thinking.

"Don't think it's likely," he said. "If it should happen, then you can tell him that we are on that job. But make him swear he'll keep his mouth shut to Barbara. She's not to know a thing."

"If he offers to help, then you'd still like it?"

"I think so," he said. "I told you he was a spry bird. He ought to help you a lot."

So much for that. Whether I was pleased or not I didn't know. Hamson might have been a police official years ago in India but that didn't amount to much. Then I realised I was being rather illogical. After all, I hadn't promised to undertake the case, so why should I object to a collaborator with whom I was never likely to collaborate? But of one thing I was sure. Hamson was no stool pigeon. If Worrack thought his role would be pumping Barbara Grays, then every instinct told me he was most damnably wrong. Hamson, whatever he was, wasn't that sort. Nor did he strike me as a gold-digger in the matter of Barbara Grays. A pure adventurer would have had far more bounce and assurance, and Hamson struck me as a man of some means and a definite stability.

In any case, I could tell myself, Barbara Grays might be a damn good-looking woman—at least in her agreeable moments—but it would have taken more than half a million to induce me to tie myself to her for the balance of my natural life. One thing in particular about her had struck me as curious and unpleasant. Though, according to Worrack, Georgina made her an allowance, she had seemed to me utterly indifferent when I had asked my question as to Georgina's whereabouts. Her attitude had seemed, in fact, heartless to the point of callousness. And then, again, I wondered if I was being just. Worrack had said that the sisters were not the demonstrative kind, and I couldn't very well have expected Barbara Grays to weep on my shoulder. Still, it was all very confusing, and when I relinquished the case—and all the time I was telling myself that that was what I definitely intended—then I pitied the official at the Yard who would have the dubious pleasure of taking it over.

I ought to have written to my wife, so to take my mind off the case and to pass the time till a quarter to four, I wrote a long letter. Then I did some spit and polish and as there were a few minutes left, tackled the *Times* crossword. It was one of the harder sort, and after putting in half a dozen clues I was stumped completely, though I should say that as mine is the hither and thither kind of crossword brain, I usually managed to finish a puzzle in well under half an hour. However, it had passed the time for me, and I set out on the ten-minute walk to Hamson's hotel. When I fumbled in my pocket on the landing to make sure I had my key, I felt that piece of paper that Worrack had given me with the address of the club. To my amazement it was a personal letter, typed and signed. Harcourt Gardens, No. 72, was the address and it began, "Dear Blunt," and went on to say that Worrack was throwing a small party that night and would appreciate my company. I didn't know what its validity would be as a method of evading the law, but it struck me as an ingenious and highly amusing effort.

Warfield's Hotel was a private affair that seemed both decorous and expensive. It seemed also to pride itself on tradition, for in the entrance hall were various pictures and engravings connected with its history, and as Benjamin Franklin had once stayed there, it doubtless did a roaring trade—I beg its pardon—sedate and prosperous trade—with Americans. Indeed, an American officer was the first person I saw there. At the bureau, presided over by an elderly lady, who I was surprised to see was not wearing mittens, I was simply told to go right up to Number 18, on the first floor.

When I tapped at the door, Hamson's voice told me to enter. He was in as unconventional a position as could be, well back in a low easy-chair and feet on the mantelpiece, smoking a filthy-looking pipe and browsing over a paper, which I spotted as the *Financial Times*.

At the sight of me he gave a look of comical dismay and scrambled to his feet. "I'm so sorry," he said. "Hadn't any idea it was so late. Let me order you some tea. And let me take your coat."

I said it seemed only a few minutes since I'd eaten that lunch, but he said he was having a cup in any case. There was a telephone with a house connection in the room, so he ordered what he called the usual, which turned out to be toast, cake, and tea.

"Very few people know this place," he said, "and thank God for that. I've had this little suite of mine for a goodish time now. And it isn't as expensive as you might think."

He was clearing the newspapers off the side table that had stood at his elbow.

"Hallo," I said. "You've been doing the *Times* crossword."

"You're a crossword fan, aren't you?" he said. "Very disappointing to-day, don't you think? I hate them when you can finish them off without writing down a word."

"Good God!" I said. "I thought it the hardest there's been for weeks."

"That's the beauty of them," he told me. "Those you finish in ten minutes would probably take me an hour."

Worrack had called him a spry bird, but that couple of minutes gave me a far greater respect for his brains. Then the tea was brought in by a maid who looked as if she'd been born on the premises, and just too late to see Franklin.

Hamson had tricked me into that meal, for he never took anything to eat between lunch and dinner. I said I wouldn't spoil good food and helped myself to some toast.

"Salt?" he said, and then made a rather dramatic pause. Then he gave me a look that was just a bit too humorous to be purely cynical.

"Bread and salt. You know what that means, eating a man's bread and salt. I wonder if I ought to encourage you—at least before I've told you why I wanted you to come here."

"It'll take something pretty startling to put me off this toast," I said, and my hand went out to the salt.

"But seriously," he said. "I didn't get you here under false pretences, but I ought to tell you something first. After that you mayn't want any tea."

"Very well," I told him with an assumption of good humour. "Get it off your chest and then I'll get on with the toast."

"I doubt if you will," he said. "The fact is—well, I had an idea to-day that I'd seen you before. It was only when that cove spoke to you at Moroni's that I knew where. And when Peter Worrack tried to explain away why he'd called you Travers."

CHAPTER IV
AND LULU

I hope I didn't flush and I certainly did my best not to gape.

"This is all very mysterious," I said.

He ignored that feeble disclaimer. "I knew you were Ludovic Travers," he said. "Before I'd been in England a month I went to the Old Bailey to hear the Craigne trial and you were the principal witness for the prosecution. You hadn't a moustache in those days and, if you don't mind my saying so, you didn't look as fit, and that's what put me off."

"Well, I'm still eating your bread and salt," I said. "And it was the policeman in you that made you attend that trial?"

"Maybe," he said. "And because I knew Craigne. Once when I was on leave I helped finance one of his shows, and did remarkably well out of it. That was before he ran off the rails."

That gave me another, even if vague, insight into Hamson's mind, and I might say, his milieu. That Craigne circle had been the same racing and gambling kind: get-rich-quick schemers, effusive back-slappers and strident-voiced, aggressive women.

"A queer gang to be mixed up with," I said bluntly.

"Not much in my line," he told me quickly. "But Craigne himself wasn't such a bad chap—then." He paused. "Like me to go on?"

"No," I said dryly. "You say I'm Ludovic Travers. Well, what next?"

"I'd like to put a question to you," he said. "It was true what you told me about being in the Service?"

"Absolutely. And about being on leave."

"Then I'll tell you this," he said. "If you'd been anything like a friend of mine, or perhaps even an acquaintance, and I'd met you to-day, I'd have asked you to do me a personal favour. You mustn't mind my harping on it, but as an old policeman I've got an inquisitive mind. I can't help putting two and two together, so to speak, and getting worried when they don't add up to four."

"I'm the same way myself," I told him. "But what are this particular two and two, and what was the answer?"

"Perfectly frankly I'm worried about Georgina Morbent, Mrs. Grays' sister. And I'm rather of the opinion that Worrack has forestalled me."

I raised incredulous eyebrows.

"My dear Travers," he told me, and the smile was definitely cynical. "Surely that wasn't much of a deduction when I'd remembered who you were? He brings you along under an assumed name, and looks damned silly when that cove calls you by your right name. And he'd fixed it for you to meet Georgina's sister—the woman, by the way, to whom I'm hoping to be engaged—and myself."

"To save argument, let's admit it," I said, and reached for the last piece of that excellent toast. "But why should you be worried about Georgina Morbent? Up to to-day's lunch other people hadn't taken any action, to your knowledge, so why should you have wished, for instance, to have had someone like myself to whom to apply for private enquiries?"

"All common sense," he said. "Not that I'm trying to be rude. I saw Georgina Morbent before she left for Ireland —left ostensibly, that is—and I happen to know she didn't go there. I know it through Barbara Grays. It's a long story but I'll tell it briefly, like this. I have a key to Barbara's flat. I knew she'd suddenly got something on her mind and that evening—she hadn't come in and I was waiting for her—O'Clauty, Georgina's trainer, rang up and I took the message, which was to the effect that in answer to Barbara's telephoned enquiry, Georgina hadn't been to Ireland.

"And there's more to it than that," he went on. "I know Worrack's been worried. And I know this. Just before she left—again I say ostensibly—for Ireland, I asked her about an engagement we'd fixed up and she told me she'd certainly be back for it, and that'd be inside a week. She didn't like her present flat, to tell the truth, and was frightfully keen on getting another, which I had inside information about. It involved a third person whose time was valuable, and who was doing us both a favour. Yet she didn't drop me a line or ring up to say she couldn't make the appointment, and an appointment she wouldn't have missed for anything."

"All that seems pretty conclusive," I said. "But what am I to do about it? Assume you were correct about Worrack having approached me, we're still at a dead end. As an old policeman, you ought to know I can't admit the fact. All I'll say is that I couldn't accept any commission from you, and if I'd accepted one from Worrack—which I haven't—then I'd never dream of divulging what it was. So there we are."

"You called yourself Blunt, so I'll be blunt," he said. "I don't ask you to tell me about yourself and Worrack because I know I was right. You've told me so a dozen times over. It's one and one and the answer's two. All I'll add is, that I'm damn glad of it. I want to be told nothing and the last thing I want to do is to intrude. On the other hand, if there's anything whatever I can do—and when I say anything, I mean anything—then you've only to ask me to do it."

"Well, there seems no more to say," I told him. "Thank you for a most excellent tea and I'll be getting along. I shall be seeing you—"

"Just one other thing," he cut in. "Give me a chance to explain why I got you here. It's a damnably awkward thing to do, but it's got to be done. If anything *has* happened to Georgina—which God forbid!—then it affects my whole life. I'm not a poor man but I'm the hell of a way from being a rich one. If Barbara comes into Georgina's money, then I'm damned if I'm going to press her to marry me. That may sound quixotic, but it's my way of looking at things, and you can take it as final. What I should do is find some pretext and cut loose altogether."

"It's not for me to comment," I said, "though I see your point of view."

"Don't go yet," he told me quickly. "There's just one other question." He hesitated, and the question had a certain hesitation about it too. "What did you think about Barbara—Mrs. Grays—at lunch to-day?" I avoided his look and he went quickly on. "How did she strike you, as a complete stranger?"

"You tell me how she should have struck me," I countered.

"Damn your subtlety," he said with a humorous exasperation. "Still, I'll tell you this and I want you to believe it. She wasn't herself; in fact she was the devil of a long way off being herself. I didn't make any comment at lunch because I flatter myself I know how women should be handled."

"And what should she have been like?"

That facer didn't disturb him in the least, in fact he seemed grateful for it.

"She's a thoroughly good sort. Always very blunt, but not damnably rude and pettish like she was to-day. And all the bilge about making herself out to be a damn selfish woman. When the blitz was full on they tell me she did some pretty fine work and she had to be forced to throw her hand in when her nerve went.

She mixes with a pretty fast crowd, I'll admit that, but then so do I. She's always liked a flutter, and I do myself, so long as I can afford it."

"What you're trying to tell me is that she wasn't herself to-day, because she's worried about Georgina," I said.

"Perhaps it is," he said, and let out a breath. I had got to my feet and he rose too, and out went his hand. "Thanks a lot for coming round. I'm afraid I've been a bit tiresome."

"You don't know how much," I told him enigmatically. "I'll be seeing you to-night?'"

"At Worrack's place—yes, if you're really going."

"Oh, I'm going," I said airily. "I like a bit of a flutter too."

He gave me a quick look at that, I don't know why. Maybe he'd looked me up in *Who's Who*, for there was one in the little bookcase, and a *Debrett*, though no scheming of mine could ever land me inside those august covers. All he did do was to say he'd be seeing me then, and could I find my way down.

There was plenty of time before I was due at Worrack's flat, so I got on with a job I'd intended to do. In my time I've often employed private detective agencies, and I've made a habit of spreading my commissions round so as to have likely helpers in all sorts of places and in order not to place myself under too great an obligation to any particular firm. That afternoon I went to a firm in Broad Street, whom I had not employed for a good number of years. A chap called Ellice—Bill Ellice—ran it; he was still there, and he recognised me promptly enough. I knew I shouldn't have to put in a plea for snappy service. All the little firms go frantic at the likelihood of getting in well with the Yard, and I took care not to let him think the job was merely something of my own.

"Georgina Morbent," he said, when he'd written down particulars I'd given him. "Anything to do with the racing man who was killed in the blitz? A millionaire they said he was."

"His widow," I said, and I could see he was interested. Maybe he thought the charges could be accordingly.

"Well, she ought to be easy," he said, and took another good look at the photograph. "Things aren't too brisk at the moment, Mr. Travers, so I'll take over the job myself."

"Good for you, Bill," I said. "And when you pick up her trail, don't let go. Follow everything up till it's a dead end. Report when there's anything worth reporting and be as long-winded as you like."

I gave him the new address and telephone number, and when I left him there was still a half-hour before I was due at Worrack's place, so I strolled on for a bit before taking the Underground. Between six and seven, he'd said, and it was about ten past six when I neared his door. As my hand went out to knock, I heard voices, and that was strange, considering the fact that when I'd done my best to listen that very morning, not a definite word could I hear. Then I saw that the door was not quite shut, and in the same moment I knew that in that room something was going on that was remarkably like a first-class row.

"Do as you damn please!" That was Worrack and he seemed to be in a tidy temper. "You bloody little fool! You don't think you can try that kind of blackmail with me?"

"And you keep your language to yourself!" A woman's voice, furious to the point of hysterics, and quite unknown to me. "You're a nice one to talk about blackmail."

"Look here, Lulu, you'd better get out of here before I do something." Worrack's voice had become ominously calm. "Get out in any case. I'm expecting a caller."

"A caller. How nice for you. And what's her name?"

"Will you get to hell out of here?"

With one hand I held the knob of the door and with the knuckle of the other I rapped loudly. The voices ceased as by magic; there was a moment's silence and then Worrack was calling, "Come in!"

"Hallo, Blunt," he said. "Didn't expect you on the dot like this. Meet Miss Mawne—Lulu to you. Lulu, this is Blunt, but Ludo to you."

She was what is known as a stunning brunette. Just about the right height for a woman and the right shape in the right places. The cheeky black hat on her jet-black hair went well with the lipstick, and she was wearing a swagger-coat that was either mink or the next best thing. Her face was pretty flushed after that scrap with Worrack, but the smile she gave him was almost coy.

"You're pulling my leg. Isn't he, Mr. Blunt?"

"I get you," I said. "Lulu and Ludo."

"Sounds like something on the music hall," she said, and gurgled.

"There you are, Blunt," Worrack said. "If that isn't an invitation to team up, I've never heard one."

I was trying to look as if I was tickled to death at the mere idea. Worrack was going on. "Lulu's our secretary at the club. One of the originals."

"I haven't met you there, have I?" she asked me, and the smile was a first-class invitation.

"I've only just got back to England," I told her unblushingly. "Maybe if I'd known what I know now, I'd have got back before."

She didn't look as if she'd fallen for that. Maybe she'd heard it too often before.

"Run along now, Lulu," Worrack told her. "You and Blunt can get better acquainted later."

He gave her a large envelope which she stuck in an inside pocket of the swagger-coat.

"See you later, Ludo?" she told me with a smile that was flattering enough to a man of my age. Then: "Cheerio, Peter!" and off she went.

I closed the door behind her but Worrack was suddenly there too. He opened the door again, stuck his head out, and listened. Half a minute went by before he closed the door.

"Well, what did you think of her?" he said as he waved me to my chair. Then he noticed the two glasses. He and Lulu had had a sherry, he said, and what about one for me? I said I would, if he'd have another.

"Well, here's how," he said, and nodded to me over his glass. "And may we never combine business and pleasure."

I took it that cryptic reference was to Lulu.

"A smart-looking wench," I said. "The club secretary, did you say?"

He'd said that because Lulu liked the title, he told me.

What she was, was a kind of secretary, spare croupier, and general receptionist. She typed the invitations, among other things, and brought them along every afternoon to be signed by him.

"You remember the old song?" he said. "The lass who

When she left the village she was shy . . . ."

I popped in with the rest.

But alas and alack
She came back
With a naughty little twinkle in her eye.

"That's it," he said. "And that's Lulu. Believe me or not, the product of a country vicarage."

"Well, the twinkle was there all right," I said. "But she doesn't seem to have gone back."

"Lulu's all right," he said. "You wouldn't think it, but she puts in three solid hours every day working in a canteen. The vicarage conscience, perhaps."

"She didn't buy that coat out of what you pay her," I told him.

"We pay pretty well," he said, and then grinned. "What she makes on her own is no concern of mine. Live and let live, that's the motto."

"What was that crack of yours about business and pleasure?"

"That?" He shrugged his shoulders. "We all have our indiscretions."

"Jealous of Georgina, was she?"

There I was, theorising again. The question had popped out and I wished I hadn't put it quite like that. He gave a grunt and smiled a bit cynically.

"Jealous as hell." He was quiet for a moment or two and was giving a solemn shake or two of the head.

"Funny how women find things out," he said. "I'd have bet that nobody had an idea that Georgie and I were . . . well, more than just acquainted, but she found out. Still, there we are." He smiled. "And let it be a lesson to you. Another spot of sherry?"

I said I'd rather not, and we got down to business.

First, I told him how plain it was that Georgina had intended all the time to go as far as Rugby, to throw everybody well off the scent, and then hurry back to town by that convenient train. I also said that I had a man on the job and we ought to know something of her movements within twenty-four hours.

"Your man can be trusted?" he asked me quickly.

"Absolutely," I said, and then began to tell him all that had been discussed between me and Hamson. He listened with an attention that could only be called strained.

"There you are," I said. "You told me he was a spry bird, and, by God! he was. A damn sight too spry for me. Some of the best deduction I've heard for years. When I tried to put him off, I felt all the time that I was simply telling him a whole lot more."

"All to the good," he said. "Don't tell him exactly what we're up to, but leave him thinking he was right." Then he was frowning away again. "What job can you find him?"

"That's for you to suggest," I told him, and just a bit frigidly. "The only assistance I might want is the kind that man of mine's doing at this moment. Hamson couldn't do that sort of thing. If anything fishy has happened, then everybody likely to be concerned knows him. He might perhaps be used for getting information out of people. They might talk to him thinking they were just passing on gossip."

I said that because I wanted him to mention again what he'd said originally, about using Hamson to spy on Barbara Grays. And the funny thing was that he made no response to that deliberate opening, though it must have been in his mind, for he began referring to her at once.

"What was his idea in telling you that Barbara was all different at lunch to-day?"

"Lord knows," I said. "Wasn't she?"

"Well, she's always a bit aggressive," he said. "A bit touchier to-day, perhaps. I admit she didn't show much of her bright side, but you know what women are. By the way, how does Hamson strike you personally?"

"I don't know," I said. "Somehow I feel I'm not supposed to like him, and yet I do. Or it may be merely respect for his intelligence. And his directness."

That side of the conversation had an air of petering out, so I pulled out my notebook and said I had a question or two to ask. For instance, why hadn't Barbara seen her sister off at Euston?

"Why should she?" he asked, and with a curious belligerence.

"Well," I said, and grinned feebly. "I just wondered why, that's all."

"Did you make a point of seeing your sisters off at the station?" he said, and then apparently realised he was being a bit abrupt. "What I mean is, that Georgina's trip wasn't any big affair. It was a casual trip to Ireland such as she'd taken before. Besides, Barbara knew I was seeing Georgie off. Just to help generally, that's all."

"I get you," I said. "But just a question arising out of that. You were pretty close to Georgina. Didn't you expect her to report her safe arrival to you, especially after what she'd said about the thirteenth and all that?"

"She said that just as the train was on the move," he said, "and I didn't have time to answer. Also, we weren't the demonstrative kind. I expected her back in under a week, and I knew she'd write only if she felt like it." He had been hoisting himself from the chair and now he was making his way to the window and fiddling with the blackout curtains.

"Do you mind if we drop this for a bit?" he said, and his voice was suddenly tired. "There's just so much I can stand at a time."

"Sorry," I said, and got to my feet. "Maybe we can have a few words later to-night."

"No, no, no," he told me quickly. "Damn silly of me. You ask me those other questions you've got in that book."

"They're not going to be too easy either," I warned him. "For instance, where does Mrs. Morbent live?"

"She had a flat in Creevy Street."

"Have you got a key?"

He didn't bridle up as I'd expected at the implications in that question.

"As a matter of fact, I have," he said.

"And have you been round there since she's been away?"

He hesitated, but only for a moment. "Once," he said. "Two days before I wrote to you."

"Notice anything different?"

He shook his head. "There wasn't anything to notice. It's a furnished flat, with just her extra personal possessions."

"What about private papers?"

"Those are in her desk," he said. "That's locked and I haven't a key to that."

"Feel like going round there now? If you've got time?"

Again he hesitated a moment, then he said that he'd rather dreaded going there again, but if I went too it might be different. It was only a five-minute walk.

On the way I told him what I'd like to find. A bank pass-book, for instance, and cheque counterfoils, and the chance of tracing any payments which might look like blackmail.

"Where did she actually bank?" I asked.

"Barclay's in Maynard Street," he said.

"If nothing turns up at the flat, would you feel like seeing the manager?" I asked him. "You could make it frightfully confidential."

He said he didn't like the idea but he'd think it over. Then I asked about a maid. What did he mean by saying that she'd taken no maid with her to Ireland? He said he'd mentioned it because I might have thought a moneyed woman like her would have been expected to have a maid. She did have one, in fact, when her husband was alive.

It seemed a long five minutes and I told him we ought to have taken a taxi on account of his game leg. He said he liked walking. It got him used to the leg and he was hoping it wouldn't be long before no one noticed he had a game leg at all. In any case we were there, he said, and stopped before the porch of what looked like the real old-fashioned type of town house, area, basement, and all. It had been made into four flats, he told me, and Georgina's was the best of the bunch and on the ground floor.

"No service meals, then?" I asked as he turned the key in the Yale lock and drew back for me to go in.

"That's why she thought of leaving it," he told me. "I believe Hamson had rather a good place in mind."

I thought of a question I'd have liked to ask but kept it to myself instead, and had a good look round the room.

"This is a superb room," I said. "Are the others like it?"

There was a smaller sitting-room, a really fine bedroom a second smaller one, and a kitchenette. In the basement, he told me, there were a married couple who did housework for the four flats but only very occasional cooking. I ventured to guess the rent as three-fifty, and he told me I was fifty shy.

Back in the drawing-room, as it was called—I'd have called it a lounge—I ran my eye over the bureau.

"Mind if I open it?" I said.

He looked surprised at that and even more so when I manipulated my piece of wire and drew the lid down. As I had tight-fitting leather gloves on I did the searching of the drawers.

Inside half an hour the bureau had been gone through with a small-toothed comb. We found correspondence from O'Clauty, and copies of her letters to him, and notes from the brokers about investments, and every kind of oddment, but never a cheque book with counterfoils that might be of any use to us. The last one of all ended towards the middle of January.

"That proves nothing," I said. "The blackmail payments might only have just begun. Or they needn't have begun at all. It's the first blackmailing demand that's always the greatest shock. Maybe she'd refused to pay and that's why he—or she—made her go for an interview, just to get her into line." Then I gave him a shrewd look. "I suppose, by the way, that she couldn't have been protecting *you*?"

"Who should want to blackmail me?" he said.

I shrugged my shoulders. It wasn't for me to say that I'd overheard Lulu talking about blackmail.

"What's worrying you?" he said.

I suppose my face had looked rather worried, for I'd been suddenly wondering if it had been Lulu who had listened behind that door at Worrack's flat that morning, and if so, where could I fit her in.

"Nothing's worrying me," I said. "All the same I'd very much like to know what money she had with her when she left for Ireland. Sure you won't see her bank manager?"

He said perhaps he would.

"Just hint as to how you're worried about her," I said, "and say you're on the point of going to the police. After all, it isn't a lot for him to reveal."

But he wouldn't commit himself to anything further, so I closed the bureau again. At least I shut the lid, for when I tried to manipulate the lock it was beyond me. But I didn't tell him I'd learned only half of the trick and I left him to think it was locked.

"There's only one vital question for us to ask ourselves," I said, as we had a last look round. "Did she come back here at all after she left here that morning? You say that nothing's been tampered with, so the answer's that wherever she did go, it wasn't to here."

A cruising taxi passed us as we came out to the street again, and I hailed it for Worrack.

"Thanks a lot," he said. "And for all you're doing. And about to-night. Make it just before nine if you can."

I said my time was my own and I'd be there at a quarter to. On my way back to my flat I was thinking of that little group of people, so like in tastes and so different in themselves, and all living within walking distance of each other, with Worrack's club the centre of the crude circle. Then I wondered about Lulu Mawne, and whether she hung out in the same neighbourhood too, and whether it was Worrack who had given her that swagger-coat.

When I got to my room I had a final clean up for the night and then rang down for a service dinner. The sight of my wireless set started me off thinking again. For the first time in a good few weeks I'd spent a day without caring two hoots about the news. Montgomery was hard on Rommel's heels, and the Russians were doing wonderful things, but as far as I was concerned there needn't have been a war on at all. But I didn't see things that way with any personal reflection on myself. After all, I'd had a busy day. But there was Worrack, who hadn't said to me when Lulu had gone, "Damn the woman! She's made us lose the six o'clock news." Had Hamson listened to the news, I wondered, and I knew for a certainty that neither Barbara Grays nor Lulu Mawne had cared a couple of hoots between them. And, as I remembered, at lunch that day not one of the three had so much as mentioned the war, as a war.

There was something, I told myself, that I had to get into my mind as part of the background of the circle with whom I would be in contact. If, of course, I undertook the case. And that, I could tell myself again, was what I had no intention of doing. It was true I had set certain enquiries in motion, but that could hardly count. And I was going to that club of Worrack's which again might come under the heading of exploration. Then I was remembering Lulu again and trying to analyse that smile she'd given me. And I was wondering something else—if that scent of hers that afternoon had been the same as I'd caught that morning.

CHAPTER V
CALL IT A DAY

As I MADE my way towards 72, Harcourt Gardens, I was wondering how Worrack's patrons—guests, if you like—would find their way home in the early hours, with petrol restrictions what they were. But that, I thought, was their headache, and doubtless there were still ways and means. I found the job of getting there bad enough in the black-out, and in spite of the fact that Worrack had given me a detailed route for the very brief walk. However, I didn't have much trouble after I'd passed the Ardrey Hotel.

There were three entrances, Worrack had told me, and use of them was timed for the sake of economy in staff. Till ten o'clock the front door, till eleven the side door, and after that the entrance through a Car Hire and Service Garage that somehow tunnelled a way under the house at the back. That business had also been owned by Georgina Morbent.

I went up four steps to the front door and very little could I see of what the house looked like, except that I judged that at one time it had been, and might still be, in a first-class residential area. But I didn't look about me long, and hardly had the bell finished ringing than the door was opened.

"Who is it, please?" a man's voice said.

"Blunt," I said.

The voice had an immediate heartiness. "Come in, Mr. Blunt. Mind the screen. That's right, sir. This way."

The door closed behind me and the unknown appeared from behind the black-out screen. He was a tallish chap, wearing a dark lounge suit. His nose was slightly snub, and he was clean-shaven, and as his voice had had some Cockney quality, there were more unlikely things, I thought, than that he was an ex-petty-officer.

"I'm Taplay, sir. George Taplay," he said. "Got your invitation with you?" Then he was grinning. "Sorry, sir. I forgot you were a friend of the guvnor's. This way, sir."

"Not very mysterious so far," I said. "No secret panels and no high-signs."

"Lord bless you, no, sir," he said. "This is a private house."

He didn't even wink. He did wave round the entrance hall from which the stairs led.

"Hamm Junction, they call this, sir. Here's where everybody comes to through any of the doors."

"Who gave it that name?" I asked, as I followed him up the carpeted stairs.

"One of the Air Officers," he said, and grinned again. "We get lots of officers here, sir."

On the spacious landing at the head of the stairs he gave me some more bearings.

"That's the cloak-room for men, sir, and the men's room. No charge, sir. Everything's inclusive. Just along there is the ladies' room."

I hung up my coat and hat, gave my hair a perfunctory smooth in the mirror, and then was ready for him again.

"Through here, sir," he said, and opened a door and ushered me through.

It was a very large room indeed; two rooms, I should say, made into one, and a quick calculation of the size said forty foot by thirty. Covering the floor, except for a four-foot surround of unstained and polished wood, was a superb carpet. Almost in the middle of the room, though just to the right as I entered, was the usual long table and the apparatus for roulette. A card table and five chairs were in the near corner, and along the far wall were small tables and one larger one set out as if in a restaurant. In the far left corner was a small bar where a foreign-looking cove in a white jacket was polishing glasses.

"Soft lights, but no sweet music," I said.

"That's right, sir," George said. "No music here and no dancing. Just a little friendly game and everything nice and comfy." His finger was pointing. "That's the guvnor's room, sir."

The door was in the far right-hand corner, and as I looked it opened, and Lulu came out. Maybe she flounced out, for her face looked a bit set. Perhaps the scrap had gone on from where I'd interrupted it that evening. But she'd had time to get into a really taking gown of scarlet and black, well-cut but not too revealing. She didn't look round, but went straight across the room and out by a door near the bar. George nodded back to me and I followed him. A quick tap at the door and his head was inside.

"Mr. Blunt, sir."

"Good," came Worrack's voice, and George was ushering me in.

"Glad you're early," Worrack told me. "Take a pew. And what about a drink?"

I said it was too early, and I might have to take a cargo aboard. I was having a quick look round the room. It was about twelve foot by twenty, at least as far as the curtain which seemed to be shutting some of it off. Its air was that of an office which had been long used and had become remarkably snug. The big desk looked somehow homely, and the two easy-chairs, and the swivel chair on which Worrack sat had an old red cushion.

"How long have you been here?" I asked.

"About a year," he said. "And three months in our old home."

Then he began telling me the lines on which the show was run. The invitations I knew about, but I didn't know that every guest paid two quid a night, which, as George had hinted, included all drinks and refreshments. A man could drink as much as he liked provided he could carry his liquor. At midnight games closed down for a friendly drink and snack, and Worrack said that was always insisted on. It brought people together and made an excellent break. The whole show closed down at three o'clock prompt. Roulette was the main game, but poker was popular, and for that players paid five bob each for cards. No high stakes were permitted, and no play at all without the club counters, and those could be purchased only to a limit of twenty pounds per guest.

"That's an innovation of only three months," he said. "We had practically no limit up till then, and allowed IOU's where we thought we could rely on the signature. Then I found things were getting a bit out of hand, so I had a quiet word with some of the people I could trust, and we hit on the present system. I must say it works well."

"Strict cash and no bad debts."

"Only one or two," he said. "As a matter of fact, there're exactly three bad debts. Two were from officers; poor devils who got scuppered before they'd settled up. Those I don't count. They're wiped out. Then there's Mouldy—Lewton-Molde—who still owes a matter of five hundred." His lip drooped. "He's *not* being wiped out."

"Haven't you got to trust a large number of people?" I said. "What I mean is, if you were raided, that invitation stunt wouldn't get you clear."

"It might help," he said. "And nobody can claim we aren't well conducted. Nobody gets ruined here." He smiled amusedly as he said that.

"And of course there's the application of a little judicious baksheesh?"

"But not so that you'd notice it," he said, and gave that same amused grin. "Also the clientele is carefully chosen. A stranger can only get in on the recommendation of someone already known."

"And the staff? You can trust them?"

"I think so," he said, and then was frowning slightly. "Lulu's been a bit restive lately. George—you've met him—is a topper. Jean's all right. He's the drinks wallah. And, by the way, we've got this."

He had swung himself to his feet and was making for the curtain. When it was drawn back I saw what looked like a smaller office. There was a closet and a wash-basin, and a huge safe. There was also a door, and it wasn't locked, for Worrack simply turned the knob and it opened.

"Private exit in case of a raid," he said. "But only about half the company would use it. The rest would stay on and support the idea of a private party."

"Where's this door lead to? The garage?"

"Lord, no," he said, and grinned. "The police'd probably follow it down to the garage where there might be some sort of cordon waiting. Those in the know would find themselves in the next house to this. That's ours too. It's been made into a couple of high-class flats. George and his missus occupy one, and Lulu the other."

When we were back in the main office he asked me if anything had happened since we'd parted. I told him it was no use being impatient, but as he'd changed to that anxious mood of his I thought I might as well ask him one or two questions.

"About Hamson," I said. "How long have you actually known him?"

"About six months," he said. "Why?"

"How long have you been what I might call really pally?" He frowned in thought. "Probably about six weeks."

"You needn't answer the next one if you don't feel like it," I said, "but did he ever make any kind of a set at Mrs. Morbent?"

"Good Lord, no!" he said. "They were just friendly, the same as everybody here is friendly."

"And when did he show that he was smitten with Mrs. Grays?"

"Ah, that," he said, and frowned again. "That'd be hard to say. You know how things are. You get friendly with people, you lunch and dine together and go places, and the next thing you hear is that they're engaged."

"I see," I said. "They just sort of slipped into everything. But they aren't engaged, though he'd like to be. Any chance of her taking him?"

"Ask me another," he said. "I've known Barbara since I was that high, but I don't know that."

A buzzer went suddenly and startled me. He grinned as his hand went to the receiver.

"No panic. It isn't a raid. Though we have a system through the garage."

I could hear a faint voice but no words. Worrack gave a couple of nods and then said someone was to be shown in.

"Mouldy wants to see me," he said, and his eyes narrowed. "You'd better pop behind there."

I nipped behind the curtains and put my handkerchief over my mouth in case of a sneeze. In half a minute I heard Worrack's, "Come in!"

"Hallo, Moldy?" he said mildly. "How are things with you?"

Ever so gently and with one finger I drew the edge of the curtain aside. Lewton-Molde was standing sideways to me, but I had a good look at him before letting the curtain slide back again. He was a good-looking chap, about six foot, and thin. His chin was the weak link in his face, and the one eye I saw had a baggy look. His voice had an irritating quality of preciousness, with a's made into e's.

"Not too bad," he said.

"Well, take a pew and tell me about it," Worrack said.

"There's nothing to say—really. . . . I thought I'd bring you this."

I heard the faint rustle of paper and guessed he was handing over a cheque.

"Thanks, Moldy," Worrack said quietly. "Two hundred and fifty." A slight pause. "I suppose it's good?"

"What the hell are you getting at?"

I dared not touch that curtain again, but my mind's eye saw the shrug of Worrack's shoulders.

"Well, things do happen," Worrack told him evenly, and it must have been some pertinent reference for Molde said no more. Then again there was the rustle of paper.

"A balance of two-fifty," Worrack said. "And now—"

"My God, Worrack, what a bloody money-grubber you are!"

"Am I?" Worrack told him, and with what I thought an ominous quiet. "But you didn't let me finish, my dear Moldy. What I was going to say was, that I'm not pressing for payment of the balance."

"You're cancelling it?"

"Well, that's what it sounded like to me."

"I say, that's damn good of you."

"Maybe," said Worrack. "Here's the IOU for the two-fifty, and God help you if the cheque isn't O.K."

Molde took that without a murmur. A moment's quiet and then his voice came with a tentative wariness.

"You're giving me the other IOU's?"

"Oh, no," Worrack told him. "But I'm not pressing for payment. I'm just holding them as a guarantee of good conduct."

"What the hell do you mean?"

"What I say," Worrack told him evenly. "I just don't trust you, Moldy. You hate me like hell, because I've made you pay and I didn't let you wriggle out of it. If you could do me a dirty trick, you would. Only, if I were you, I wouldn't! Any trouble here of your making, and you bet your ruddy life I'd find out, and I carry out my original threat. I take these IOU's to your father?"

"My God, what a swine you are!"

"Another crack like that," Worrack told him, "and I'll take them personally to-morrow."

I could hear him getting to his feet, and there had been such a fierceness in his tone that I risked the moving curtain. But his back was towards Molde and all I saw was his hand push back a drawer of the desk into which he had doubtless slipped those IOU's. I let the curtain fall again.

"Think it over," Worrack told him calmly. "You'll come to see that you're getting a damn square deal."

I heard Molde moving towards the door, and then his voice came rather suddenly, perhaps because of the abruptness of the question.

"Any news about Georgie?"

"News?" asked Worrack quietly.

"Well, people are beginning to wonder," Molde said. "What do you mean?"

"Well, she said she'd be away a week and nobody's heard a word about her. And there was that business I told you about."

"Quite a little mystery you've been concocting," Worrack told him, and his voice had a dangerous sound. "You've been opening that mouth of yours a bit too far."

"God's my witness—"

"Shut up!" A moment and the voice was almost normal again. "What the hell's Georgie to do with you, in any case? Her business is her own. And neither yours nor mine. And remember this. If I get wind that you're doing any more chattering, I'll reconsider those IOU's. And now get to hell out of here."

The door closed. I peeped out.

"It's all right," Worrack said. "I think I've got his mouth shut."

"He sounded a nasty piece of work," I said.

"Yes," Worrack said. "Did you notice that little bit of blackmail he was trying? Give him the IOU's and he wouldn't say what he knew about Georgie."

"He sounded to me as if he'd do the hell of a lot of mischief if he only had the pluck."

"He's got the pluck all right," Worrack said. "Outside this room, I mean. That's why I want you to get a move on. The only way to counter a swine like him is to show him the truth."

"Was he, by any chance, a particular friend of Mrs. Morbent?" I asked.

"She rather liked him," he said. "God knows why. Women have these queer sort of pets."

The buzzer went again. Worrack nodded into the receiver and hung up with a curt O.K.

"The show's starting," he said. "We might as well go in. Any counters you buy, by the way, are dummies."

"The hell they are," I said. "A small flutter's just up my alley."

"Have it your own way," he said, and grinned as he opened the door. "And if you want to pop in here during the night—just do. You'll find a drink in that cupboard."

Most of what happened that night is of no concern to this story, but a few things are definitely relevant. There were about a dozen people in the main room when we came in, most of them standing round the bar. Worrack seemed very popular, though I saw at once that his policy was to keep himself just a bit aloof. To be the avuncular and presiding genius was his role, and he played it unobtrusively. Nobody came in after eleven o'clock. Hamson was there, and he seemed very pally with, of all people, Lewton-Molde, for they were hobnobbing in a corner over a couple of drinks. Barbara Grays was there, and I must say she greeted me in the most friendly fashion. If I had not known her I should have described her geniality as very near the flirtatious, though maybe it was all due to the friendly atmosphere of the whole room.

For Worrack had not exaggerated when he had emphasised that side of his club. I saw no haggard faces, clutching hands, or spasms of despair, which the moral tales of one's youth impress on one as the dreadful accompaniments of the gambling vice. I saw only one person who seemed rather concerned when things went wrong, and she was Molde's girl—the one who had been with him that afternoon at Euston. She was a platinum blonde, neatly gowned and with a face something like Garbo's, though the last one in the world to wish to be alone. When I had a word with Hamson about her, he said her name was Scylla Payton, and except that he thought she had money, that was all he knew. He also said that, as I'd probably noticed, she had plenty of IT. I gave a hypocritical heigh-ho, and said that sort of thing had long ceased to worry me. One thing I did notice about her, by the way, was that she had spatulate finger-tips, and rather ugly I thought they were. She must have thought so too, for her nails were unvarnished. Lulu's—she was croupière for the first hour and a remarkably efficient one too—were an intense purple that clashed, to my eye, with the scarlet gown.

Generally, the crowd might have been called mixed, but there was never a soul that hadn't a moneyed look. Some of them, one could gather, regarded the chips as peanuts, and there was plenty of ragging of the earnest ones who had come provided with systems. Service men were there, but in mufti, and the soul of the party was a naval commander —hailed as Tubby—who was just back from six months at sea. It was Tubby who deftly flicked a cigarette lighter at the bottom of an evening paper which one fat and prosperous, but very genial, gentleman was reading, and when it went up in flames there was tremendous applause. Tubby had a girl with him, and she wasn't his daughter.

Usually about twenty people were there, and Worrack had hoped to make up for me a poker four or five, but as things were, we all played the roulette table. I pottered around on the red and black, and my extemporised system went so badly that even Lulu's smile had a sympathy in it. Occasionally someone would look round and call for a drink, and Jean would give a *"Bien, m'sieu"* and be over with it. Which brings me to my thrill of the evening.

Since my system was a simple one, I had leisure enough to study my fellow-gamblers. Hamson, Barbara Grays, and Molde and his girl were the ones who particularly interested me, and it was about Molde that I became aware of something peculiar. He suddenly grew anxious about something in the neighbourhood of the bar, and every now and again would give a quick look round. Then, without having received any order, Jean was bringing him a drink.

"Your veesky, m'sieu."

"Thanks," he said curtly. Then I saw his eyes lift towards Scylla, who was facing him across the table. A moment or two and she rose.

Now there was nothing peculiar about her leaving the room. People were always getting up and disappearing, and Tubby had informed me in an audible whisper that a visit to the summer-house was the surest means of changing one's luck. He himself was winning and he wasn't going to stir, he told me *sotto voce*, even if his bladder was like a Zeppelin.

I got up and strolled over to the bar.

"A drink, m'sieu?" Jean asked me.

"A small whisky and soda," I said, and had a good look at him at close quarters. He was over fifty, flat-skulled and with a florid, upward-sweeping moustache that made him the very spit of the boulevardier of stage or screen.

His eyes were decidedly shifty.

"What's your part of France?" I asked as I took the drink.

He shrugged his shoulders.

"Me, m'sieu? I am what you call ceetizen of ze vorld."

"The devil you are!" I said amusedly, and finished the drink at a go. "We must get together some time."

I gave him a friendly nod and turned back to the table. Then I changed my mind, for I was suddenly feeling a bit sticky and a wash, I thought, might brighten me up. I remember I did look round as my hand went out to the knob of Worrack's door, perhaps because I'd instinctively wondered what people would think if they saw me making free use of the office. But all eyes seemed to be concentrated on the revolving wheel, and even Jean happened to have his back to me.

Inside the room I gave a gasp, and the gape of my mouth must have made me look a first-class idiot. Scylla Payton was at Worrack's desk, and I'd disturbed her in the act of going through the drawers. So intent was she on the job, I'd slipped between her and the door before she really saw me. And was she startled?

"Lost something?" I asked amiably.

She had whipped the top back and was standing with hands on it, and behind her, eyes tense and glaring. I was still smiling pleasantly, and then her hand went suddenly out to the switch and the room was in darkness. Before I knew it her arms were round my neck and her lips were on mine.

She held me so tightly that even if I had wished to disturb that moment, I should have had to wrest her away by force. Then at last that kiss ended. The lips moved upwards towards my ear.

"You won't say a word?"

"Devil a word," I said.

She kissed me again, an even more luscious effort that time, and then she had gone, and I heard the rustle of the curtain before her. A moment or two and I turned on the light. In the mirror above the wash-basin behind the curtain I saw with sudden horror the lipstick on my lips and cheek. When I'd washed it off I looked round and found that the lights in office and curtained annexe were operated by a two-way switch.

I didn't feel like going back for a minute or two, and just when I was really going, Worrack came in.

"Hallo," he said. "Had a drink?"

"Came in for a clean up," I said.

He opened the door again, had a quick look out, then took out a key and locked it.

"I just had a word with Hamson outside," he said quietly. "I think he was on the look-out for me. What do you think he asked me? Did Molde owe me any money!"

"You mean he shouldn't have known?"

"Not that," he said. "I gather that's fairly common property. But wait for what's coming. I said I thought everyone knew it, and he asked if Molde had paid up. I said he had, more or less, and to-night. Then he was a bit persistent. Apologised and all that, of course. What did I mean by more or less. I said he was to keep it to himself but he'd coughed up two-fifty, and the balance was probably being cancelled. I thought he made a bit of a wry face. And that's all."

"I get you," I said. "You think Molde touched Hamson for the money and got the whole five hundred. Molde paid you two-fifty and now pockets the rest. He's playing with some of it to-night."

"That's what it looks like," he said. "But why should Hamson lend Molde money? Molde stinks."

All I could say was that the situation was interesting and I'd do my damnedest to look into it.

"Did you know the outer door was open?" I said. "I tried it when I was in there."

"It's left open," he said. "George and Lulu might want to use it to slip along to their flats."

Then he said he saw what I was driving at. But there was no need to worry about an unexpected raid that way through the garage. George's brother was the manager and the warning system was highly efficient.

"But why shouldn't Molde have slipped up that way?" I pointed out. "He saw you put the IOU's in a drawer, and your desk isn't locked."

He didn't notice that slip; he was too amused.

"So you were peeping, were you?" He chuckled. "But I didn't put them in the drawer. I put them in this breast pocket and Molde saw me do it. What I put in the drawer was a paper fastener and Molde saw me do that. If you want to know where the IOU's are, they're in the safe." That was a facer, but he didn't know that.

"You can really scare Molde with them?" was what I asked.

He shrugged his shoulders. "The old man's on his last legs, they say, but he'd certainly cut him off with a shilling." He shook his head. "And yet I don't know. Molde's more than I can sum up. There's a look about him sometimes that makes me positively scared. I shouldn't laugh," he added as he saw my look of amusement. "His reputation's about as unsavoury as I know. It's only the snobs who put up with him. I let him come here because I wanted my money back. And he does attract a certain kind of customer."

I went out then and he followed in a minute or two. Nobody seemed to have noticed my absence, perhaps because it was near midnight and the quarter of an hour break. That was quite a jolly affair. Jean had already laid the tables, and was bringing sandwiches and snacks, and Lulu and George helped him with the drinks. People settled themselves haphazardly at the small tables, and the talk was largely the luck of the night. Tubby spun a questionable yarn that was received with shrieks of mirth. Worrack was there, at what might be called the high table, and Lulu and George joined him as soon as Jean could cope with all the drinks. It seemed to be considered a kind of honour to be asked to that table, for Tubby went over with alacrity when Worrack called him. I didn't hear any of their conversation, except the opening gambit, which was when Tubby said, "How's the game leg?" I was at Molde's table, of all places, making small talk and being most attentive to his girl. Then Barbara Grays called me over to hers. The fat genial gentleman had just given her a Stock Exchange tip and she wanted to ask me what I thought of it. Perhaps I was pleasantly excited by the drinks I'd had, but I didn't see the significance of that till far too late.

The game was resumed, and I must say I was surprised when three o'clock came so soon. Then there were hilarious partings after the settling up, and Lulu was taking notes of those who were turning up the following night and of any guests they proposed to bring. At half-past three only Worrack and I were left, and he had nothing to do but switch off. We parted at the front door, for our homeward ways were divergent.

As I strolled along in the light of the young moon I recalled his question as to what I had thought of things.

I had been right, I thought, to say it had been a damn good evening. So it had been, though I had lost a couple of quid's worth of chips and had insisted on standing them. Perhaps the drinks inside me made me so tolerant and made me put myself in the place of the rest of us who had tempted chance. After all, I said, when one goes to the races and bets quite unrestrained by law, the preliminaries cost the same couple of quid that Worrack charged, and with no drinks and supper thrown in. As for his two hundred a week profit, it didn't seem excessive to me considering Georgina's original outlay and the number of guests over whom the profits were spread.

But that night I couldn't do any serious thinking. As soon as I got into bed I did wonder what Bill Ellice might have discovered, and then when the bed was pleasantly warm I began thinking of the amorous Scylla. If it wasn't the IOU's she was looking for in Worrack's desk, then what in blazes was it? And where did the shifty-looking Jean come in? Then just when I began thinking of that minute or two of darkness in Worrack's office, I had some bad luck for I went off to sleep.

CHAPTER VI
OUT GOES HE

THERE WAS a telephone extension by my bedside and it was the shrilling of the bell that woke me. I stirred, became aware of what the noise was, hooked on my glasses, grabbed the receiver and glanced at my wrist-watch, and all practically in the same moment. I thought it was midday, but it was only eight in the morning.

"Hallo?" I said sleepily.

"That you, Mr. Travers?"

"That you, Bill?"

"Ellice speaking," he told me formally. "I've got some news for you, sir, but I'd rather you heard it direct."

"Where're you speaking from?"

"The office," he said.

"Right-ho," I said, "but give me a quick outline."

"Well, I got on the trail at once," he said. "Had a bit of luck and found the taxi-driver. It was that red hair that did it. He drove her to Richmond."

"Richmond!"

"That's right, sir. The White Rose Hotel, and she'd booked a room beforehand. She stayed the night, and paid for another night, though she knew she was leaving before that night, so to speak."

"Let's get it straight," I said. "She arrived on the 13th and slept there the night of the 13th. She left the next day. Where to and when?"

"I know when but not where," he said. "A car—a private one I should think—came for her just after dark. About six o'clock. I'd like to go into it all with you, sir, then I'll know what lines you want me to work on."

"Right-ho," I said. "I'll be with you in an hour. That do?"

I hopped out of bed, rang for a service breakfast, had a shower and dressed. To my joy I hadn't the trace of a hangover, maybe because I'd tried the old Army dodge of taking a Number Nine or its equivalent before setting out for Worrack's place. That was pretty good, considering the atmosphere of that room and the usual circle of smoke, dry throat, drink, and then more smoke.

As a matter of fact my mind was unusually clear as I ate my meal and reviewed that little matter of Molde and Scylla. What I was utterly flummoxed over was what she had been looking for in Worrack's desk, for the rest seemed easy enough.

It explained something that had very much puzzled me. I had heard Worrack tell Molde to get to hell out of the office, and he'd made no bones about showing what his opinion of Molde was. That was why I had been surprised to see Molde having a chat with Hamson, and looking afterwards quite at home at the roulette table, and not turning a hair in the presence of Worrack. Surely, I'd thought, he must have the devil of a thick skin to hang on after what Worrack told him. What he should have said was: "Get to hell, eh? All right. So I will. And you'll never see me in your ruddy club again."

Now I knew why Molde had swallowed all that Worrack had had to tell him. There was something in the possession of Worrack—and not the IOU's—that he most desperately needed, and he and the wench had come prepared to get it. Jean had been nobbled. He had given the high sign that Worrack was out of the office for a safe time by bringing the unasked-for drink, and Scylla had done the rest. As for my easy promise to look into the matter—though not the matter that Worrack thought—well, I stood about as much chance of finding out what Scylla was looking for as I did of being made Chief of Hitler's staff. I couldn't even make a flank attack through Jean, for it was a certainty that the reasons that had been given him were far from the real ones.

If—and why—Hamson had lent Molde that pretty hefty sum of money was something else I could not yet begin to work out, nor, strangely enough for me, could I hit on a theory. Then I suddenly realised something else. It was still less than twenty-four hours since the whole thing had started. Twenty-four hours, and it seemed already like days. But that day, I tried to assure myself, would see the last of my efforts. A loose end or two might be tied—hearing what Ellice had to report, for instance—and then I could tell Worrack with a perfectly good conscience that the case was regrettably of a kind which I did not feel myself competent to handle.

The taxi got me to Broad Street well on time, and Ellice was waiting for me.

"Good work, Bill—so far," I said. "But what's holding you up? Not being able to trace the car that called for her?"

He said he'd like to tell me the whole story, which wouldn't take five minutes. It didn't. At the Richmond hotel he'd made discreet enquiries on the plea that the lady was urgently wanted back in town. Luckily he mentioned no names and so was in no quandary when he found out she'd registered under the name of Mrs. Graves. The room had been booked by telephone two days previously.

She slept at the hotel that night, as he'd told me, and then the next morning she had a visitor. When the desk clerk said, "What name, sir?" this caller said she'd know. He was a man slightly below normal height, and sparely built, and he spoke with what the clerk described as an Irish accent. Mrs. Graves had a small suite consisting of sitting-room, bedroom, and bathroom, and the caller spent a good hour with her and left about an hour before lunch.

Mrs. Graves had all her meals in her room, and she rang down to the office to say she'd be leaving that evening soon after dark; a private car, of which she was to be warned when it arrived, would be calling for her. That car duly drew up. The hall porter went out at the tooting of the horn, and a voice said that it was the car for Mrs. Graves. The voice was foreign in quality, and that was all that could be said about it. The trunk, which had been brought down in readiness, was put in the back of the car, which was a black or dark saloon, and naturally the porter didn't think of taking its number. Mrs. Graves had already settled her bill, and went out to the car at once. The porter heard no greetings. The car, as far as he was concerned, simply drove off, and he found his tip waiting for him at the desk. As for the direction the car went, he had no idea. The hotel is approached by its own circular drive, and where it went after leaving the drive it was impossible to say, or to check.

That was all, and I didn't need to put many questions.

"There's one vital thing," I said, "and I shan't blame you if you don't know it. It's this. Mrs. Graves, as she called herself, told the hotel people that she'd be leaving on the Thursday at dusk, shall we say, and that a private car was coming for her. *When* did she say that? Before the caller came on the Thursday, or after?"

"After," he said promptly.

"You're dead sure?"

"Dead sure."

"Don't mind my being persistent," I said, "but why are you sure?"

"Because I put two and two together, like you are now," he told me with a grin. "It was the visit of that Irishman that made her change her plans. She'd booked the rooms for two nights."

"I'll agree," I said. "But how did she get in touch with the private car or the people who sent it?"

"There was a telephone in her room."

"Agreed, but did she report the use of it when she paid her bill?"

"I didn't think of that," he told me regretfully. "But something I did think of. I asked if the accent—described as foreign—of the man with the car was really an Irish accent. The porter insisted it was foreign. His idea was that it was French. He'd fought in France in the last war, by the way."

"Good work," I said. "But you'd better clear up that matter of the room telephone and you might see if it's possible to trace the call. And now take this name and address. William O'Clauty, Gilland Lodge, County Dublin."

He repeated it as he wrote, then was asking if that was the caller. I told him all I knew—with reservations.

"No possible chance of your getting over there?" I said.

He shook his head. "I could fake a letter," he said, "but there'd be the devil to pay if I got caught. I daren't take the risk, Mr. Travers."

"Any means of finding out where O'Clauty was at the relevant times? When he crossed and when he went back?"

"That's easy," he said. "A man in Dublin will do that for me. Might cost a packet for telephoning, though."

"You get the information," I told him, "and I'll do the worrying about the cost."

I strolled back as far as Piccadilly, for it was a glorious morning; as fine a spring day, in fact, as I'd ever known, even if it was still winter. I didn't do any thinking, except in one direction, and even then I didn't know if it would be discreet to ring Worrack up. And I doubted if I'd get him. There was that business with Georgina's bank manager on which he was supposed to be engaged.

In Piccadilly I treated myself to a coffee at Moroni's and then took the Tube. Before I had been in my flat five minutes, there was a ring at the bell, and who should be there but Hamson.

"I've come to throw myself on your mercy," he said, and with a disarming smile.

"Heave away then," I told him.

"Lewton-Molde seemed rather attracted by you last night," he said. "He told me you looked a very good sort and he was angling for further acquaintance. Said he was probably at school with your brother."

"Maybe he was," I said, "except that I never had a brother."

"I thought not," he said. "Still, he was very importunate, so I gave him your address, which I got from Worrack. Then my conscience smote me and I thought I'd slip round and give you the tip."

"Thanks," I said dryly. "And when's he likely to roll up?"

"I should say at about an hour before lunch," he said. "That's when he usually blinks out on the world. Unless he's very anxious indeed to make your closer acquaintance."

My eyebrows lifted. "What's his racket?"

"I wouldn't like to say," he told me, and then gave a slight grin. "I don't know the gentleman well enough, and you're too wily a bird."

"Glad you think so," I said, and wondered if I dare ask him a certain question. Not that one about the money but something a bit trickier. Then I decided not to, and at that moment the telephone bell rang. Hamson got to his feet but I told him to sit tight.

It was from Worrack. He'd had bad luck at the bank, he said. The manager knew him but managers are punctilious to the point of exasperation. All he had induced that one to do was to have a quick look over the account. The manager had done so and had then grudgingly stated, and in the very closest confidence, that no recent payments had been out of the usual run.

"I tried passing the buck to Barbara," Worrack said "and when she gathered what I'd been doing, she was absolutely furious. I mean furious. Blue, blazing mad. Speechless too—after a bit. Just slapped back the telephone."

"You didn't mention me?"

"Good God, no!"

He must have gathered something from the non-committal nature of my other remarks, for he was asking then if I was alone. I said I wasn't, then told him Hamson was with me.

"Good," he said. "And this for your private ear. I've decided I can't stand all this any longer. Some time to-night I'll pass on something that'll interest you. I don't give a damn about Barbara."

"Pass it on where? At the club?"

"That's right," he said. "And I'd be obliged if you'd give Hamson the same tip. Tell him to be there."

"Anything else?"

"No," he said. "Except that I'd be glad if you could find Hamson something to do. You know, along the lines we discussed."

"I remember," I said vaguely.

"Any news from your end?"

"No," I said. "But there certainly will be to-night."

I heard him let out a quick breath. "Sure you can't tell me now?"

"Quite sure," I said, and, "Right-ho, then. See you to-night. Trust me to give you any information when I happen to think fit."

"That was Worrack," I told Hamson casually.

"He's up and about early?"

"Yes," I said, "and he's anxious for me to find you some sort of job."

"Fine," he said. "Got one in mind?"

I shrugged my shoulders. I hoped he didn't think me too casual but I wasn't thinking about him. The gesture was one that put the onus on Worrack for intruding on what was my own jurisdiction. Still, if Worrack wanted Hamson to help, I did have a job in mind.

"The first condition I lay down is that you ask no questions," I said. "You just do as you told and trust me to give you any information when I happen to think fit."

"Suits me," he said.

"Then find out this," I said. "When does Jean come on duty at the club?"

To my surprise he was whipping out a small notebook. I repeated the instructions slowly.

"Find out what time Jean has to report for duty at the club and especially at what time he reported on the night of Thursday the fourteenth of January. Also, if he can drive a car, and anything further that's likely to be useful."

"Anything else?" he asked when he'd got that down.

I told him that Worrack had as good as ordered me to tell him that there might be a certain disclosure at the club sometime that night, and he was to be sure to be there. While he was nodding, the door bell went, and his look turned to a grimace.

I motioned to him to sit tight. Half a minute and Molde was coming in.

By daylight he didn't look so good. If he wasn't a dope fiend, then my name was Blunt. Did I tell you that he had the air of some patrician trifler with the arts? Hair rather long and brushed well back, and a general air of the slovenly intellectual. His colour was bad and there was a faint scent of pomade about him, and his fingers had little nervous twitchings.

"Morning, Blunt," he said, and then appeared to have caught sight of Hamson. "Hallo, Hamson; you here?"

"Any objections?" Hamson asked amusedly.

I broke into my last bottle of sherry and poured three tots. Molde plunged straight into the object of his call. I said my brother hadn't been at that particular school—I daren't mention its name—but probably he was thinking of my cousin Charles. That'd be it, he said, and I couldn't help giving Hamson a surreptitious wink. When he asked after Charles, I said he was soldiering in North Africa.

We talked about the war for a minute or two, then he said he would be going, and would I lunch with him some time. I said I would, and I asked if I'd be seeing him at the club that night. He said he rather doubted it.

Hamson said he'd be moving too, so I accompanied the pair of them to the hall door and saw them go off together in the direction of town. Then Frank, the hall porter, hailed me. He was a cheerful, garrulous soul.

"The gentleman found you then, sir? I knew he was making a mistake."

"Found me? What do you mean?"

"Well, he asked me for a Mr. Blunt and I said we hadn't no one of that name. Then I asked him to describe the gentleman, sir, and I knew he meant you. It's Major Travers you want, sir,' I told him. 'No it isn't,' he said, 'his name's Blunt.' 'You go up to the flat, sir, and enquire and I think you'll find I'm right,' I said. 'What's his Christian name?' he said, and I told him. Then he was shrugging his shoulders. He might have told me he was wrong, sir, mightn't he?"

"He certainly might," I said. "Very good of you, Frank, all the same."

If that wasn't a piece of bad luck, then I don't know what would be. I knew very well why Molde had made that flagrant excuse to see me. Scylla had told him about that contretemps in Worrack's office, and his visit therefore had been exploratory. But a visit to Blunt wouldn't have mattered. What was most devilishly exasperating, and indeed dangerous, was that he knew now that my name wasn't Blunt. He knew, in fact, that it was Ludovic Travers, and it seemed only reasonable to anticipate that before many hours had passed he would know precisely who Ludovic Travers was.

"Damn the whole case!" I said, and knew only too well that the annoyance should have been directed against my incompetent self. Nothing was wrong with the case; what was wrong was the equivocal, butter-fingered way I'd handled it. But to blazes with it in any case, I said, and tried to settle down to my crossword. Just as I'd ordered a service lunch, the telephone went. It was Bill Ellice, calling up from Richmond.

"Something fishy about that business, sir."

"How?"

"When she paid her bill she didn't say a word about a telephone call. On the other hand, she took a stroll in the garden that afternoon and I guess she'd done her 'phoning from outside. There's a sub-post office with a call-box, not two hundred yards away and that's where she did 'phone from."

"Then it can't be traced," I said.

"Afraid not," he told me. "It could hardly have been a long-distance."

"Well, see what you can do about it," I said. "And do your best to trace that car. A needle in a haystack, I know, but do your best."

That afternoon I strolled along to the Yard to see if there was any news of George Wharton. Something told me to go to a certain department and ask guardedly if there was anything known about Molde, then I thought it too dangerous. Hamson I might have enquired about, perhaps, with a hint at a confidence trick, but I gave that the go-by too. Then I went to Moroni's in case any of the crowd should be there, but there was devil a soul I knew. Then I walked all the way back to my flat, because what was wrong with me was too much wondering just what it was that Worrack was about to disclose that night, and whether even the disclosure would be either a red-herring or a fake.

Before nine o'clock I was ready to push on to the club, and that was far too early. I had not heard from my wife, so I decided to ring her up and make it a party to party call. Then I poured myself a beer and settled down to waiting till I should be rung by Exchange.

It was half an hour before I found myself speaking to my wife. A letter was in the post for me, she said, and I said the same. She might be getting local leave before I went back to duty, she said, and we agreed to fix something up. I said there was a strict rule about keeping to three minutes but did she happen to know a Mrs. Grays by any chance.

"Has she a sister, Georgina?" Bernice asked.

"That's right," I said.

"But you know her, darling," Bernice was trying to point out. "Wasn't she on that hospital committee of yours, just before the war? You must remember her, darling! A bit aggressive but awfully nice when you got to know her."

I said I'd just remembered and then, before she could ask any more questions, the time indicator began, and all I could do was make a hurried and husbandly conclusion and hang up. Then my fingers went to my glasses.

"Oh, my God!" I found myself saying aloud. "What the hell's going to happen next?"

Still, it couldn't be helped, more bungling on my part though it was. I knew I'd seen Barbara Grays somewhere, but that didn't matter now. There was some excuse for my forgetfulness, after three years and more of war, and with hospitals consisting as they did of scores of women and perpetual change. Not that that mattered either. What *did* matter was that yet another person knew precisely who I was.

Then I gave a gasp of something like horror. Bernice's habit of wifely eulogy! The way I'd had to administer gentle reproof about her admiration for my talents so guilelessly and publicly expressed, but rarely I'm afraid in my private ear. No wonder Mrs. Grays had asked my opinion on that Stock Exchange tip! Bernice had doubtless told her I was a financial wizard. And that, in another of my many spheres, I was the mainstay of Scotland Yard! In fact, it was a million to one that Barbara Grays had spotted me the very moment I had entered Moroni's with Worrack the previous day. That was why she had been so annoyed and damnably off-hand. Blunt indeed, I thought grimly, and, oh, my God, how I hated that name!

I'd mooned so long over those introspections that when I realised it was past ten o'clock, I had something of a new horror. Then, before I could get clear of the room, the telephone went. It was Ellice again.

"Sorry, sir, but I can't get any further down here."

"Keep on trying for just one more day," I said. "Anything from Ireland yet?"

"There couldn't be till late to-morrow," he said.

That was that, but another five minutes had gone down the drain. Then I took a wrong turning in the black-out and it was a quarter-past ten when I got to the club. Still, I found the side door and George let me in.

"Mr. Worrack expecting me?" I asked. "If so, I'm a bit late."

"You don't call this late, sir," he told me cheerfully. "But here's your invitation, sir. No, nothing to pay."

As we went upstairs he told me that Worrack wasn't feeling any too fit. He'd been in the office and then, as soon as things were started, he'd gone out. George thought it was for a breath of air. He had little nervous fits at times, he said. Just a hangover from that Dunkirk business, and a spell of fresh air did him good. George also told me that I was the twenty-first to arrive.

The first thing I noticed on entering the main room was that Tubby and three other men were playing poker. Roulette was in full swing, and I recognised most of the previous night's crowd. Barbara Grays spotted me and gave me quite a nice smile. My tail wagged at that, because I thought I knew something—that she hadn't really been annoyed at my duplicity in using the name Blunt. After all, if Bernice had given her my life history, then she should have known that I couldn't very well be seen in that room in my own name. Maybe she was being charming to me to show that she regretted that display of petulance at the lunch at Moroni's.

Hamson was there, sitting between Tubby's girl and Molde. Molde I remembered, had said he wouldn't be there, but he was, and Scylla was facing him as usual across the table. George had sold me ten pounds' worth of chips. I took up a position behind Scylla, and once more fooled around on red and black. At about half-past eleven Worrack came in. He didn't come over to the tables but went straight through to his office, and from the quick look I had at him I thought he looked tired and ill.

There was no point in my going to the office, for I knew he'd send for me and say what he had to say in his own good time. Thinking about that, and puzzling my wits over what it could be that he had to reveal, brought me a bit of luck, for I'd doubled a pound stake on the red and forgot to remove it, and red turned up again. Then, just before twelve Worrack came out and Jean began laying the tables. The wheel went round for the last time and when we closed down for supper, Molde buttonholed me and began talking about my non-existent cousin Charles. He talked quite a lot, and his hand seemed even more unsteady than usual. I thought he'd probably forgotten to give himself a shot of whatever his particular dope was, before coming out. At any rate I couldn't dodge him, and I found myself at the same table with him. Barbara Grays had been sitting there, and again she smiled at me as I sat down.

What with passing the salmon mayonnaise to Barbara, and trying to keep an eye on Worrack, and listen to Molde, still babbling in the conversational hubbub of the room, I was pretty busy. I saw Jean bring a long drink to the high table, and Worrack take a pull at it. He was rubbing his eyes as if they were tired, and then he sort of roused himself to make some reply to Lulu, who was sitting by him. Hamson was there too, taking a seat at Worrack's left hand. George was at the bar, talking to Jean about something, and Jean was shrugging his shoulders and apparently expostulating. I also saw Hamson beckon to Scylla, who came across to him and stood talking for a minute or so, but she didn't sit down and that showed she wasn't intending to stay.

I hope you have got that lay-out, for it is highly important. George and Jean at the bar; Molde, Barbara Grays and myself at two tables removed from the high table, and at the high table Worrack, with Lulu on his right and Hamson on his left, and Scylla standing by Hamson. Other people don't matter, except perhaps Tubby. Though he swore blind that he knew nothing about the mouse, I'll always think he had his own reasons for the denial.

It was a genuine mouse, caught alive in a trap, probably, and brought along that night for a spot of fun. What Tubby didn't deny was that he was the first to see it and give the tally-ho.

"Hi! Look there! A mouse!"

That was Tubby, and when we looked, or tried to look, we knew he wasn't pulling our legs. I spotted the mouse nipping along the wainscot past Barbara's chair, and was fool enough to holler the fact and in a moment there was pandemonium. Lulu let out a shriek and hopped on a chair. Scylla went one better. Her shriek wasn't so shrill but she nipped up on the table, frock clutched tight round her knees. There were shrieks of delight from the men, and in the general din followed the chase of the mouse and the bandying of jokes.

Why did I notice Worrack? Because he was the only one who was outside the spirit of that rag. He made never a move when the two women shrieked, and then after a couple of seconds maybe, his head went forward into his cupped hands. Then his hand went out towards the drink, and slowly and gropingly, as if he was half afraid to take it. He seemed to clutch the glass and drag it reluctantly towards him, and when his lips went to it he changed his mind. Then he swayed in his seat, and it was then that I knew he was ill. Two men were in my way as I made for him, but I brushed them aside. Worrack had slumped back in his chair, mouth agape, and just as I reached him he was falling sideways to the floor.

CHAPTER VII
ON THE SPOT

WHAT HAPPENED, and all inside a couple of minutes, I can't really tell you. As I told that Inspector, I'd have needed six sets of eyes and then a few more to keep up with things, and half a dozen hands to note them down. I know that instinctively I let out a yell and waved my arms. What with that and my six foot three I must have looked rather ridiculous, and I knew that people thought me some new variation on the old joke, for there was a different kind of laughter and even more noise. But Hamson had got to his knees and was staggering to his feet with Worrack in his arms. That quietened them.

"Please!" I said. "Quiet everybody. Mr. Worrack's been taken ill."

It was no more than ten foot to the office, and Hamson was nearing it, Worrack in his arms. Lulu was flying across to open the door, and after the sudden hush a new babble began. Barbara came by me as my fingers went to my glasses; she was almost running, and something made me follow her.

The door had closed upon Hamson almost at once, but just as I caught up with Barbara, it opened and Hamson was ushering—pushing, I might almost have said—Lulu out to the room again, and her fingers were frightenedly at her mouth.

"What is it?" Barbara asked, and she looked scared too.

"Nothing much," Hamson told her curtly. "Keep everybody out of here if you want to help."

He drew me in, closed the door and then was nodding back. I saw Worrack lying in the swivel chair, mouth still agape.

"Have a look at this," Hamson said, and was drawing back Worrack's eyelids. A quick look at me, and then he was prising open the mouth.

"Poison?" I said, and I had never said anything more lamely.

"Looks like it." He thought for a moment or two. "Nip out and get that glass he was drinking from."

I looked back from the door.

"Is he dead?"

"Afraid so," was all he told me.

There was a crowd round the high table. Molde was sitting in Worrack's chair and Scylla was by him, hands on his shoulders, and I remember I had to move her aside to reach the glass. I don't know why but I left the glass alone for a moment. There was no need to call for silence, for there wasn't a sound in the room and everyone appeared to be watching me.

"Mr. Worrack's very ill," I said. "Everybody had better cash in his chips. George, you see that nobody leaves."

I had seen him making for me, and pretty scared he looked.

"Is he bad, sir?"

"Worse than that," I said. "In fact, he's dead."

"Oh, my Gawd!" His eyes had bulged and then Tubby was pushing him aside. The murmur of voices died away.

"What are you getting at, Blunt?"

"Nothing," I told him mildly.

"Well, you're acting as if something fishy had happened. Do you mean he's killed himself?"

"I mean nothing," I said. "What I've said I've said."

"To hell with that." He gave a look round. "If you're going to call in the police, then some of us ought to be on the move. It's going to be pretty awkward for some of us here."

I knew it was that girl he was thinking of, but somehow he got my goat.

"You stay here, and like it," I told him. "Isn't it going to be awkward for me too? Who the hell are you, in any case?"

What he ought to have done was clip me under the jaw. Probably he was far too taken aback. I'm a mild-looking soul and he was looking as if he'd been suddenly savaged by his pet rabbit. Also I was ignoring him and putting my handkerchief round the glass. As I moved off with it, Barbara was clutching my arm.

"He isn't dead. You're fooling!"

"I only wish I were," I told her, and when I moved on to-wards the office door I had the queer feeling of being extraordinarily alone, with all those people back there and the new quick murmur of voices that suddenly arose.

Hamson took the glass carefully from my fingers and had a good sniff at it.

"Don't recognise it," he said. "What do you make of it?"

I had a good sniff too.

"Something very faint," I said. "Reminds me . . . what the devil is it? Something like new-mown hay. But very faint."

"It's a new one on me," he said. "But why the devil should he want to do himself in?"

"God knows," I said. "Maybe the strain had got too much for him."

"But what about that communication he was making to you to-night?"

"Who knows?" I said. "Maybe there wasn't any communication. Maybe he intended to do himself in. That's what he was talking about, and why he wanted me to be here."

That knocked him endways. He took a turn or two up and down the room, and he was shaking his head.

"Whatever he died of, there's one thing we've got to do, and quick," I said. "And that's ring the police."

"My God, yes!" he said, and stopped his prowling. Then he was giving me a rather queer look.

"When they come there's one thing I wish you'd do for me. Keep quiet about my police service. There's no point in dragging that in."

"No point at all," I said, and didn't think too much of the request at the time. Somehow it seemed something of the same kind of argument as Tubby had begun propounding, and there wasn't any sense in reminding him that most of us would have things we wanted to conceal.

"Another thing," he said. "Oughtn't we to take a quick look through his pockets? We don't want too much dirty linen washed."

"Don't get you," I said.

"Well, there might be something incriminating about some of the people out there," he said. "Molde, for instance. He may be a wash-out, but he's entitled to a certain amount of protection."

"Molde be damned," I said. "You know as well as I do that nothing ought to be touched."

Then as I moved over to the telephone, straddling Worrack's body to do so, I told him something else.

"You get outside and tell them the truth. Say the club's closed down after to-night. Say they've got nothing to worry about. Spin any yarn you like."

I thought he might cut up rough, but he didn't. He gave me another quick look and then he went out. Before I'd found the number of local police-headquarters—and I didn't give the universal call for reasons of my own—I heard him calling the room to order.

In less than five minutes George was showing in an Inspector Brontway, and two plain-clothes men with him. They came up through the garage and so had no idea what was beyond the office door. Hamson, by the way, had not returned.

I gave quick explanations and he had a look at the body. Then he had a sniff at the glass, poured the remaining brandy-soda into a bottle from his bag, and then put in the glass and my handkerchief with it. I told him the handkerchief was mine and handkerchiefs were rationed.

"You'll get it back, sir," he told me reassuringly. "And let me see, sir. The name you gave was Blunt. Christian names?"

I told him I'd come to see the dead man. A business appointment. As there was a gaming-room outside there, the dead man had suggested I should give a *nom de guerre*, so to speak.

You can guess the kind of look he gave me. Then he was opening the door and leaving it ajar behind him. The faint sounds ceased, and then he was back again.

"A gaming-room, eh? But *you* didn't come here for that."

"No," I said. "I did have a flutter to pass the time till Mr. Worrack here might be ready for me. That's all."

"I see. You did have a flutter."

I took a look at one of his men. His eyes shifted from mine. I expect he thought the net of the Law had already enmeshed me, and good and proper.

"And your real name, sir?" the inspector was asking.

"Travers."

He spelt it out as he wrote so that I might correct if necessary. Then he wanted my Christian name.

"Ludovic," I said.

"Ludovic Travers," he repeated slowly. Then the most comical expression came over his face. The pencil stopped writing.

"Ludovic Travers," he said. "Not *the* Ludovic Travers?"

"Looks like it," I said, not wishing to seem too eager.

"I recognise you now, sir," one of his men said. "I remember seeing you with Superintendent Wharton."

"Maybe," I said. "But there's the telephone and you've only to dial the Yard."

Another minute and we were all as thick as thieves. I ventured to tell him, with the air of one man of the world to another, what the club was and how it was run, and I showed him my own invitation. Mine, of course, as I told him, was just a blind to disguise the real object of my visit.

"Would you mind telling me what you did come here for?" he asked me.

"To tell you the truth, I don't know," I said, and felt I was getting into deeper water. "I believe it was about a financial investment. That's my real job, you know."

"Financial investment," he said. "Then he wasn't losing any money. He didn't do himself in for financial reasons, if you get me. But why couldn't he see you in the daytime, sir?"

"That was my fault," I said. "I was too busy. He said it was urgent and would I see him here." I shrugged my shoulders gracefully. "I didn't see why I shouldn't. Provided, of course, no one knew who I was."

Just then the police doctor arrived. I left him to the Inspector while I did some pretty quick thinking. My previous night's visit might get out and then I'd look a bit of a liar. But think how I might, I couldn't find a way of wriggling out of that.

"Poison all right," the doctor was saying, and then the Inspector let him have a sniff at the bottle. All he did was grunt, and that told me he didn't know what the poison was.

"You'd better get it sent along to the Yard," he said. "We may find something else at the P.M."

"Whatever it was, it was pretty quick," I said. "From the time he took the first swig at it to the time he dropped wasn't more than five minutes."

"Some of these new atropine groups are fairly quick," he told me. "What was his general health like?"

I told him what George had told me. I also mentioned the leg, and who he was exactly.

"The son of an honourable, was he?" the Inspector said. "That's right," I said. "The grandson of a peer, if you like." I thought that information might do us all a bit of good.

The finger-prints were taken, and that was when it all seemed so unreal. Somehow I expected Worrack to sit up or groan or something. That he was dead seemed unthinkable.

"His prints on the glass," the Inspector said, "and no one else's. Smudged a bit, sir, where you had that handkerchief."

Then he told one of his men to go through the pockets, while he made a note or two. I didn't see any sign of those IOU's of Molde's, but I did run my eye over the keys and saw that they included those of the safe.

"Now, sir," the Inspector said. "You've no knowledge of any reasons why he should commit suicide?"

"Never a reason," I said. "On the contrary. Why, for instance, did he want me to come here? It couldn't have been because he wanted me as a witness to his suicide."

"That reminds me," he said. "What about witnesses?"

I said I knew those who might help, and my view was that the rest might go home. After all we had their addresses. I said, too, that to save time and to be helpful I wouldn't mind making an announcement.

"What sort of announcement?" he said, and when I told him, he said that would suit him fine. Then he told the doctor to hang on for a bit and we went into the main room.

Once more there wasn't any need to call for silence. "Ladies and gentlemen," I said. "The Inspector here doesn't want to cause any of us any undue inconvenience. Provided George has your full names and addresses, everybody may go except the following, who might be able to throw some light on things."

The list of those who had to stay was: Hamson, Lulu, Scylla, Jean and George. Scylla probably meant that Molde would hang on too. I also added that if anybody else had anything that seemed of even the slightest importance, would that person stay on too.

"Where was he actually sitting?" the Inspector asked me.

I showed him, and then before he spoke I knew what was missing. For he was frowning away at the table, then looking under it, and finally all round it and along the wainscoting.

"Just a minute, sir," he said, and nipped off back into the office.

I could have told him he was wasting his time. No bottle or anything that might have contained poison had been in Worrack's pockets. Then as I moved my foot, what should I see against it but something like a small capsule.

"Look," I told him as he came frowning back. "That what you're looking for?"

He picked it up gingerly, using a pair of forceps. It was a capsule of a kind, a flimsy affair of what looked like stout cellophane, and it looked as if it had been much trodden on. He sniffed it, then put it under my nose. The same scent of new-mown hay was there.

He took it into the office and I watched the room gradually clear itself. George was doing manfully, shepherding the witnesses to a table next to Worrack's.

When the Inspector came back I said that if he liked, I'd be Worrack and I'd place the witnesses just where they'd been at the crucial times. When I looked up at Jean he seemed the most uneasy witness of the five. Doubtless he still had plenty of work to do, and he was about to lose a good job.

"This man we can soon get rid of," I told the Inspector. "It was you who mixed the drink, Jean?"

"*Oui, m'sieu.*"

"Talk English," I said. "We're not all citizens of the world. But you saw him mix the drink, George. What happened exactly?"

George said nothing happened. Mr. Worrack, who was looking very ill, asked Jean for a stiff brandy and a very little soda. That was what Jean mixed. Then he put it on a tray and carried it over.

"You go with Jean and bring the brandy bottle," I said. "Make sure it's the right one."

That didn't take a couple of minutes. I gave the Inspector the bottle and asked in a whisper if Jean might get on with his work. Best, I thought, to keep on the right side of the Inspector and let it appear that I was only his mouthpiece.

Then we got down to the reconstruction. The mouse, by the way, had long since been butchered, and was lying on one of the tables. But the whole thing didn't take long. George brought me the drink in Jean's place, but water instead of brandy and soda. I took a good pull at it, and then put my head in my hands. Lulu said she hadn't noticed that because she was looking for Scylla. She'd been trying out a system that interested her and she wanted to ask her how it had worked.

And so to the mouse. George said that for a mouse to get into the room by ordinary means was unthinkable, and I backed him up by saying someone had brought it in for a rag. Then we got to work on that part of the reconstruction, and it was far from a success. Lulu burst into tears when we came to the point of Worrack's collapse, though only after she'd said again that she'd seen nothing unusual in his behaviour, as she'd been far too busy worrying about the mouse. Scylla, very pale and nervy, said much the same, but I noticed that when she did her act on the table she didn't draw her frock up to a height well above the knee. Hamson said that what with the shrieking women and his own interest in the mouse, he hadn't noticed a thing till Worrack fell back on him in the chair.

"Well, that doesn't get us much farther," the Inspector said disappointedly. Then he said it looked as if I was the last one to see him alive.

The last thing I wanted to do was to attend an inquest, and luckily Hamson stepped in.

"He was alive when I picked him up," he said. "I know that for a certainty, for his eyes moved and I thought he was trying to say something to me. I wouldn't be certain, mind you, but I think he passed out just as I got him into the office."

"Had he any relatives?" the Inspector asked generally. No one knew of any. Hamson gave me a look and then suggested that a Mrs. Grays, whose address he gave, was probably his closest friend, and she might know. Then the Inspector said he wouldn't keep anybody much longer, and if they'd kindly sit down, he'd be back in a few minutes. George and I went with him into the office.

Who should be in the office but Molde. When the Inspector raised his eyebrows at the sight of him, his man explained. Mr. Molde was waiting for one of the ladies, and as he'd thought he wouldn't be allowed to wait in the main room he'd come to the office to wait instead.

"I'm engaged to Miss Payton, one of the witnesses," Molde said.

"The lady who mounted the table," I whispered.

Brontway's man had something else to say. "I was emptying the safe, sir, and came across this envelope with this gentleman's name on, and he reckons it's something he gave the deceased to keep for him."

"Mind if I have a look?" I said, and there was Molde licking his lips and nervously blinking his eyes as he watched me.

I guessed it was those IOU's and the feel of the envelope confirmed it.

"It's all right, Inspector," I said. "I know about this. It's Mr. Lewton-Molde's all right."

The Inspector had a look at the name on the envelope and then handed it over rather grudgingly.

"This isn't in order, you know, sir. Still, if it's all right it's all right."

"There's no reason why you shouldn't wait in the cloak-room," I told Molde.

"I don't think I'll wait after all," he said. "Unless Miss Payton's coming almost at once."

I don't know what happened, because the Inspector took him over and went through with him to the main room. He was back in a minute, though, and without Molde, and found me looking at the contents of the safe. The books of the club principally, but also a foolscap envelope which interested me, for on it was written:

Will.

P.W.

"Made his will, had he?" the Inspector said, and had a good look at the sealed envelope before putting it in his pocket. Then he rubbed his chin and gave a quick look round at George, who was still stolidly waiting.

"I don't like to commit myself, sir, but everything seems pretty straightforward. I suppose you've got nothing else to suggest?"

I said I hadn't, except that he could trust George to help all he could. George would now be in charge, subject to the Inspector's orders.

"What about calling up to see me in the morning?"

I said I could manage that at any time he liked, and we agreed on ten o'clock at the station. As we went through to the main room I gave George a cheerful good-night, but his own good-night was pretty glum. Outside the door the Inspector shook hands and said he didn't know what he'd have done without me. I'd have liked to give a snappy come-back, like, "You're telling me!" but all I said was that I'd been glad to help. Then, as I made for the far door, I had a quick look at the waiting witnesses. They looked a rather bedraggled lot. Lulu's eyes were red and Scylla had probably been crying too. Hamson was in an attitude like Rodin's Thinker, and Jean, still at the bar, had shot me a look and then turned away.

It was a cool night, and in a couple of minutes my brain was icy cool too. I knew how dangerously thin was the ice over which I had just been skating, and though I had always been willing enough to lie unblushingly in the cause of justice, I couldn't remember an occasion before when I'd lied to get myself out of difficulties of my own creating, and the thought was not a happy one. Already I was wishing it was morning and that I was seeing the Inspector again, for I'm one of those people who believe in attack as the best defence. Or maybe I should have said, like those people who can't stay indoors in an air-raid but have to get outside and see the bomb that gets them instead of merely hearing it. I found one consolation for myself. Even if I did have to attend an inquest, this was war-time, and paper was rationed, and the Press would give little publicity to the matter of poor Worrack.

Still, I thought out some questions the Inspector might ask me, and found the right answers. I also thought of Molde and the ghoulish use he'd made of Worrack's death. I wondered how he would react to that good turn I'd done him, and whether he'd now be asking himself just what I knew about those IOU's. I thought about Worrack's will, and wondered what was in it. I also wondered if Georgina Morbent's name would in some way come into things. Somehow I couldn't see how that could be avoided. Barbara Grays would probably say that Worrack had been worried over her mysterious absence, and Brontway would have his suicide reason. Or wouldn't he?

It was a quarter to two when I got to my flat. I poured myself a beer and stretched my long legs out from the easy-chair, and it was then that I realised again that Worrack was dead. Worrack dead, I said gently to myself, and I knew that I had liked him. A white man if ever there was one, and the kind of whom I'd have been pleased to make a friend. It was in that moment that I knew he had never committed suicide. Not for the hackneyed reason that he'd left no farewell message, but just through a lively, and to me very real intuition, and the fact that he could never have asked me so urgently to come to the club that night for the sake of being present at his death.

It was curious how tired my brain suddenly went as I thought of that. Then as I got into bed I realised something else. Othello's brief occupation had gone! I was a private enquiry agent without a client, and yet I didn't know if I was sorry or glad. I ought to have been glad and yet I wasn't, for the whole business had done nothing but land me into difficulties and now most of the difficulties had solved themselves. Instead of my having awkwardly to resign from the case, the case had resigned from me.

CHAPTER VIII
A NEW EMPLOYER

IT WAS JUST SHORT of nine o'clock when I woke, and long before I'd dressed that case was fretting my mind. Cool day confirmed what the night had insisted, that Worrack's death was no suicide. If it was murder, I asked myself, then who had committed it? Had Jean, unseen by the trustful George, dropped that dope into the brandy? If so, how had the capsule got near Worrack's table? Then even that was easy. Jean, I thought, could have palmed it, and then have dropped it when he brought the drink.

If Jean didn't put in the dope, then who did? It was true that as soon as he had brought the drink Worrack had had a long pull at it, but there was plenty left in the glass —a thin, pint glass it was—to take the poison. And where did the mouse come in? Was it let loose designedly or had it been a lucky chance for the murderer? At any rate, three people could have dropped that poison in, in the excitement of the moment, with everyone's eyes on Tubby. Hamson, Lulu, and Scylla were the three. What motives, I asked myself, had any of them, and strong enough to be worth, or demand, Worrack's murder?

No sooner did my breakfast arrive than I began on Hamson. He didn't fit at all, as far as I could see. If he was out for Barbara's money—assuming first that he knew Georgina was dead—then I didn't see why Worrack should be an obstacle to the marriage. Or did Worrack know something about Hamson? Worrack, as I remembered, had been insistent to me that Hamson should be at the club, and he had virtually forced me to tell Hamson that that night he was going to make a disclosure. The line then would be to enquire into Hamson's past and find out if he was all he made himself out to be, for if he had something vital to conceal, then there was no need to look farther for the murderer.

And Lulu? What about her? Maybe she hadn't an idea about the disappearance of Georgina Morbent. If she had an idea, it might be that Worrack had parked her somewhere. Had installed her, if you like, in some handy spot. Lulu, I told myself, had certainly been Worrack's mistress up to the time of Georgina's arrival. There had been that scene I had overheard, and the mention of blackmail. Lulu meant to get Worrack back, and had threatened him accordingly. Then, when she found she could not get him back, she had told herself that if she couldn't have him no other woman should.

And what about Scylla? If she had done anything it had been as the confederate of Molde. And yet, dangerous though the IOU's were from the point of view of Molde, how could he have foreseen that he would have the faintest chance of recovering them? He had not seen Worrack put them in the safe. And also I remembered that Scylla's actions at the time of the appearance of the mouse had been absolutely in character. She'd outdone Lulu in the matter of screaming, and she'd taken care to show not only her uncommonly graceful legs, but her equally graceful knees.

Scylla, I told myself, was a highly unlikely candidate. But if it had been Molde himself, then things might have been different. There was one who was capable of anything; but he hadn't had an opportunity. To my certain knowledge he had never been within a table or two of that drink, nor had any of his actions been suspicious. True, he had chattered a great deal, as if he was nervous about something, but that was somehow in character too. And perhaps, as I thought at the time, he'd forgotten to give himself a shot of his own special dope.

Then I realised, with a queer jolt, that all that thinking was a waste of time. What in hell had it to do with me? I was out of things, except as a chance witness, and an unimportant one at that. All I had to do was to respect implicitly all Worrack's confidences, wriggle out of the rest of the mess, and then keep my mouth shut. But, thank God, I fervently told myself, it had not been George Wharton who had walked into Worrack's office! Not that a senior Superintendent of Scotland Yard would have been called on to handle anything like a case of suicide. Still, the thought was a relief all the same.

I finished my meal, and I hadn't too good an appetite. It was then twenty minutes to ten, so I rang Bill Ellice's office. There was no answer, so I guessed he was not yet back from Richmond. A quick squint at myself in the glass, and I set off for Inspector Brontway's office.

As I walked towards Knightsbridge that perfectly lovely morning, the sun was shining and the air so good that I couldn't possibly feel any depression, even when I remembered that, since poor Worrack had gone, I should have to pay Bill Ellice. But that didn't worry me, and I even got a minor kick out of the realisation that with Bill still in, I hadn't lost all interest in things. I didn't even worry about what he would think when I told him that he was being called off.

Brontway was not in, but I was told he was expected at any minute. He had just rung up to say that if he was late I was to be kept till he got back, so they parked me in his office. Though my eyes were everywhere about me I saw nothing relative to the previous night's tragedy. It was half an hour before he actually appeared, and he was full of apologies.

"Couldn't see that Mrs. Grays," he said. "Some people don't get up till it's time to go to bed. When I did see her I had to get things out of her with a corkscrew."

"The visit worth while?" I asked idly.

He seemed to think it was. She'd said there were no relatives, except a distant cousin or two. She'd also told him about what she'd described as Worrack's infatuation for Georgina, and how it was her view that she'd gone off with some other man. There was motive enough for the suicide, and as it appeared that George, after I'd left, had told about Worrack's being nervy and none too fit, everything looked well in the bag.

"What about the will?" I asked.

"Everything left to that Georgina woman," he said. "Five hundred quid to Conroy. He must have made a packet out of that club of his."

Conroy, I gathered, was George, but I didn't ask.

"Something in the will about a bomb being likely to drop," he was going on, "and if he outlived that Georgina, then everything went to Mrs. Grays, except that Conroy got a thousand."

"Anything to that secretary, Lulu Mawne?"

"Not a thing," he said.

"Well, that seems to have everything settled," I remarked. "Everything set for the inquest?"

That was the following morning, he said, and he wouldn't be wanting me.

"No point really in bringing my name into things at all, then," I said casually.

He said he didn't think there was, and then I was just about to ask him if he'd come out for a quick one, when the doctor came in. He nodded to me, but none too genially. Brontway told him he needn't mind me. Mr. Travers, as he put it, was pretty well known to the Yard.

The doctor said that the poison was duropine, one of the new atropine class, and he gave me a what-did-I-tell-you look, as he added that the Yard analyst had confirmed it.

"Damn smart work on your part, doctor," I said guilefully.

"Quick working stuff, is it?" Brontway asked.

"Yes, and no," the doctor said. "It depends on the dose."

"Then Worrack had enough in him to kill a mule," I said, "for he went down as if he'd been pole-axed."

"Where did he get the poison from?" Brontway wanted to know.

The doctor explained, and highly interesting I found it. Duropine was one of the drugs the Nazis used as a stimulant; for doping troops, in other words. Strychnine is a tonic in minute doses, as he reminded us, but deadly dangerous in large ones. Very well, then; what was happening was that the dope-fiends had become aware of the properties of the new drug and were using it to supersede coke.

"Where do they get it from?" asked Brontway.

"Where did they get coke from?" the doctor asked, with a shrug of the shoulders. "Where there's a demand there'll always be a supply."

"But wouldn't it do a dope-fiend in, in time?" persisted Brontway.

"Not at all," the other said. "De Quincey got accustomed to drinking enough opium to have killed the three of us twice over. And what about the Tyrol arsenic-eaters?"

"Would that capsule have held enough to knock out Worrack?" I asked, and the doctor said that most decidedly it would.

Well, that was that. I didn't see any point in hanging about, so I said good-bye to the pair of them, but added for the Inspector's benefit that I thought of slipping round to that club place to recover a pair of gloves I'd left there the previous night.

"May see you again some time, sir," he said.

I said I hoped so, and then we'd have a drink. But I was due back from my leave before long. Then, of course, I had to impress him with the fact that I was now in the Army, as I'd intended all along. In fact, when I left the station I was on pretty good terms with myself. Thanks to a little finesse, I complacently told myself, I'd wriggled plumb clear. All that remained now was to close down on Ellice.

But whether I should soon be finished with the case or not, there was one thing that Brontway had told me that intrigued me very much. Why should Barbara Grays have told him that Worrack had been infatuated with Georgina? The word meant "overcome by foolish passion," so the dictionary said, and I knew that much because I'd wanted that definition for a cross-word puzzle. But even if Barbara Grays had not used it in that strict sense, yet the fact remained that the accepted connotation of the word had in it something meretricious and transitory. In other words, Barbara had told a deliberate lie, and, in doing so, she had cast a slur on Worrack, who was supposed to be a very good friend.

Then I thought again. That business of Lulu. If Barbara knew about that—and such things had a way of getting out—then mightn't she have come to regard Worrack as something untrustworthy where women were concerned? Something of a Don Juan, in fact? If so, then her tale to Brontway had a certain basis of truth. But what about that other tale, that Georgina—her own sister, and a sister to whom she was indebted—had probably gone off with some other man? I had made the suggestion myself to Worrack, but as an outsider and objectively; coming from Barbara Grays that suggestion to Brontway seemed not only uncalled for, but deliberately malicious.

What, then, was to be made of Barbara Grays? Surely she couldn't be mixed up in her sister's disappearance, and when I said disappearance I knew I meant death or even murder. Yet various facts stood out. Her conduct throughout seemed to me to have been extraordinarily callous, and she was the one who stood to profit most by her sister's death. On the other hand, would she not, if in any way guilty, have pretended to be distracted at Georgina's possible death? Surely that elementary idea of concealing guilt must have occurred to her. Bernice, as I recalled, had spoken of her as a good sort when you knew her.

Then I recalled something else, that there I was, invoking a whole series of tortuous theories about a case with which I should soon be finished. I also realised that I had just passed the front door of the club.

I rang, and after a wait of two or three minutes George admitted me. The police had only just gone, he said, and he'd had orders to admit no one except the staff. I told him I was privileged, I also said that ostensibly I'd called for a pair of gloves I'd left behind. He winked as he let me in.

"Your name Conroy, isn't it, George?" I asked.

"That's right, sir."

"How'd you first run across Mr. Worrack? Between ourselves."

"There's nothing confidential about that, sir," he told me. "I was his colonel's batman—full corporal I was then —and when the colonel was killed and Major Worrack took over, I did for him too. With him at Dunkirk, sir, and that's where I got my little packet."

His packet was a lump of shrapnel in the belly. It didn't trouble him much, he said, but he had to be careful over what he ate.

We stood for a time in the deserted room. Table and chairs had been stacked, the roulette apparatus put away, and the bar front drawn down.

"A bad business this for you, George," I said.

"I'm all right as far as that goes," he said. "It's him I shall miss. I thought the world and all of him, sir."

"And he did of you," I said. "I can't tell you how I know, but you'll be finding out. What's happened to Jean, by the way?"

He grinned, and that should have told me something. "Oh, him. He's been paid off, sir. He won't have any trouble in finding a job."

"A queer-looking cove," I said.

"People liked all that parley-vooing of his," George was going on. "Used to give the place a romantic, foreign sort of air, if you know what I mean."

I thought I did, but I missed the whole point of what he was saying, and it was not till days later that I knew just what he had meant.

Then as I was turning to go, in came Lulu. She gave me a casual hallo.

"How are you this morning?" I asked solicitously.

"Not too bad," she said. "Sorry I made such a fool of myself when that policeman was here."

"You did nothing of the sort," I assured her. "I thought you did uncommonly well. But what are you going to do now?" I asked, and waved a hand at the empty room to show what I meant.

"Oh, I'll get a job easily enough," she said.

"I bet you will," I told her, and then held out my hand. "Well, cheerio, Lulu. I hope some time I shall see you again."

She gave me one of her old fascinating glances at that, and when I looked back at the door with George, she gave me a little wave of the hand. There, if I wanted one, was a secretary who wouldn't be too scrupulous about combining business with pleasure.

George went to the front door with me, and we wished each other good luck. As I came out to the main road I saw a pub, and as my throat was like a cross-section of Libya, I had a beer. There was a telephone kiosk there, so I tried Ellice's office again. He was there all right and pawing the ground. Twice in the last hour he'd rung me and had no reply.

"Nothing from Richmond," he said, "but the straight tip from Ireland. Our friend crossed over on the Tuesday night boat from Belfast to Liverpool, so he got to town at about one o'clock. He went back on the Friday night boat, same route."

"Good work, Bill."

"Want me to follow him up from Euston?" he said. "And back from Richmond if I can?"

"Sorry, Bill—no," I said. "What you've found out is all we wanted to know. Thanks a lot and send me in your account and I'll drop you a cheque."

I knew by his silence that he was a bit flabbergasted at that. When he did speak it was to hope he'd given satisfaction, and if there were anything else at any time he'd be only too pleased. Things were rather slack and he wasn't so particular as he had been. I said I'd remember it, thanked him again, and rang off.

So there was I, rid of the case and clear of what, with Worrack's death, might have become for me an extremely awkward situation. As a sign of my emancipation I took my time about strolling home, and then I had a go at my *Times* crossword. Before I'd been at it ten minutes, the bell rang and in came Molde.

"Morning, Molde," I said, not too pleased. "What brings you along?"

"Just popped in," he said. "I'm not staying a moment. Got to lunch with some people. Most frightfully good of you, last night. By the way, is your name Blunt or Travers? Rather pointed of me, I know, but that policeman chap alluded to you as Travers."

"Travers is the name," I said. "I didn't think it would have done for me to show up at Worrack's place as Travers, so he and I agreed I was to be Blunt."

"Well, it was frightfully good of you in any case," he said, and then twiddled a bit with his green pork-pie hat. "What I can't understand is why you were so decent. I mean, why you did it."

"Surely that's simple," I said. "You said something was yours and it had your name on it. If it was a question of you and the police, well, I had to stand by you. Anything special, was it?"

"Only some rather private papers—deeds really. I haven't a safe and he was always frightfully obliging. A bad business about poor old Worrack—what?"

I said it was. He twiddled with his hat again and then said he'd better be going.

"How's Scylla?" I asked him at the door.

"Absolutely prostrate," he said. "A frightful shock, all that business. She didn't get away till nearly three."

"Well, I hope to see you both again some time," I said, and he repeated his vague invitation for a lunch, and that was that. I returned to my puzzle, finished it, and then had a second look through the news. Then the telephone went. It was Hamson.

"Sorry to worry you, Travers," he said, "but are you doing anything in particular?"

"It all depends," I said guardedly. "Just what is it you want?"

"Could you have lunch with me? I know it's a late invitation, but I'd be awfully obliged."

I put my foot promptly down. No use fooling around on the fringes of the case.

"That's the one thing I just can't do. As a matter of fact I'm busy all day."

"A pity," he said, and I thought I heard him heave a sigh.

"By the way, I've done that little job for you," he went on. "The one about Jean. He was due on duty not later than eight-thirty each night. Not earlier because he was supposed to leave everything in order each morning when he left. And about that special night you asked for, he was on duty on time."

"I'm most grateful," I told him. "Afraid, though, it's been a waste of time."

He seemed surprised, so I explained how, *if* I'd been working for Worrack, that was a thing of the past. He appeared to understand.

"A bad business, that," he said. "And it reminds me of something. I know it sounds a bit of a coincidence, but a pal of mine was asking me only last night about a reliable detective agency. Nothing in your line. Just the old divorce stuff. I give you my word, by the way, that it's absolutely genuine."

"If you want a reliable chap for your friend, I can give you one," I said, and gave him Bill Ellice's address and number. I also said I'd rather his friend didn't mention my name.

"I'm tremendously obliged," he said. "What about lunching with me in the near future? Can't be to-morrow on account of that damnable inquest."

I said it was good of him, and I'd see. Maybe I'd give him a ring. In any case, we'd be meeting somewhere. Then, as an afterthought, I said I'd be grateful if he'd forget any ideas he might have had about my ever working for Worrack, or anybody else for that matter.

"Worrack?" he asked tactfully. "Who's Worrack?"

That was that, and I promptly rang down for a service lunch. I also thought I was several kinds of a fool to go on being a hermit, so I ran my eye over the movies and matinees, and that afternoon I treated myself to a show. Then I had a quiet little tea at Fuller's, and as the sun was shining gloriously, I walked the whole way home.

Frank hailed me as soon as I stepped inside the hall. "Been looking for you, sir. This came for you while you were out. I signed it, sir, so perhaps you will let me have your signature."

"This" was a large envelope, addressed to L. Travers, Esq., and marked PRIVATE and URGENT.

"Who brought it, Frank?" I asked when I'd signed the book.

"Special messenger, sir. Most particular he was."

I gave Frank a tip and went up with the envelope. It was a good-quality envelope, so I opened it carefully with a knife. The first thing I saw was a wad of banknotes, and then a second wad. On top was a letter.

Dear Travers,

I know you to be a man of honour and that is why I am trusting you implicitly in a certain matter. Before you read any further I know you will respect any confidences about to be made and will afterwards burn this letter. Mr. Worrack was a friend of mine and I do not believe he took his own life. In fact I have strong reasons which I am unable to divulge for thinking he did not do so. In any case I know, and again I cannot divulge my source of information, that you are the one to discover the truth. What I beg of you to do, then, is to find out all you can without revealing any discovery to the police unless you are forced. I leave it to your honour to decide that.

Will you therefore regard me as your backer in the matter, and as evidence of my own good faith I enclose £100 in notes to cover any immediate expenses. While I do not suggest any line of action, I believe the attached may prove of interest to you. I would also add that I trust you implicitly to keep to yourself anything whatever that you may find discover, reporting it only to me.

If you agree, will you insert in the Personal Column of the Daily Telegraph *the following:*

READY. *Accept your offer. T.*

If you cannot accept, simply say "refuse" instead of "accept" and I will thereupon arrange for the return of the contents of this envelope. But I beg of you to help.

And I would also ask that if at any time you suspect who is the writer of this letter, you will give no hint that you know. I forgot to add that if you accept, further expenses will be sent if you intimate your wishes in the Personal Column.

Yours gratefully,

READY

That was the most extraordinary letter I'd ever received in my life, and even the first reading had made me gasp. When I'd read it a second time I did a bit of quick wondering. Hamson had written it, I thought, and had worded it craftily and so out of character that I could never connect it with him. Then I switched. It was typewritten, except for the signature, and that was neatly hand-printed. Lulu had typed it. She would be interested in who had poisoned Worrack. Yet I didn't know. Whoever had written it had done the job sufficiently well to bamboozle me entirely.

The notes, all in fivers, were attached to the letter by a clip, and I made them the £100 that had been mentioned. Then I turned my attention to the second enclosure, also held by a clip. First was a half sheet of paper on which was typed:

HIGHLY CONFIDENTIAL

and beneath that was a pawn-ticket! Attached to that was £90 in ten-pound notes!

Do you know what a pawn-ticket is like? If you don't, here is a drawing of that one.

Pawned with
COWAN, CLEETE & CO.,
229, CARTER ST.,
SOHO.

2110

Emerald ring, gold setting . . £90 0 0
(ninety pounds)

Ivan Markovitch,
273, Yeovil St.,
London, W.2.

The serration at the bottom showed where the pawn-broker's counterfoil had been torn off. That gives him a duplicate, and he also makes an entry in his ledger. And in case you don't know it, here is an important fact. In spite of the name on the ticket, the law assumes that the *holder* of the ticket is qualified to redeem the article pawned.

My free hand had gone to my glasses, even if there was still something I had missed. All I guessed, and bewilderedly enough, was that I was to redeem the ring with the ninety pounds. Charges, of course, would be paid out of the expense and retaining fee. You may think me slow in the uptake, but it was only then that I realised just what it was that I had to redeem. An emerald ring, pawned for ninety pounds and maybe worth double at least. Georgina Morbent had had such a ring!

A moment or two, and I was telling myself that there couldn't be a shadow of doubt. The clue to Worrack's death lay in Georgina's disappearance, and I'd know more about that when I'd found out about the ring. Another moment, and my fingers were at my glasses again and I was nervously moistening my lips.

As Syd Walker used to ask, "What would you have done, chums?" I won't tell you—yet—what I did, but I will say this. The money had no interest for me. I am far from a wealthy man, but I'm the very devil of a way from a poor one. For my amusements and hobbies in life I've always been prepared to pay handsomely, and here, in a dramatically reopened case, was something that had fascinating prospects. Dangerous prospects, too, as I knew, and I told myself I'd be a fool to get myself in wrong with the Yard if my activities leaked out. In fact I was in the very devil of a quandary, and it was not till the morning that I'd made up my mind.

CHAPTER IX
HERE ENDETH

IN THE MORNING, as I've said, I made up my mind, but I reached a decision by devious routes. Don't forget—and I don't think you are likely to forget it—that I'm not the least bashful about making theories. In my judgment, and it's not wholly as an armchair critic, the three rules for winning most things are, attack, then attack again, and then attack some more. In detective work theorising is attacking.

Long before I went to sleep I'd done some theorising about my employer, that is if I accepted the offer. I had the letter before me, and for an hour at least I tried to visualise various certainties about the one who had written it. Hamson was my first favourite. At one minute I was dead sure he had written it, and then I'd be not so sure. I hadn't quite credited, for instance, that yarn of his about wanting the name of a detective agency for a friend. Probably it was right, but if it wasn't, then why should he want to employ me? But my main objection to Hamson as the writer of the letter was that to me the letter showed signs of having been written by a woman.

I switched to Lulu, the rectory offspring whose urban education had been only too well completed by Worrack. She was my second favourite, displacing Hamson, that is.

It seemed to me that she might have had a better chance of acquiring that pawn-ticket—wheedling it out of some admirer, for instance—than Hamson, for how on earth he could have acquired it I had no idea. Doubtless, too, she had the money, for her salary must have been good and, as Worrack had cynically hinted, there were pickings. But I had two objections to Lulu. One, a very small one, was that the letter was not too well typed. Mistakes had been made and erased; in fact it was not a good advertisement for Lulu as a secretary. But that might have been designed, and to throw one off the scent. But the second objection was far more important, that the letter showed unmistakable signs of having been written by a man.

Then I had my brainwave, and just when I was thinking of Scylla. A man *and* a woman might have concocted that letter, so why not Scylla and Molde? Something told me I was on the scent. Scylla, according to Hamson, had money; and Molde, whatever I may inadvertently have led you to believe to the contrary, very definitely had brains. Scylla had them too, and quick-working ones, as I'd discovered that night in Worrack's office. But if those two were behind the letter, then every intuition told me that behind it was something crooked.

What could the scheme be? Obtaining through me information for the purposes of blackmailing someone? Making the £190, in fact, a lucrative investment? It couldn't be anything so foolish as luring me to the pawnshop to pay ninety pounds for a fake ring. A scheme so devious as that would mean not only that the pawn-ticket was a forgery but that the pawnbroker was the one who would get the ninety pounds. And the ninety pounds wouldn't be mine!

That was what I thought overnight, and when I woke in the morning it was all clear again in my mind. But setting aside that letter, and whoever had written it, I now had a new thought that was something of a resolve. Worrack had been murdered—of that I was sure—and I had liked him, and I was going to do my best to get the one who had got him. As for my unknown employer, well, I had the whip-hand. I could insert that acceptance in the newspaper, and then go blandly on in my own way. It would be for the employer to make the next move. In fact, if I wished I could force him, or her, or them, clean out into the open.

But I had also a last remnant of caution. Without going into the reasons why I should be a fool to involve myself farther in a highly complex and dangerous case, I made a bargain with myself; tossing, if you like, the coin of an event. To begin with, the pawnshop might be risky. What I would do would be to look up Ivan Markovitch—a phony name if ever there was one—and if anything suspicious arose, then I would insert the notice. If Ivan was a genuine person, then I would go no farther.

After breakfast I looked up Yeovil Street in a large-scale map of the town. There were three of them altogether, so the useful appendix told me, but the others were far removed from W.2. It was at about half-past nine when I left, and as it was again a perfect morning I decided to walk. My own views on Yeovil Street were that it would be a turning off a larger residential street, and that Number 273 would be a tobacconist's or other accommodation address. But when I reached it, after ten minutes' walking, I found it to be a fork from the main road and quite a high-class residential street in itself. Quite modern and expensive-looking flats were there but never a sign of a shop.

I began walking slowly along the side with the odd numbers until I came at last to Number 147. Then something peculiar happened, for the street forked into two new streets and neither was a continuation. Upwell Street was the name of one and Aukland Crescent the other. So I guessed that Yeovil Street had one-way numbers, and crossed to the other side. The first house was 148, but to my exasperation the second wasn't 149. It was 146, and after that came 144.

Along the road was a milkman and I asked him about it. He said there wasn't a 273. The last number was 148, and so it looked as if Ivan had given a faked address. Then I another idea. What if one of those big blocks of flats had one that was numbered 273? Hardly likely, perhaps, but worth trying. And just as I arrived at what was undoubtedly the biggest block, a taxi was going away and the hall porter who had helped with the luggage was still on the pavement.

"I expect it's a ridiculous question these days," I said to him, "but you haven't got a flat available here?"

"Not a hope, sir," he told me.

I shrugged my shoulders gracefully. "No harm in trying. How many are there here, by the way?"

"Exactly eighty," he said. "You wouldn't think it, sir, but there are, and they're not cubby holes at that."

That was the end of Yeovil Street for me. There certainly had been something fishy and a bet was a bet, especially when made with one's self. But as I walked back I decided on my new itinerary. A personal call in Fleet Street, I thought, and then to Soho and the pawnshop. All very simple, or wasn't it? It wasn't.

"Young feller-me-lad," I told myself, "you've got to watch your step. You can go into that pawnshop and collect the ring, but how much farther will that get you?"

I stopped where I was and looked at the palm of my hand as if the ring were in it. How far would that have got me? Not an inch. All I could do was to insert another notice—"Goods in my possession," or something like that, and then wait for the writer of the letter to make the next move. But that wasn't according to my book. I wanted a description of Markovitch, and I'd have liked to know if a platinum wrist-watch and a platinum cigarette-case had also been pawned. I wanted action, in fact. The correspondence method of carrying on the case looked hopeless from the point of view of a man who had only ten days' further leave left in town.

And how was I to get the information I wanted? I hadn't the least idea but it did seem to me that I might have a better hope of both bluff and bribery if I changed my mufti for uniform. So I altered my course for the flat again, and when I had changed I took a taxi for Fleet Street, for the morning was getting along.

The notice was handed in for the Personal Column and would appear, I was assured, in the next morning's issue. The taxi had waited and I finally paid it off at Piccadilly Circus. Then I reconnoitred, and when I'd located the pawnshop I went to a little place nearby for a coffee and a think. What I decided was to let action wait on event. On me I had my B.2606—the Army Identity Card—which might serve for bluff, and the wad of notes which might be useful as persuaders.

The pawnshop was a dingy one, even for a dingy street, though the rare sun did give it colour. In the windows were genuine rubbish and faked *objets de vertu*, and there was also a grilled window behind which were pieces of jewellery whose value I had no time to assess. The place was empty when I went in, pawn-ticket in hand. Though I'm blind as a bat without them, I'd taken off my glasses at the very last moment, and it was not till I'd had occasion to put them on again that I had a good look at the man who came up to me behind the counter. He was about fifty, rather shabby, certainly Jewish, and as wide-awake as they make them.

I cast a long look round the shop; a look suspicious and official. I hoped that would get me somewhere; and then at his, "Yes, sir?" I gave him a quiet look too.

"You Mr. Cowan?" I said.

"No, sir, I'm the manager. What is it you want?"

I put on my glasses and then counted out the notes, with a five-pound note for charges, and gave him the ticket.

"You have a ring of mine, I think?"

He gave me a quick look, then went off to somewhere at the far end of the counter. When he came back there was no fuss or bother. I signed for the ring as Ivan Markovitch and that was that. Then I gave another mysterious look round the shop. Next I produced my wallet and let him have a surreptitious look at my B.2606.

"I'd like to ask you a simple question or two," I said "If you want my *bona fides*, here they are."

I flourished the card under his nose, so that he could see it, photograph, official stamp and all.

"Just imagine," I said, and smiled craftily, "that I'm a Security Officer and making a confidential enquiry or two. And giving you my word that everything's strictly between you and me?"

I had taken out the wad of fivers and had put them carelessly in the tunic pocket.

"Depends what the questions are," he said, and shot me another look. "We aren't supposed to answer questions."

"In a court of law you are," I said. "But you and I don't want that. Besides, I don't want to know very much. Just a description of the real Ivan Markovitch—the one who pawned the ring."

He shook his head, though with a definite regret as I fingered the fiver.

"Sorry, sir, but it can't be done. You ought to know the Law about that. Besides, Mr. Cowan handled that."

I found another fiver and then put the rest carefully back in the breast pocket of my tunic.

"Think again," I said. "Or do I have to go and see Mr. Cowan?"

He shrugged his shoulders and spread his palms, but his eyes never left those two fivers. When at last they did, it was to have a quick look round. His voice lowered.

"You're sure this won't get me into any trouble?"

"I give you my honest-to-God word," I said, and fingered the notes. "These notes aren't marked," I added. "Look at them for yourself."

He was motioning mysteriously, and I made my way round the counter to a kind of office.

"I'll tell you about Markovitch," he said. "But even if you offered me a hundred quid I wouldn't tell you any more. Not that I've got anything to be afraid of."

"I never suggested it," I said, and waited.

"He's a Russian refugee," he said. "Connected with the Embassy, so he said. We've done a little business with him once or twice before. Jewellery belonging to himself, and his pals; you know how it is with those Russians."

"I know," I said helpfully. "Living from month to month on what they have to pawn. But what's he actually like?"

"Tall," he said. "Not as tall as you. About six foot, I'd say. A short black beard. Speaks fairly good English."

"Age?"

He shrugged his shoulders. "Over fifty. About my age perhaps. You never can tell with those foreigners."

"Any other distinguishing features?"

"He wears glasses," he said. "Looks a gent too."

"No scars, disfigurements, or anything?"

He shook his head, then remembered something. "Only that he's got hair on the back of his hands. Thick hair. Like some people have on their chests."

I held out the fivers, then appeared to change my mind.

"You've earned your money," I said. "Maybe some time you'll be willing to earn some more, on the same terms. But just a little assurance first. I've promised all this is strictly between you and me. It is—on one condition; that you've given me the straight dope. If I find this description, for instance, isn't genuine, then I take back what I've promised."

He swore by all that was holy that it was genuine, so I paid up. I also thanked him and told him he needn't worry. I thought of giving him my flat number, in case Markovitch called again, and then I thought better of it. A matter of a minute and I was outside again, and strolling back towards Piccadilly Circus.

As I turned into Coventry Street a taxi drew up to the pavement ahead of me. Who should get out but Hamson and we almost collided.

"Hallo," I said, "where have you sprung from?"

"The inquest," he told me.

"Of course," I said. "What happened?"

"The usual," he said. "Suicide in a moment of mental aberration, or words to that effect." Then he was giving me a shrewd look. "Would that have been your verdict?"

"Don't know," I said. "God forbid that I should judge anyone, let alone poor Worrack. But the funeral. Any subscriptions wanted for flowers or anything?"

He shook his head. "Poor old Peter wouldn't have wanted any fuss. But what about having lunch with me now?"

"Can't be done," I said. "Got an appointment with a bloke in about ten minutes. Been fooling around this morning," I added with what I hoped was insouciance. "Been grubbing round the Soho antique shops."

"Didn't know you were a collector," he said. "Get anything worth having?"

"Not really," I said. "Just one odd bit of jewellery."

"You must show it to me some time," he said. "I won't keep you now. Ring me up when you're free for lunch. I'm always in till ten in the morning."

I said I would, and we parted. Of one thing I was sure, that that reference to Soho and jewellery had left him stone cold. Unless I was the world's worst judge, it was not he, then, who was my new employer. Then I thought of something else, and circled round the Circus again. Down below I waited for an empty telephone kiosk and then rang Bill Ellice. Not that I had many hopes of finding him in; but he was.

"Hallo, Bill," I said. "Major Travers speaking."

"Oh, hallo, sir."

"Tell me, in the very strictest confidence, if since you rang me last any new business has come your way."

"Funny thing but it has! You mean I've got to thank you for it, sir?"

"Forget it," I said. "That's the last thing I want to talk about. But not very much in your line, is it?"

"Don't know, sir," he said. "Some of that divorce stuff can be pretty good. This one looks that way."

"Glad to hear it," I told him. "Good luck to you, Bill. Keep all this under your hat."

Well, that made Hamson out to be genuine enough. In fact I thought I'd been rather a fool to put him on my list at all. But I didn't do any more speculating, for I was suddenly feeling most damnably hungry. As I made my way to a place I knew, I all at once realised that I ought to do something about that ring and my employer. Maybe I ought to hurry to the *Telegraph* office and have my insertion altered.

READY. Accept your offer. Goods now in my possession.
T.

That, I thought, would meet the case. Then I changed my mind. Why rush my hurdles? Better by far let READY make the next move.

After lunch I went to a movie; one of those French pictures that are stimulating and provocative, and well out of the Hollywood rut. It was rather late for tea when I came out, but I dropped into a handy tea-shop for a cup before going on to the library. As I thought about the picture I'd seen I realised that another of my theories had gone west.

Jean, the French bar-tender, had been the corner-stone of a very pretty theory, and round him was to have been built—had I gone on with the original case—some possible solution of the disappearance of Georgina Morbent. Jean, I had thought, was the driver of the car that called for her after dark at the Richmond Hotel. It was a silly theory from the beginning, as I now knew, and the only reason, perhaps, why I had been taken with it was the idea that Georgina must have given Jean his job at the club and therefore knew him well enough to take him into her confidence.

But since the visit to the pawnshop it seemed reasonable to think that the driver of that car had been the elusive Markovitch. Was there such a person, I wondered. A dark beard can be faked and so can a foreign accent. But height could not, and when I cast about in my mind for someone of the height of Markovitch, I knew that both Molde and Hamson would fit the bill.

Then I had to smile at myself. I'd made up my mind to let things happen to me, through that notice in the paper, and I wasn't going to rush my hurdles, and yet there I was, theorising again when every theory I'd already produced in that case had been a waste of time. That theory, for instance, that Georgina had been alive, and that it was she who was listening behind the door in Worrack's room that first morning I met him. She couldn't be alive, I now told myself, for if she'd have thought as much of Worrack as he'd hinted that she did, then would she have kept out of the way when she knew he was dead? Or didn't she know he was dead?

There I was again, and so to keep my mind off things I gulped down the rest of my tea, paid my bill, and went off in the direction of the library, for if I was going to spend a domestic evening I'd need something to read. As I made my way along Regent Street I happened to glance in a jeweller's window. It was a firm with whom I'd done a little business in the past, so on the spur of the moment I walked in. An elderly man who knew me, but whose name I'd forgotten, came over to attend to me.

There was no one there but we two, so I took the ring from the fob pocket of my slacks and asked him if he'd give me a very rough idea of its value. He took one of those little spy glasses from his waistcoat pocket and squinted at the stone. Then he checked up more closely against a strong light.

"A very nice ring, sir," he said. "Very nice indeed. I suppose you don't want to sell it?"

I said I didn't. I also saw that he had been wary enough to suggest that before putting on a price. Then he said it was worth £250. Possibly more. High-class stuff had gone up enormously in value.

"How much do I owe you?" I asked him.

"Nothing at all, sir. It's a pleasure."

I thanked him and put the ring carefully back.

"Just give me a bit of private information," I said. "You know me, but suppose I'd taken this ring into a pawnshop where they didn't know me. Would it have been the duty of the pawnbroker to insist on enquiries before accepting it? Or even to have reported it to the police?"

He smiled rather dryly. "Depends on the pawnbroker, sir. I'd say that not one in fifty would have refused it, unless of course the person who tried to pawn it couldn't reasonably have owned anything so valuable."

That again was that, and it didn't tell me very much, except that Markovitch might have got far more money for that ring if he'd played his cards rather differently. From that it was easy to deduce that he couldn't play them differently. He had had to put himself at the mercy of the pawnbroker because any other method of raising money on the ring would have been too dangerous.

Theorising again, you see, and in full blast, but though I was aware of it, I couldn't stop myself. The train of thought was too attractive. For instance, did Markovitch expect to redeem the ring later and then make its value when things were less dangerous? Was the pawnbroker, in other words, merely a handy custodian? If so, why had Markovitch been such a careless fool as to lose the ticket? Or was it Markovitch—a fake Markovitch—who had sent me the ticket? Because it was too dangerous for him to get the ring out of pawn? That was it, I thought excitedly. I was merely an errand boy. I'd done Markovitch's dirty work for him, and he'd find some means of getting me to hand over the ring without his having to betray his identity. And, I told myself, I was damned if I was going to permit that. The ring, I believed was Georgina's. I could prove it, if occasion arose, by a confidential call on her sister, and no fake Markovitch or any other person was going to have that ring without giving me a good, sufficient and clean-out-in-the-open reason.

I stopped theorising then, not because I'd come to a cul-de-sac but for quite the opposite reason. A promising vista lay ahead and it was I who held the cards and had to play them rightly. Masterly inactivity, that must be the policy. READY must make all the moves and I'd make the counter-moves. A long business perhaps, and yet I didn't know. Inside a week, with any luck, I ought to force his hand. Unlike the importunate widow who wearied by her much asking, I'd drive READY frantic by being dumb.

Frank readily agreed to send a *Telegraph* up each morning with my breakfast and I promised to bring it down in under an hour, when I came through on my usual walk. I'd have preferred one of my own, but Frank said it just couldn't be done.

When the paper came the following morning I found that notice of mine at the head of the Personal Column, and that was all for the moment, because I couldn't expect any sort of reply till the next day's issue. So, in strict compliance with my overnight resolve, I set about planning my day. A long stroll in Hyde Park, I thought, just to see how things were looking there, for with the marvellous weather we'd been having, crocuses should be out and there might even be early daffodils. Then lunch at my club, where I'd been a stranger for months, and after that and a yarn with any old acquaintances there might be about, I'd plan the rest of the day.

It was just after half-past ten when I was handing Frank back the *Telegraph*. He said I needn't have hurried, for it belonged to a Mrs. Somebody who never woke till midday. Then he said it was a pretty horrible business about that head.

"What head?" I said.

"That woman's head that was found," he said. "They reckon the police have got a clue, though."

Frank loves murders and divorces, and before I could dodge him he had found me a newspaper of the baser sort.

"There it is, sir. Much the same as was in the papers last night."

SEVERED HEAD OF WOMAN
DRAMATIC DISCOVERY IN LONDON PARK

Those were the headlines. I ran a casual eye over the rest without actually seeing a word.

"Pretty ghastly, as you say," I remarked, handing the paper back.

"I hope they find the one what did it," Frank told me grimly. "Red hair, they reckoned, she'd got, so that ought to make it a bit easy."

I was just moving off, but that stopped me in my tracks. But I didn't like to ask for the paper again, so as soon as I got outside I was looking round for a taxi. I was lucky enough to get one, and in ten minutes I was at my club.

Papers of all sorts were there, and I found one with the discovery spread on the front page. This is what I read:

> A dramatic and horrible discovery was made yesterday morning by Mr. James Gullage, a park-keeper in Hyde Park. Under a seat near Spouter's Corner he found a parcel and when he opened it he was horrified to find the severed head of a woman. A policeman happened to be in sight and Mr. Gullage immediately called him. It is understood that the police have a highly important clue and sensational developments are expected. (See below.)

Below was an interview with Mr. Gullage, but chiefly padding, for he had obviously had the matter taken out of his hands by the policeman. He did say, however, that the head was that of a "lady" and that she had the most beautiful red hair; what, in words certainly faked by the reporter was "the most silky and striking auburn I have ever come across."

When I laid the paper aside I found myself polishing my glasses. It seemed to me a certainty that that head was Georgina Morbent's, and as my mind flashed back to all I knew and had been told, something like horror came over me. A head, I told myself, but no limbs; though doubtless they'd be found later. There were a dozen things I wanted to know. How had the severing been done, for instance; how long had the woman been dead, and what was the clue that the police had found?

I got to my feet. With my pull at the Yard it shouldn't be too difficult to find those things out and even to get a look at the head itself. Then I sat down again. At all costs I must keep myself clear of what had happened. If the head was Georgina Morbent's, then before I knew it I might find myself somehow involved, and there might be the very devil of a lot of things I'd find it uncommonly hard to explain. But though I changed my mind about going to the Yard, I couldn't settle to anything. That visit to Hyde Park wouldn't be politic either, and my morning generally had been knocked cock-eyed.

Then it struck me that that discovery might be having an even more terrific effect on READY, and that he wouldn't wait for a communication with me in the next day's *Telegraph* but might even risk a telephone call to my flat. So out I went in search of a taxi.

I had been back about ten minutes, mooning restlessly about, when the telephone went. My heart began to race as I grabbed the receiver. But it was only Hamson.

"Pretty ghastly news," he began. "I suppose you've seen it?"

I preferred to lie doggo and asked what news. He told me.

"How're you sure it's Georgina?" I asked.

"Barbara's identified her," he said. "The poor girl's absolutely prostrate. I've just left her now."

"Horrible," I said. "Do tell her how desperately sorry I am."

That was about all, but it left me more restless than ever. It took the appetite from my lunch and I made up my mind to go to a show and get my mind off things. Let READY telephone if he wished, but I shouldn't be there. Maybe he'd open out a bit in the morning's *Telegraph*.

I found a show I rather wanted to see, and then just as I was going out, the telephone went again.

"Hallo, hallo," a voice said impatiently.

Only two words, but I knew that voice at once. It was George Wharton's!

Part Two
THE OLD MASTER

CHAPTER X
A SLIPPERY TRACK

DO YOU KNOW George Wharton? If not, and you meet him, let me give you a word of warning. What you will see will be a tall, heavily built man, with a slight stoop and a huge walrus moustache. If he dons his antiquated spectacles and peers benignly at you over their tops, you will know him for a kind father and a perfect husband. Something wistful in his eyes may tell you that he is probably henpecked by a wife who doesn't understand him. Subsequently you may describe him—women often do—as an old dear. That impression of yours may explain why I call him an old humbug and it may account for that other 'old' in the Yard's nickname of the Old General.

What of the real George? Well, there isn't one, for George is always playing a part and revelling in it. Like Voltaire's Frenchman, he can't even stir his tea without a stratagem. Did you ever see one of those music-hall magicians who can produce for you out of a miniature bar contraption with one tap any drink you call for, from milk to absinthe? Well, George is rather like that. He can turn on his tap and produce anything, from crocodile tears to the pure milk of human kindness. He does everything with such gusto and a perfection of showmanship— at least, that is his own private opinion. His speciousness would swindle Uriah Heep, his wheedling would have been the envy of the sirens, his tenacity would make Bruce's spider seem a yellow quitter, and his wrath would make Hitler's mouthings sound like a B.B.C. poetry reading. Some of that explains the 'General' in the nickname.

I have long seen through his little tricks, however; the way he keeps pieces of information and discoveries to himself, and then produces results which are expected to astound you, just as if you didn't know that up his sleeve he had kept not only the ace of trumps but a couple of pairs of spare packs as well. There's the way he'll invite and even beg me to theorise, and then ridicule my efforts. Then, when later I analyse results, I find it is one of my derided theories that he has worked on, but craftily altered and manipulated to look like some inspiration of his own.

The devil of a man to work with, you might say. But don't you believe it. Working with George may be exasperating at times, but it's very good fun. Like being at a theatre, except that George wants to play all the parts. But don't imagine he's any kind of a buffoon. Ripe and fruity, yes; but a man doesn't become a Superintendent at the Yard except by hard work and merit. At a necessary moment George can lose his stoop and draw himself up with a dignity that somehow reminds you of the awful majesty of the Law, its long traditions, its incorruptibility, and its remorselessness of patience. I laugh at him, but when I expose his weaknesses, it is because I don't want you to miss the best part of him. But there's no man for whom I have a greater regard, respect, and admiration. As for my wife, she loves him. She once remarked that she'd love to have him stuffed.

It was just half-past two that afternoon when, with an outward imperturbability, I entered George's room at the Yard. Never had his smile been more endearing or his handshake so hearty.

"Well, well," he said. "It's good to see you again."

"And you, George," I said.

I should tell you that over the telephone he'd said he'd heard I'd been asking after him, but he'd been away on a job and had only just got back. He'd also got out of me that I had ten days more of my leave, and that I wasn't doing anything in particular. Then having fixed a place and time he'd rung off.

"So you're just on the look-out for something to do," he said. "Not that I've got anything much."

"A pity," I said, and smiled cynically.

"Yes," he said piously, and then I knew something was coming, for he was taking his antiquated spectacles out of their still more antiquated case, and adjusting them well down his nose in the most convenient place for peering over their tops.

"The fact is," he said, with a mildness that was meant to be deceptive, "I happened to hear you were in town in a rather different way." Then he was peering at me. "What I might call a remarkable way." He shook his head regretfully. "A way I'd never have thought of."

"Damn you for an old humbug," I burst out at him. "Why the hell can't you say what you mean!"

"There you are!" He threw up his hands in simulated grief. "There was a time when you talked like a gentleman." He shook his head again. "I'm afraid the Army's done you no good. In fact I'm sure it hasn't."

"And why?" I asked amusedly.

"Well,"—he spread his palms again—"the way you lose control of yourself. And frequenting gaming houses. I ask you."

I cursed Brontway under my breath for the double-crosser he'd doubtless been.

"Oh, that," I said, and still amusedly. "I'm afraid you've got me pretty badly wrong."

"I hope I have," he told me unctuously.

"Blast you, George, will you listen," I told him exasperatedly. "If it's my morals you're worried about, you might at least hear my side of the story before crediting other people's. I could tell you a thing or two, too."

"Oh?" he said, and shot me another look over the tops of his spectacles.

"Yes," I said. "What I gather is that you're in charge of that severed head business, and you've discovered the trail leads back to a Peter Worrack who committed suicide. When you dug into that you came across my name. Sorry, you were horrified to come across my name."

That caught him in the wind. "I don't know about that," was all he could say.

"Well, it's my guess and I'll bet you a new hat it isn't very far out," I said.

Then I told him my story, and he actually swallowed it. I'd happened to run across Worrack, etc., etc.; the same tale, in fact, that I'd told Brontway, with a trimming or two in George's special line. I told him that I knew Barbara Grays through that hospital committee, but so little that I'd forgotten all about her when I met her again. I added that Worrack had hinted that he was worried about the sister's long absence without a word to a soul. As for that gambling den, I told him that it was a highly respectable place.

"You were all breaking the law, weren't you?" he snorted at me.

"No doubt," I said. "You're not a Galahad yourself, if it comes to that. What about that ticket you had for the last Irish sweep? However," I went on, "I'm the last one to cast a stone. All I will say is, the next time you want to call me into your study like a ruddy headmaster, make sure of your facts."

"There you go again," he said, and raised his hands as if appealing to high heaven. "Can't you take a joke. Anybody but you'd have known I was pulling your leg."

"Splendid," I said. "That's what I'm doing. Pulling your leg. Now, what about your telling me a few things. How far have you got?"

"Nowhere at all yet," he said, and then as a sop to me: "That's why I could have leapt into the air when I heard about you from that chap Brontway."

"I'd have liked to see you," I told him. "But what have you done?"

"Well, I saw that head, and what was found with it. I can't show it to you because it's being gone into." He went over to the side table. "But here's the brown paper it was wrapped in, and the string that tied it."

"No blood," I said. "Was the head cut off after death?"

"Yes," he said, "and a good bit after death—so I'm told. But here's the funny thing. The paper was double, the same as it is now, but between the folds was this."

What he gave me was one of those invitations to the club. That one was made out to Mrs. Georgina Morbent, and the date was the 10th January.

"Pretty much of a gift, wasn't it?" I asked. "It told you who she was, and it led you straight to Worrack."

"Right enough," he said. "What I've been wondering, though, is why the information was given. Talk about a gold salver?"

He had been peering at me over the spectacle tops again; an obvious invitation to theorising.

"Surely someone wanted you to go straight to Worrack."

"Yes," he said craftily. "But when? Before Worrack died, or after?"

"I get you, George," I said admiringly. "You think the head ought to have been discovered before, and it ought to have led to Worrack. If it was a plant, then someone was trying to frame Worrack. If it wasn't, then Worrack was just too careless."

"That's what I've been thinking," he said. "The head was put somewhere and nobody found it, as they ought to have done. So it was shifted to where it was bound to be found."

"Then the one who shifted it must have known that Worrack was dead," I pointed out. "What was the point in casting suspicion on a dead man?"

"That's one of the things we've got to find out." He began putting his spectacles away, their purpose having been accomplished. "After that I had the sister identify the head. A nice woman, that Mrs. Grays, even if she is mixed up with that set." He had been about to say "gambling set" but remembered in time.

"What did she tell you about the sister's absence?" I asked.

It appeared she had told George that same tale as had been told to Brontway. George appeared to be believing it, and I didn't disillusion him. She had naturally mentioned the Irish visit, so George had got hold of O'Clauty, who was crossing at once.

"He won't be here till to-morrow afternoon," he said. "Then we'll see him."

You'll appreciate the dilemma I was in. There were so many things I wanted to know and yet each question I put had to be most carefully worded for fear I should make a slip. The track wasn't a slippery one, it was just sheer smooth ice. But I saw no harm in asking why he wanted to see O'Clauty, and why a telephone conversation wouldn't have done as well.

"How do we know he's telling the truth?" he asked me.

"He says she never went to Ireland, so the sister told me, but there's only his word for it. Oh, no," he said, and shook his head reprovingly. "Short cuts don't pay. I'd like to run my eye over this O'Clauty. For all we know, he may be a bit of a surprise."

I could have added that O'Clauty was going to produce rather more than a surprise if he told George about Richmond.

"Have you got any suggestions?" George was going on.

"I don't know that I have," I said, and was doing some more quick thinking. "What does strike me is this. If this Mrs. Morbent did go off with another man, then why did he murder her?"

"Just a minute," George cut in. "Isn't that getting on a bit too far? The fact that there's a severed head doesn't prove she was murdered. She may have died on this man's hands, so to speak. For some reason—if he was a married man, for instance, or had to avoid scandal—he had to dispose of the body."

"A good job, was it? I mean the cutting?"

"Fair," George said. "It wasn't done by an expert. But to get back to that theory of yours. What's wrong with this? Worrack found out about that man and her, and it was he who did her in."

"As good as any other theory," I told him guardedly. "Also it gives a stronger motive for Worrack's suicide. But let's assume she was murdered, and that the other man did it. Why did he do it?"

"To get himself out of an awkward hole," he suggested, but as if he didn't believe it himself.

"Maybe," I said, and then popped in with some of the things I was itching for him to get at. "But suppose he'd intended to do away with her from the first, and he thought it worth while for other reasons. What jewellery did she have on her, for instance? A wealthy woman, going off with a man, should have taken a pretty valuable lot. And money? What about that? In fact—though heaven forbid I should teach you your job—I'd ask the sister about the jewellery and see her bank manager about the money."

"As a matter of fact," he began, and I knew from his honeyed tone that he was going to do a bit of showing off, "I did ask the sister about jewellery, and she gave me a likely list. It's being circulated to all pawnshops and jewellers straightaway."

I went hot and cold all over, wondering if my friend at Cowan & Cleet's would come forward with information.

"What you don't know, probably, is that this Mrs. Morbent did start off for Ireland," George told me. "Worrack saw her off, and the date was the 13th of January. Now you know why I want to see O'Clauty. Worrack would have been the man to know what jewellery she was wearing."

"He wouldn't have known what she was carrying in her bag," I said. "But what about her will? Got the details yet?"

"Yes and no," he said, and I gathered he'd extracted something from Barbara Grays. George would always boast that women witnesses were putty in his hands. "What I was thinking was that I'd see the solicitors now. I've got the address and her bank too. I wondered if you'd like to see the bank manager for me."

"Certainly, if it's any help," I said. "When do I go? Now?"

"No time like the present," he told me briskly. "Here's the address. I'll ring up to say you're coming."

In less than twenty minutes I was in the manager's office, and we were telling each other what a horrible business the death of Georgina Morbent was.

"A charming woman, Mr. Travers," he told me. "Of strong opinions, mind you, but always charming."

"That makes us both all the more eager to see justice done," I said portentously.

"Indeed it does," he said. "Of course, everything's strictly in confidence."

I said that naturally it was, and with that he began to unloosen. On the 11th January Mrs. Morbent had called at the bank, and she had done two significant things. She had cashed a cheque on self for three hundred pounds, and had taken it all, except fifty, in one-pound notes. Then she had asked for her pass-book and had waited till it was made absolutely up to date.

Now, when I used the word "significant" I meant to me and not necessarily to him.

"A large amount for her to draw out?" I asked.

"Oh, no," he said. "But I think it was unusual for her to draw it in one-pound notes."

"She kept a large balance?"

"Roughly about five thousand," he said. "Not a lot for a woman in her position. The cheques for her trainer, a man named O'Clauty, were often rather large, particularly in the summer, when there was no racing."

"How did she find racing? A ruinous business?"

He smiled amusedly. "The scale she raced on wouldn't have made a great deal of difference whatever happened. She was a very wealthy woman. But as a matter of fact she lost very little. O'Clauty is a very shrewd man, so I'm told."

"Well, you're a busy man," I said, "and so am I. I can't see her pass-book or the cancelled cheques to January the 11th, but I can see a statement, and that amounts to the same thing."

He rang through for it to be made up and then I asked another question.

"Did she keep her jewels with you?"

He said they were in the strong room. Mrs. Morbent had kept them there for a year or two, since during the blitz in fact. If necessary he could give me a list.

"It's another kind of list I want," I said. "The list of that wasn't in the strong room."

He did a bit of thinking. She was not a woman who relied on things like jewellery for her charm, he said, and she rarely wore anything. A wedding ring? No. But the last few months she had worn a beautiful square-cut emerald ring. She had shown it to him and he had admired it. Then he remembered the platinum cigarette-case, solid and valuable, and lastly the platinum and jewelled wrist-watch, quite a simple affair, but in perfect taste like all her things, and certainly very valuable too.

The statement came in and we had a look at it together. It covered a period of four months, and most of the payees were easy to check up on. Rent of flat, for instance; O'Clauty's account, cheques on self, payments to dressmakers and hairdressers, and small cheques to Worrack. One or two cheques looked like payments to casual firms and didn't need checking. One to a Madame Montrose for instance, for eleven guineas and one to a W. M. Chataway, for five guineas. The first might have been a modiste, and who the other was he had no idea. In any case the amounts were so small as not to be worth worrying about.

As for the credit side, there were dividends, cheques drawn by Worrack, and at least three from a firm of bookmakers. They also needed no explanation, so I put the statement in my wallet and rose as if to go.

"A highly confidential piece of information," I said, lowering my voice. "We couldn't help wondering about blackmail. I'm glad to see that nothing in the statement suggests it."

He smiled rather grimly. "She wasn't the sort who'd have stood for that sort of thing. I pity the man who tried to blackmail her." Then he was looking a bit aghast.

"Not that I'm suggesting anything of the sort, of course. I couldn't conceive of her doing anything that would lay her open to blackmail."

"I know," I said, "But we have to look at things from all angles."

Another twenty minutes and I was back in George's room. I didn't expect him there, but it appeared that, unknown to me, he'd already rung the solicitors and had merely had to call round for a copy of the will and to put any questions arising therefrom. It was like him to want to know what I'd found out before telling me what had happened to him.

When I told him about the jewellery, I found the three articles tallied with what he'd wormed out of Barbara Grays, and I ought to have been exasperated when I discovered also that the three articles were those about which enquiries were being made. But I wasn't. I was only scared stiff when I thought again about my pawnbroker friend.

"Doesn't it look to you as if Worrack gave her that ring?"

"Quite possibly," he said, and pursed his lips. "If he did, where does it get us?" he asked, and gave me a glare.

"I'm only trying to be helpful," I told him amiably. "But what about this? She took out her pass-book so that she could destroy the cancelled cheques. There was a payment—or payments—she didn't want traced, if anything happened to her. But not being too knowledgeable, she forgot that a statement would give the show away."

"Has it given it away?"

"Don't be so damn superior," I told him. "It has given her away. It's told us that she drew two hundred and fifty pounds in one-pound notes. What woman's going to be bothered with a wad like that? What she was going to do was pay them over to someone who didn't want the payment traced, as fivers and tenners could have been."

"Blackmail?"

I shrugged my shoulders. If so, as I pointed out, then it was a first payment. He said the sister ought to have noticed some change in her, and it was a pity she couldn't be questioned, but she'd had a kind of breakdown from shock.

"What did you find out?" I asked.

It turned out to be little more than I knew already, except for one quite dramatic thing. A week before that supposed trip to Ireland she'd changed her will. It had been a rush affair and she'd made a significant remark to the lawyers, that there were more unlikely things than that she'd be changing it again in a few weeks. At the same time, she'd had the property conveyances rushed through for Worrack.

The will itself was very short and simple, and at her own insistence. Twenty thousand to Worrack, five hundred and the flat to George and the same to Lulu, the balance to Barbara Grays, and the two horses to O'Clauty, with a special condition that Amber King was not to be sold unless he'd won either the Cheltenham Gold Cup or the Grand National.

"What do you make of it all?" George wanted to know.

"That obviously she knew she was soon going to be in a dangerous spot," I said. "That she was likely to die, in fact. Also that she had, say, a fifty-fifty chance, and if she was lucky she might be changing the will again."

"Just as I read it," he said. "It puts us up a bigger gum-tree than ever."

I threw in my old theory of a possible hasty marriage, and how she'd repented when she met Worrack, and how it was the blackmailer she was going to meet.

"Anything's worth trying," he said. "But two-fifty's not much of a blackmail payment."

"Some people would think it so," I said.

He said he'd get Somerset House to work and that'd settle the marriage business.

"And what now?" I asked hopefully.

Nothing, he said, for the moment. He had notes to write up, and a man or two to see. What I might like to do, however, was to turn up at the club that night. Nine o'clock sharp.

"What's happening?" I asked. "The club's closed down, isn't it?"

"Opening for one night only," he told me with a chuckle. "The old gent"—that was the complacently disparaging way he would sometimes allude to himself—"had a brainwave. I saw Conroy, that manager chap, and he gave me the list of those who used the place most. I went over it and picked out a few. A half-dozen or so, and they've been asked to turn up to-night."

"What's the idea?" I asked. "A reconstruction?"

"All in good time," he told me exasperatingly. Then in his mildest tone. "As a matter of fact that's where I'm off to as soon as I've written those notes. I don't suppose you'd like to come along?"

"Since you ask me so earnestly, I don't think I would," I told him cynically, and picked up my hat. "In any case I'd rather get home before the black-out."

"Well, see you at nine," he said, and held out his hand. A huge and yet flabby sort of hand it was, and I'd never seen him looking so much like a church deacon.

CHAPTER XI
WHARTON AT WORK

I ARRIVED AT the front entrance of the club on the stroke of nine. Another man came up at the same time, the prosperous-looking gent who'd given Barbara Grays that Stock Exchange tip, though I didn't recognise him till George Conroy had let us in.

"What's on, George?" he was asking at once.

"Just a special night, sir," George told him. "A few things to clear up."

"What's the idea?" he demanded of me when George had left us at the head of the stairs.

I shrugged my shoulders. He gave me a suspicious look, remembering, no doubt, how helpful I'd been to Brontway, so there wasn't any more conversation. Inside the main room there seemed to be about eight people, and I recognised them all. Lulu, Hamson, Molde and Scylla I'd expected to see, and Jean perhaps, who was standing forlornly by the closed bar. There was also a lean man, a theatre magnate I learned later, and a jovial-faced little man who was something in the City. The roulette table was bare, but the green shaded lights were on above it, and chairs had been placed. The rest of the room was as I had seen it last.

Naturally, there was an air of restraint. Hamson gave me a nod and remarked helpfully that he saw they'd dragged me in too. Lulu gave me a wan smile, and Scylla a decidedly nervous one. Molde, who'd been standing by her chair, made for me and was wanting to know what it was all about. Before I could do more than shrug my shoulders, Wharton was making a dramatic entry, with George, from Worrack's office.

"Ladies and gentlemen"—up went his hand—"I must introduce myself. Superintendent Wharton of the Criminal Investigation Department." His features softened in a smile that I can only call roguish. "But don't let that alarm you. Whatever may have gone on in this room, there aren't going to be any prosecutions. I give you my word on that. No!"—and he struck an attitude that was perfect Mark Anthony. "What I've asked you here for is to see if any of you can throw any light on that terrible affair of Mrs. Morbent. Ladies and gentlemen, I know that I shall have your co-operation."

I don't know why I didn't applaud. Perhaps I was wondering what the swindle was going to be, and in half a minute I knew—at least some of it. George Wharton explained that he was going to put two questions to us and they would be answered in strict confidence. To ensure that, the answers would be written down on sheets of paper that would be handed round, and with the same kind of pencil. The statements would be unsigned and then they would be folded and collected. Just like a ballot, and just as secret, he said. What he was interested in was the answers, not the writers.

George got us seated round the roulette table, and then Wharton handed out the sheets of paper and the pencils.

"Now ladies, and gentlemen, please write a figure in the top left-hand corner, and opposite it put your answer. If you haven't anything to write simply leave the space blank. You are all ready? Then the question's this, preceded by a statement. It's no secret that the late Mrs. Morbent was a very close friend of the late Mr. Worrack. Shall we imagine, for the purpose of this test, that she was engaged to him? Very well. Here's the question I'd like you to answer. Do any of you know of any other man in Mrs. Morbent's life within the last month, shall we say? That's all, ladies and gentlemen, and I leave it to you to know what kind of man I mean."

We looked furtively at each other and then some of us began to write. In under two minutes Wharton was ready for his second question. It was an easy one. Was there anything—anything under the sun—that any of us knew or could remember, that might throw any light whatever on the murder of Mrs. Morbent. You will notice that he made no bones about the word murder.

I was pretending to write, but now and again having a surreptitious look round. The two women seemed to be taking things very seriously. Molde was biting the end of his pencil. Hamson caught my eye and gave a quick shrug of the shoulders. Jean was looking puzzled and kept looking round, but there was nobody who was taking it as any kind of joke. The business was too grim for that, and Wharton was towering above us like an usher.

"Don't be afraid of putting down anything that mayn't seem very important," he reminded us. "I'll be the judge of that. And don't forget that everything's strictly confidential."

Nobody seemed to have anything else to write, so he told us to fold our papers up; then he collected them himself and deposited them in a large envelope. Then he whispered to George, who had not been asked to write, by the way, and after that he made his final announcement.

"That's all, ladies and gentlemen, and I'm very grateful for the trouble you've taken. If anything should subsequently occur to any of you, I rely on you to communicate with Scotland Yard. Every confidence will be respected."

It was not till the room had cleared, except for George and Jean, that he and I went to the office.

"Now we'll see what we've got," he said, and shot the papers out on the table. "You hold them to the light and you'll see a number in one corner."

"What's that for?" I wanted to know.

"Did you notice how you were sitting?" he said, and when I said I didn't: "A pretty nice detective you are! In alphabetical order, that's how you were sitting."

"Rather sharp practice, wasn't it?" I told him.

"Why should it be?" He glared. "Everything's in confidence, isn't it?"

"More or less," I said, and got on with the job, which was to call out the number on the paper—previously written in invisible ink—to George who then told me the writer's name, I wrote that on the paper under the number.

"We've got all their prints," he told me when I'd finished. "They might come in handy some time. Now let's check up what's been written."

Most of the remarks were negative, such as: "Regret I can't find anything to say." Of the positive ones, three only looked at all promising.

Parsons (the lean man). "Why were all sorts of yarns told us when we asked after Mrs. Morbent? Someone must have known she wasn't absent in what I might call a regular way. We all thought very highly of her and that's why we asked."

Wharton and I agreed that there was nothing to follow up in that. The question involved far too many theories.

That either Worrack or Barbara Grays had been concerned with her death, for instance, or if there was any truth in the views they'd expressed that at any moment they'd always expected Georgina to turn up out of the blue or send news of herself.

Scylla. "Why did Mrs. Morbent come so rarely to the club when everyone knew it was really hers? Was she having an affair with another man when she knew P. W. was safely parked here?"

"What's your opinion of that?" George asked me.

"A bit of feline playfulness," I said. "If Worrack was manager, then she was letting him get on with the job."

He made a note in his book and then we had a look at the third communication.

Lulu. "Isn't it a fact that the sisters had at least one bad quarrel and so violent that Mrs. Morbent was ill after it? Ada Grant, the maid, might tell you a thing or two, and why was she dismissed?"

"That's very definitely cattish," I remarked.

"All the better," George told me with a chuckle. "I like to see them with their claws out and spitting. That's when you hear things. But what sort of a maid does she mean?"

I said I thought a personal maid. Then I let out a bit more.

"Don't let him know the source of your information," I said, "but that chap Hamson might tell you something about all that. He is supposed to be friendly—very friendly indeed—with Mrs. Grays."

"Yes," he said. "George told me all that."

Then he was putting the papers away, and the envelope in his overcoat pocket. From his manner I thought something must be in the wind, and it was. He opened the door and called to George to 'bring him along'.

'Him' was Jean. Wharton nodded amiably at him, said he was sorry he'd had to waste an evening, and then was asking for his full name. Jean, who had looked decidedly nervous, told him with all the aplomb in the world that the name was Jean Carpentier.

"You are French?" Wharton asked. With the same deceptive gentleness.

Jean shot me a look, and then remarked that he was a citizen of the world.

"Capital!" said George. "I'm a bit of a cosmopolitan myself. You speak pretty good French?"

"Naturellement, m'sieu."

Wharton, who speaks better French than any Englishman I know, burst suddenly out into a literal torrent. I'm not too bad myself, but I didn't catch even the drift of a quarter of it. I did catch a couple of phrases that were indelicate, to say the least of them, and concerned with the pulling of people's legs.

"What do you say to that?" Wharton asked him when the half-minute oration was over.

Jean said nothing. He was looking like a deflated blimp. Even his moustache had wilted.

"Show me your identity card," Wharton said, and still quite amiably.

"I have not him with me," Jean said, and shrugged his shoulders in regret.

"I don't know that it matters," Wharton told him, and now his eyes were beginning to narrow. He frowned and rapped his skull with his knuckles. "Let me see if I can remember. John Carpenter's your name. You were what they call a stooge to Carl Pellet, the French comedian, and you worked the Continental halls with him, and here too. Then the French authorities collared him for drug peddling, and you were out of a job. But you found one. In—let me see—in 1937 you got two years for trafficking in drugs and procuring. I hope that's right?"

Mild though the words were, the look was now a glare. Jean had shrivelled to nothing, and with a contemptuous gesture Wharton turned away. Then he was shooting me a quick look as if to see how I'd taken the exhibition.

"You've got his address?" he asked George. George said he had it.

"Then clear out!" Wharton suddenly roared at the barman. "And if I want you, see you come at the double."

Jean fairly scrambled out of the door.

"A nice sort of character to employ," Wharton told George.

"We didn't know all that, sir," Conroy said. "Fairly kidded us, he did. He was straight enough with us, sir." Then he was adding lamely that all that parley-vooing had gone down very well.

"It probably did," Wharton told him curtly. Then he gave one of his special glares. "Any dope peddling going on here?"

"Here, sir?" George looked positively horrified. "Never, sir. I'd swear to that on my dying bed. Anything of that sort, sir, the guvnor'd have jumped on with both feet."

Wharton gave a grunt. "Let's hope you're right," he said. "Better try over the reconstruction. I don't want to be here all night."

I was booked for the reconstruction, which followed the same lines as that which I'd demonstrated with Brontway. It didn't take long, with only the two of us to act and Wharton to look on. All the time I was wondering just why Wharton was considering it necessary, now the verdict of suicide had been brought in. I was wondering other things, and you may have been wondering about them too. Why had Hamson written nothing positive on his paper, for instance, when there was so much that he knew? Probably he knew very much more than he had imparted to me. Was he trying to keep absolutely clear of things, *and himself out of danger*? Or was it out of some mistaken idea of loyalty to myself?

And Molde, why had he written nothing positive either? Never a word about seeing Georgina Morbent at Euston that late afternoon; and if that wasn't important, what was? He couldn't be keeping quiet out of any loyalty to myself. I doubted if Molde had any loyalties at all except to himself, and any to spare, maybe, to Scylla.

Wharton expressed himself as satisfied, and said he'd be going. Conroy was given effusive thanks, though doubtless in his mind there would long remain the vision of Wharton's less unctuous moments. In a couple of minutes Wharton and I were groping our way in the black-out. He had said he'd walk to my place and take the Tube from nearby, and at the first opportunity I asked my first question, with a little bit of sugar on the pill. George always had a sweet tooth.

"What a memory you've got, George! If I'd had one as good I'd have been a millionaire by now."

He chuckled. "Or been in jail. But he was easy meat, Jean Carpentier!" He snorted. "Who could forget a face like that."

"Why that reconstruction business?" I asked. "Don't you think that inquest verdict on Worrack was correct?"

"Why shouldn't I see things for myself?" he fired at me, and I knew the answer was an evasive one. A grunt or two and he was grudgingly adding more. "Besides, that duropine stuff is pretty tricky. All those variable action poisons are." Another grunt. "Does that get you anywhere?"

It didn't, though obviously it should have done. But George wraps things up pretty shrewdly when he has a mind, and before I could comment he was shifting ground.

"A fi'pun note to a pinch of horse-dung there was peddling going on in that place."

"Then it wasn't to Worrack's knowledge," I said. "Conroy was right. He would have been furious. Say and think what you like, but he kept that place clean."

"That's all you know."

"Have it your own way," I told him. "But let's come out in the open. Assume Worrack was murdered—poisoned in fact. You think Carpenter found the stuff that did it?"

"Possibly," he said, and I was thinking of the night when Jean had given the high sign that sent Scylla to Worrack's office. "That is, if I thought anything of the kind."

I let out a sigh. "Why were you so keen on getting people's prints?" I said. "Were there any on the brown paper the head was in?"

"Devil a one," he said. "But that isn't to say prints won't turn up somewhere later on."

"Why was the head put where it could be found?" I went on. "That's something that interests me. Will the rest of the body be found in various pieces too?"

"Very interesting, that head," he said. "You mean to say you haven't any ideas?"

"Plenty," I told him. "It needed only the head to identify her, for instance. Also, finding the head meant telling the world she was dead, and without telling what she had died of. Therefore we can presume she died of something that affected the rest of the body."

"Not bad," he said. "In fact, it's pretty good. It'll sound even more good if the rest of the body doesn't turn up."

"A man's job very definitely, don't you think?"

"If you mean the cutting up, then I do," he said. "But that isn't to say a woman wasn't concerned in what happened before."

That was fair enough, and then we came to the fork where he would turn right for the Tube station. I put my last question.

"Come clean out of your shell, George, and give me a straight answer to a straight question. Do you or do you not think the two deaths are connected?"

He grunted and I could almost feel his brain hedging. "Don't you think so?"

"I do," I said. "You and I have seen the long arm of coincidence stretch pretty far, but I don't think there's any stretching this time. Bluntly, I think you're up to the neck in two murders."

"The more the easier," he told me grimly, and came to a halt. "Isn't this my way?"

"That's right," I said. "Keep straight on and you can't miss it."

Out went his hand. George loved a ceremonial parting. "Well, thanks for what you've done. I'll be ringing you in the morning about eight."

"I'll be listening," I told him.

He came nearer and his voice lowered dramatically. "You said something about the head telling the world she was dead."

"I did."

"Very interesting," he said. "When she was dead the sister could inherit, and not before. And the gentleman friend. Lucky for him too, if he marries her."

I imagine he nodded a last good-night, but I didn't see it, for he moved off before I could say a word.

The next morning I was dressed before half-past seven, and I went down at once to see Frank, all agog to read what there was for me in the Personal Column of the *Telegraph*. There was nothing at all!

I ordered a service breakfast through Frank, and then knew I had been a bit impatient. Why should I worry if my correspondent was taking his time? In a way, it made things easier for working with George Wharton. So long as I respected all confidences, I could actually give George an occasionally prod and turn his interests in the directions I wanted them.

Just as I was finishing my breakfast he rang up.

"I think I've located that maid, Ada What's-her-name," he said. "It means going out to Bedford so I may be a bit late back. What about you meeting O'Clauty and taking him to my office?"

"And questioning him?"

"What else did you think I meant?" he growled at me.

That was all, and it suited my book very well. In fact I hoped George would be so late back that all the pow-wow with O'Clauty would be over. As things turned out, the wish came almost true.

I didn't have any difficulty in spotting O'Clauty as he came through the barrier, even if he wasn't wearing breeches and leggings, and chewing a straw. In the taxi we told each other what a terrible affair it was, and then he told me about himself. I shall make no attempt to imitate his accent, rich and fascinating though it was, and he was what I'd call a Whartonian personality too, all showmanship and blether.

He had been head lad to the trainer of Colonel Amber's horses, he told me, and had known the sisters since they were knee-high to a bee. The Colonel had left him a legacy, and as the trainer had died at the same time, he had taken over the stable and had moved to Ireland. Leppers were his speciality, he said, and many's the tip he might be able to give me if I was a racing man.

He said he'd had a wee bite on the train, but a drink would do neither of us any harm; so I stopped the taxi just short of the Embankment and we got out and had one. Mine was a beer and his a double Scotch. No soda, he said, and when I was passing him the water he was taking just a quick gulp and a swallow, and that was the last of the whisky.

"Nothing like a wee nip or two to put life into you," he said, so I had his glass recharged and hastily gulped down my beer, Then we walked the rest of the way, with him telling me the beginnings of his story. He had received a private letter from Mrs. Morbent, asking him to come to London and meet her at that Richmond hotel, and the letter warned him not to breathe a word to a soul about the visit. He hadn't got the letter on him, he said, but when he got back he would send it, if he could find it.

"Mind ye," he said, "if I'd known then what I know now, I'd have run to the police that fast that you'd never have seen the whisk of my tail."

After he'd seen her at Richmond, that was, and it was as we were entering Wharton's room that he was telling me that. By the time I'd got someone in to take down a formal statement, Wharton appeared. You'd have thought O'Clauty was his long-lost brother by the way he grasped his hand. But the smile went off his face when he heard about Richmond.

"What did she have to say to you?" he asked.

This is a summary, and put in a better order than that in which O'Clauty told it. She explained the confidential letter by saying that she was having a holiday on her own, and didn't want to be disturbed by anybody or anything, and that holiday might last a few weeks. Then she said she'd got him over to go into the programmes of the two horses. O'Clauty outlined them and she agreed, though she did suggest one change.

"A rare knowledge she had," he said with a quick side-ways nod of appreciation.

That took some time, and when it was over she told him again that if anything happened to her the horses would be his, subject to conditions. He laughed at her.

"Away with you now," he told her. "It's an old man like me who should be after talking like that. And if it's them bombs you're thinking about, sure there's nothing to stop you coming over to Dublin for a wee while."

She smiled and shook her head as if she knew better, and that was all, for O'Clauty left immediately afterwards. When Wharton asked if he'd stayed on for a day or two, he gave quite a detailed account of his movements before he left for home.

"It's a terrible business," Wharton said. "All I can say is that it's done you a bit of good."

"Good, are you saying?" burst out O'Clauty. "Here's my hand and the whole arm of me, and I'd cut it off myself if she was alive again."

He began talking about the two girls, and how he had mounted them on their first ponies, and Wharton was asking him about Mrs. Grays. O'Clauty praised her to the skies, but it was clear that there had been no one in his eyes like Georgina. She was free and outspoken, he said, and the devil of a one for a bit of mischief or adventure, and one gathered that in those things the elder sister was lacking.

Just when it seemed that Wharton had finished with him O'Clauty remembered one vital thing. Miss Georgina had re-minded him as he was leaving that the visit was strictly con-fidential, and then a brilliant piece of intuition by Wharton brought to light a tragic error. What she said to him was that if anybody rang him up or wrote—to Dublin, that is, where they'd think she was—he was to say she was there and staying with friends. What he got into his head was that she'd said he was to say she wasn't there. In fact, as he confessed, he wasn't paying too much attention to those last words of hers.

On his way to town he did begin to think and he realised he hadn't got her orders clear. There was something about not actually being in Dublin but staying with friends, and he made up his mind that he would ring the Richmond hotel and get her to explain it all again. Unfortunately he met some friends and it was late that night when he did ring up, only to find she'd left the hotel. The next morning he rang up her flat and she wasn't there. Then, on thinking things over, he decided that what she'd meant was for him to say she wasn't in Ireland. In any case, he didn't think it important on account of the whims she had and the pranks she played, and the foolish way she'd been talking about dying before himself.

"A bad business, as you say," Wharton told him. "Supposing she did tell you to say she was in Dublin or near it, then the truth might have come out sooner. Not that you've anything to reproach yourself with."

O'Clauty was a bit cheered at that and Wharton asked him, as one sportsman to another, if those two horses of hers had any class. O'Clauty rose in their defence. Amber Prince was as good a lepper as a man would want in his stables, and worth twelve hundred if a penny. But Amber King, there was the grand horse for you! Miss Georgina had laughed at three thousand for him. After the war he'd be brought over to England and the Cheltenham Gold Cup was as good as his. But not a word about that to a soul.

"Well, we're most grateful to you," Wharton said when the enquiry was at last over. "Whenever we want you I suppose you'll be only too glad to come over?"

O'Clauty hedged. He was a busy man, but he'd do what he could.

"That's the worst of you citizens of the Free State," Wharton said with an ersatz chuckle. "We've practically got to get an extradition order if you cut up rough." He turned to me. "Rather lucky for us that Mrs. Morbent was English, and the will's English, so to speak."

O'Clauty gave me a deliberate wink. He knew well enough the force of the threat that Wharton was suavely hinting at. But the devil of a bit it troubled him. O'Clauty probably had up his sleeve just as many packs as George, and probably better marked.

"What do you think of him?" George asked me.

"His story sounded genuine enough," I said. "He's a crafty one undoubtedly, and smooth-tongued, but I think he was telling the truth. He's told us plenty. You've only to get to work at that Richmond hotel to find out where she went."

"To *try* to find out, that's what you mean," he told me with one of his glares. "But a funny business all round. Wonder why she was so secretive? Had all her plans laid too."

"How did you get on with that maid?" I asked him.

He snorted contemptuously.

"A morning as good as wasted." He lugged out his notebook. "She entered Mrs. Grays' service as personal maid two years ago. Says there weren't any rows between the sisters, except one." He had put on his spectacles and was peering at me over their tops. "That was about a week—couldn't get it any closer—before Georgina went away. Georgina called at the sister's flat—nothing unusual in that—but this maid heard their voices raised. I think she tried to listen at the door. In any case Mrs. Grays came rushing out of the room and the maid was at the door. Says she happened to be going past. Mrs. Morbent had been taken ill, and Mrs. Grays was rushing to the bathroom for sal volatile. She sent the maid back to the bedroom with a flea in her ear and when Mrs. Morbent left, which was in about half an hour, she accused the maid of listening at keyholes and sacked her on the spot."

"She paid her?"

"Oh, yes. Quite generously, so the maid said." He peered at me again. "What do you make of it?"

"Was there a quarrel?"

"According to her—yes. The voices were raised. That was the significant thing."

"Well, where's it get us?" I asked him.

"Don't know yet," he said. Off went his glasses and his tone had a honeyed mildness. "That Mrs. Grays is better, they tell me. What about you calling on her this afternoon?"

CHAPTER XII
TOUGH GOING

WHEN I TAPPED at the door it was the voice of Barbara Grays that told me to enter. She was obviously waiting for me, for I had rung her up and made the appointment. Two differences struck me at once. Now she didn't look in the least dowdy or slovenly, in fact the simple dark green frock she wore made her look, to a man's eye, both neatly and uncommonly well dressed. But her face was much paler than when I had seen it last, and there were dark rings beneath her eyes. There was a glint of red in her lightish brown hair, and I hadn't noticed that when her hat was on.

"You're sure you're better?" I asked solicitously.

"Very much better," she told me. Her voice, though subdued, still had that clear hard quality, and it reminded me of something of which I had then no time to think.

"And you can stand talking about . . . well, unpleasant things?"

She gave me a quick look. "If they're necessary," she said, and with the same quietness.

I began by alluding to what I'd said over the telephone, and the reason for calling myself Blunt.

"I'd forgotten that hospital committee we'd worked on," I said. "Most regrettable of me. I believe you know my wife too."

She said she knew Bernice well. I said that she'd probably let on at some time about my occasional working with New Scotland Yard. She said Bernice might have done so, but she didn't remember it.

Then she was putting a question of her own. "Is it right that you're now in the Army again?"

I explained all that, and my leave, and how the police, for reasons of their own, had called me in. In a very unofficial way, I hastened to add. She asked if that wasn't unusual, and it struck me that she was rather too anxious to unravel the position. Another thing was striking me, too, that while she hadn't asked me, then or over the telephone, just why I was calling on her, she would very much like to know.

Well, we cleared up all that, though there still seemed to be questions that she would have wished to ask. Then I got down to business.

"I want you to give me your solemn word," I said, "that what you and I are going to talk about will be implicitly secret. I've been asked to come here, as I just said, to make certain enquiries, but I do ask you to believe that I'm also coming as a friend. I shall have to make a report, but what I tell the police is entirely up to me."

"By all means let it be confidential," she said, and then, with a little frown. "But aren't you being rather mysterious? I mean, what have I to fear from the police?"

I told her, and in a couple of minutes she was nervously moistening her lips. I gave her a picture of the Law—impersonal, implacable, and untiring, working mole-like and bringing to light things that were buried deep. Already they'd had O'Clauty over and interviewed him, and it was something in the trainer's favour that at the mention of his name her strained expression relaxed and she smiled.

"In the eyes of the police everybody's suspect," I said. "Two people have died and the Law won't rest till it knows just how and why. Putting it bluntly, you're a suspect."

"That's an insult," she said, and drew herself up.

"Not to the police," I told her patiently. "Everyone with the faintest possible motive is a suspect. In their eyes the fact that you inherit a very large sum of money is a good and sufficient motive."

Her lips had clamped tightly down and she was shaking her head. "Then I've nothing to say," she told me, and the lips clamped to again.

"To them, perhaps no," I said. "But to me, perhaps yes, considering we've agreed that I'm here to help you. Take that maid of yours—Ada—whom you dismissed. She's been questioned too."

Her eyes opened wide and I could see she was scared. "But what could she possibly tell them?"

I gave her the gist of the maid's story and how it lent colour to a theory that the sisters had been on bad terms.

"Preposterous!" she said, but I could tell she was very relieved.

Then she gave me her version. Voices had not been raised. Georgina had had a casual fainting fit, and the maid had been most flagrantly caught in the act of listening at the keyhole.

"Wouldn't you have dismissed her?" she asked me.

"Under those circumstances—yes," I said. "But did your sister often have those fainting fits?"

That made her think, and quickly. Once or twice before, she said, but never in that flat where we then were.

"Well, it shows you the methods of the police," I said. "But there's another thing, and still between you and me. Why did you lead the police to believe that your sister had gone away with some other man? Some other man, that is to say, than Worrack?"

Again she shot me a quick look. "Because I thought it might be possible, of course."

The defiance showed uneasiness and I followed it up. "But every piece of evidence in the possession of the police shows that your sister wouldn't have looked twice at any other man than Worrack."

"You don't know women," she told me, and her lips clamped together again.

We didn't seem to be getting much forrader, and I was wondering if I had better go. Then I decided to do something for which I'd come, if only tentatively, prepared.

"Very well," I said, "but now I must again ask for your implicit confidence. This ring. Did it belong to your sister?"

The lips parted, and it was at me she was staring. Then she slowly held out her hand.

"Yes," she said. "How did you get it?"

"That I'm not prepared to tell you, at the moment," I said. "What I will say is, that I'm also not prepared to tell anything about it to the police—unless I'm forced."

"What do you mean by forced?"

"This," I said. "I got possession of the ring in a highly confidential way. It was pawned, and I have a description of the man who pawned it. That's all, so far, and I'm saying nothing to the police. But they're making enquiries at all pawnshops and jewellers about any jewellery in your sister's possession. Sooner or later they'll stumble on that pawnshop where I found it. Then I may be forced to speak."

I had held out my hand and she had given me back the ring without a word.

"I've got to talk to you in deadly seriousness," I went on. "I'm convinced that there are things you can tell if you wish."

"If you're not going to believe me, there's no point in saying anything more," she told me, and with an offended reserve.

I let out a sigh. "Why quibble? I repeat that there are things you could tell me, if you wished."

"Why should there be?"

I shrugged my shoulders. "I hate to say it, but because some of the things you've already said are so far from the truth."

She got to her feet at that. I sat tight.

"Don't you think you'd better go?"

I could have told her that that tragedy queen stuff only made things look even more suspicious. What I did say was that if she didn't believe I was there to help her, then perhaps I had.

I got to my feet, heaved another sigh, and picked up my hat. But I did smile in the most friendly way as I held out my hand.

"Good-bye, Mrs. Grays. I do hope you'll soon be absolutely better."

I saw then that there was something she wanted to ask or say, so I made my way to the door a slow one. At the door itself she was halting me.

"Oh, Mr. Travers."

"Yes?" I said, and smiled and waited.

"Perhaps I've been too hasty. And I haven't thanked you sufficiently."

"Regard the thanks as given," I told her.

"That's sweet of you," she said, and smiled wanly as she shook her head. "But thank you again for keeping everything—well, just between us two."

There was never a suspicion of coquetry in the voice or the smile.

"You can rely on me," I said, and rather lamely, and then was turning again to go.

"But something else." She hesitated. "If you discover anything"—she was moistening her lips—"anything against—I mean, derogatory in any way to my sister, will you tell it to me first?"

"And not to the police?" I said. "Yes. I think I can promise that. But I hope I shan't. I just can't think your sister was that kind."

Then I knew that I'd dropped my first real brick. Her lip puckered and she was turning away.

"I'm so sorry," I began, but I was too late. As I turned again I could hear the catch in her throat, and as I gently closed the door I saw her head between her hands and heard the sound of her tears.

Before I had gone a hundred yards I passed a little tea-shop. It was nearing four o'clock, so I turned back, and over my modest tea I began to think about Barbara Grays. The first thing I realised again was that I had seen a woman utterly different from the one who had lunched with Hamson that day at Moroni's. Maybe it was the shock that had made her different, and yet I didn't know, for the change seemed spiritually deeper. But that she could have been concerned in even the remotest way with the death of her sister seemed to me incredible. On the other hand, that she knew infinitely more about it than she had even unconsciously hinted, seemed incontrovertible.

What had I learned from that brief interview? I took out my notebook and jotted a few ideas down. First, there was more in that Ada business than had met Wharton's eye. That the maid had been listening seemed fairly certain, but the main thing about which Barbara Grays had been anxious was to know just how much she had heard, and if Ada had imparted what she had heard to the police. Therefore, the talk between the sisters had been specially confidential, and from that it was not unreason-able to assume that the talk had been concerned with the tragic event that followed.

Barbara Grays' conduct with me that afternoon had through-out been highly peculiar. I don't mean such trivialities as that she had not asked me to have tea, though she knew both me and my wife. That might have a certain significance, but it stood out far less clearly than other things. At that lunch she had shown a complete and almost callous indifference to her sister's dis-appearance, but that afternoon it had been plain to me that she had for that sister a deep affection. There had been the ring, le-gally as good as hers, which she handed back to me without pro-test, and with practically no questioning. Then I remembered that she had never asked me why I was calling on her, but had left it to me to do the explaining. Queer deviations from the usu-al and conventional, and yet again significant. There was some-thing else, though as yet it was only an impression, or even more vague than that. Something, in fact, was telling me that she and Hamson were no longer on the same terms, and my belief—still purely intuition—was that he had cooled off.

One thing, and not relative to the afternoon's interview, had rather puzzled me—how Lulu could have known of that quarrel of the sisters and the dismissal of Ada. But as I was jotting down the headlines of the facts which I proposed to disclose to Whar-ton, I thought I knew the answer to that. Lulu must have been the personal go-between, in business matters, for Worrack and Georgina. To get from the club to Georgina's flat meant prac-tically passing Barbara's, and Georgina might therefore have used Lulu for little errands concerning the sisters on Lulu's way back. She must have happened to call at Barbara's flat that day after Ada's dismissal and have learned the story from Ada her-self. That was a theory in which I had no great faith, and yet afterwards it turned out to be perfectly correct. Ada had told the story and naturally it had been a heavily biased one.

I made my way back to Wharton's room and wrote out the report of the call on Mrs. Grays. Wharton, an old Inspector friend of mine told me, was well on the job. Men were short, but he had scrounged half a dozen for work on the case, and it looked as if there might soon be something doing.

Just as I was going to leave him a personal message, that I'd be at the flat and he was to ring me up if he wanted me, in he came. He had a quick look at my report, grunted, and put it in his notebook. Then he was giving me a glare.

"What do you think's happened at Richmond?"

"Lord knows," I said.

"When Richards"—that would be Detective-Sergeant Richards, and it was the first intimation that he was to help on the case—"started making enquiries, what do you think he found? Someone else was there a day or two ago and up to the same thing!"

"Good Lord!" I said.

"What's it mean?" he said, and threw up his hands. "Why should anybody go making enquiries?"

"Well, there is something that strikes me," I ventured. "As that report says, I don't think Mrs. Grays had anything to do with the sister's death, and I do think she was more worried about the disappearance than she made out. Why shouldn't she, or Worrack, have had enquiries made?"

"Yes, but how did they know she'd been to Richmond!" I gave a Whartonian grunt. "Sorry," I said. "That didn't occur to me. But why shouldn't O'Clauty have let something out? He's a natural bletherer."

"That's an idea," he said. "I'll see him to-night and find out."

He made a note and then was clicking his tongue. "Don't know which way to turn. I want to see each of those people individually we had at the club. Then I've got a little surprise for you." He glanced at his watch, an old-fashioned turnip which he carried in his waistcoat pocket. "That won't be for another few minutes. And something I want you to do. We've found out about the jewellery. The pawnbroker's come forward and he'll be here in about half an hour. I'll get you to see him for me and take a statement." I was glad he wasn't looking at me, for my face went a glorious scarlet. That shock, after the discovery of Bill Ellice's activities at

Richmond, had been too much, but as I blew my nose I managed to tell him that I'd certainly see to the pawnbroker.

"I've got to get along to Richmond," he said. "And something else. I've had a report on that head. They can't say how long she's been dead. A fortnight, perhaps, at a rough guess. The body had been embalmed."

My eyes fairly popped at that.

"When I say the body, I mean that the head had been embalmed, so probably the whole body was. Just ordinary embalming fluid pumped in. Some arsenical preparation or other, the same as they use to preserve corpses for the dissecting table."

"You mean, a doctor did it?"

"Not necessarily," he said. "An undertaker might have done it, or a medical student. Anyone who had the stuff and knew the ropes." Then he was peering at me from under his shaggy eyebrows. "Do you see anything else?"

"Don't know," I said, fingers at my glasses. "Except perhaps, that whoever killed her hadn't any means for quick disposal of the body, such as burning, for instance. Burying might have been too dangerous."

"Just how it struck me," he said. "The devil of it is, it doesn't get us very far."

Then there was a tap at the door. A sergeant looked in with, "Carpenter's here, sir. Will you see him?"

"Yes, and make it quick," Wharton told him.

That was the surprise he had in store for me, and a surprise it certainly was. So was Jean himself, and I can't somehow help calling him that, for he had shaved off his moustache and when he took off his hat I saw that he had altered his hair, combing it straight back instead of in the middle, a method which had made his skull have a Gallic kind of flatness. He was wearing what looked like his best clothes, and the plain-clothes man who brought him in was carrying a heavy suit-case.

"What a surprise!" said Wharton, up to his cat and mouse tricks straightway. "What's been happening?"

That question was to the plain-clothes man.

"Picked him up just as he got off the bus at King's Cross, sir."

"Really?" said Wharton. "Well, you can wait outside. Mr. Carpenter and I are going to have a little friendly chat."

Jean took the chair that Wharton indicated, and he was making no protests, at the moment. But his eyes did go towards that suit-case.

"So you were doing a bolt," Wharton told him. "Like to tell me what the idea was?" Then he was leaning forward with a glare. "And none of that grimacing!" A quick change to a benevolent smile. "Or would you rather talk to me in French?"

Jean shrugged his shoulders, and the gesture had both humility and helplessness. Then he said he had lost his job, and as he had a bit put by he thought he'd treat himself to a holiday with a sister at Peterborough. If a munitions job presented itself, he'd take it.

"Name and address of the sister?" asked Wharton.

Jean made heavy going of that, but at last got something out. Wharton pressed a buzzer and picked up the 'phone.

"Take this, please. Urgent. Get Peterborough and Inspector Frost personally if you can. Ask him to verify the following person and find out if she has a brother named Jean Carpenter."

Now I knew that that was all bluff. George was speaking to nobody because he had not connected up. But Jean didn't know it. Before Wharton could say another word, his hand was going out.

"Yes?" said Wharton.

Jean said he'd remembered now that the sister had moved from Peterborough. He'd have remembered that in the train, but it wouldn't have mattered, as he could have stayed with friends.

"All right. Give me the names and address of the friends," Wharton said imperturbably.

Jean was flummoxed again. Wharton gave him a look and then got to his feet. I was expecting a roar, but all he did was to push the desk bell. In came the plain-clothes man.

"Take him away," he said. "Say I'll see him again later. And search him. Bring me the key to that case."

"The case is unlocked, sir."

"You can't do this to me," burst out Jean. "I haven't done a thing."

"Pleased to hear it," Wharton told him mildly. "Hang on for a minute," he said to the man, and then was unfastening the straps of the case. Then he was rummaging carefully among its contents, and all at once I saw his eyebrows raise.

"Ah, what have we here? Patent medicines?"

He had two small packets, and both had been opened. In one were small whitish pellets, and in the other capsules like that which had been found by Worrack's table.

That was the end of Jean, but he still made something of a fight of it. The packets had been given him by a friend to keep for him and he even gave a name and description.

"Too bad," Wharton said. "Of course you don't know where we can lay our hands on him?"

Jean said he didn't, but wherever he was he was a dirty double-crosser. Wharton motioned to the man to get outside again.

"Look here, Carpenter, I'm going to give you just one chance," he said. "You're in possession of certain drugs that come under the Act. Your trying to bolt is against you, and your record too. In other words, you're in a nasty spot. I know how you got this stuff, by the way. These pellets are what the Nazis dope their men with. These other little chaps just put a man to sleep for ever when he's badly wounded. You got them from a Navy man, who picked them up from an officer taken from one of their submarines. Or from a soldier on leave perhaps. Duropine, that's what they are; the same stuff that killed Mr. Worrack. Did you supply it to him, by the way?"

Jean swore by all that was holy that he'd never parted with either a pellet or capsule. He'd bought the stuff in a pub and from a soldier, on spec., but it was unknown to him, though he'd sampled one of the pellets, and he'd regarded the deal as a bad one.

"Too bad again," Wharton said. "It's going to get you a couple of years. It may even get you hanged. And that's a pity. If you'd come clean I might have done a few things."

To cut a long story short, he got Jean where he wanted him. But again the story, even if this time true, was very far from the whole truth. Jean swore that he'd never parted with either a pellet or capsule except once, and then only to oblige a certain gentleman. The gentleman was Hamson!

"Well, tell us all about it," Wharton said with a quick glance at me.

The story was convincing enough. Hamson must have been to the inquest, where he had heard about duropine. Jean had happened to meet him the same afternoon and had asked about the inquest. Hamson had described the capsule, and the astonished Jean had thought it like those he had bought from the soldier. So that night at the club he had brought one for Hamson to see.

Wharton called in the man again. "Wait outside with him for a minute," he said. "He can have his bag."

Then he was speaking through, and this time genuinely. "The man Carpenter. He's been turned loose, but have him tailed. Report if he does any telephoning."

In came Jean again.

"Well, I believe what you've told me," Wharton said. "But God help you if I find out it's a lie. Got any money?"

Jean said he had.

"Then fix yourself up for the night," Wharton said. "Report here at nine in the morning and that may be the last I want of you."

He nodded curtly and out Jean went.

"A pretty good liar, eh?" he said to me.

"He may be telling the truth about Hamson," I said. "The only snag is Hamson's telling him about the capsule. Still, everyone was very friendly at the club."

"I'll lay Carpenter's been peddling that dope for weeks," he said with a snort.

"You're going to question Hamson?"

"Not yet," he said. "If Carpenter telephones, it's ten to one it's Hamson. But why worry? We know where everybody is."

"But if there's anything fishy about Hamson, then Carpenter will tip him off," I pointed out.

"Let him," he said, and lugged out his watch again. "Here I am, blethering with you when I ought to be half-way to Richmond."

I helped him into his overcoat, and he gave me final instructions about the pawnbroker. When he'd see me again he didn't know, he said, but if I'd leave my whereabouts with Frank, then he'd let me know if there was anything urgent on hand.

It was an anti-climax seeing that pawnbroker, even if it did have its interesting moments. It was my friend, thank heaven! and his eyes fairly bulged when he saw me in Wharton's chair.

I told him that what had passed between us at the shop was just as confidential as ever. I hinted, too, that he had nothing to fear, and that five minutes or so would settle the business in hand.

It took just ten minutes. A formal statement as to the pawning was taken down. The three articles had been pawned at one and the same evening by Markovitch. One had been redeemed by Markovitch and the other two he had brought along, and I gave him the necessary receipts. The watch had been pawned for forty pounds and the cigarette-case for thirty. There followed a detailed description of Markovitch.

"In fact," I said, as I rose, to show the interview was over, "the three articles were pawned by this Markovitch and Markovitch redeemed one of them, the ring."

He assured me unblushingly that that was correct. I thanked him formally and out he went. The room wasn't hot, but as soon as he'd gone my forehead was, and I was mopping it with my handkerchief. Another hurdle successfully negotiated, I could tell myself, and then was wondering how much longer my uncanny luck would hold.

CHAPTER XIII
THE DRY BONES STIR

I woke at seven the next morning and tried to drop off to sleep again, but it was no use. My brain was far too active, for it had picked up again the two thoughts that had last been in my mind. One concerned that clear bill of health I'd given Wharton about Barbara Grays. I'd also assured myself that she could never have been concerned in the death of her sister; and all the time I'd been forgetting something. Why, on that first morning when I had met him at his flat, had Worrack hinted that Barbara Grays had a pretty strong motive for being behind the disappearance? Surely the charge must have had some basis of fact. What, then, had I missed? Somewhere there must be a clue to the discrepancy.

I had also thought about Hamson, and once more Worrack came in. Worrack had almost forced some sort of co-operation with Hamson upon me, and I still didn't know why. The death of Worrack had relieved me of that particular incubus, but only after I'd given Hamson one small commission—to find out something about Jean. And now it appeared that Hamson had continued to be interested in Jean, according to Jean's own yarn to Wharton. But whatever Wharton thought of the yarn, I didn't credit it. What I believed was that Jean had sold Hamson dope long before that inquest, and that the yarn had probably been concocted between the pair of them. If so, it looked as if Hamson was pretty heavily involved in the death of Worrack, however innocent he might be of any share in the disappearance and death of Georgina Morbent.

Before eight o'clock I was dressed and ready for breakfast, so I went down to have a look at Frank's *Daily Telegraph*. Once more there was never a message for me, and in a rather petulant mood, perhaps, I told myself that I'd give READY another twenty-four hours—forty-eight, since it was a Saturday—and then myself announce that I was withdrawing from the case. That would bring READY out into the open and produce some action.

That was what I was beginning to want—action, and spelt with capital letters and followed by a couple of exclamation marks. Before the forty-eight hours had gone I was certainly going to get it, though I didn't know it then.

I had just finished breakfast when Wharton rang up. "Can you be here at nine-thirty? Shan't keep you long, and I'll have seen Carpenter again by then."

"Did Carpenter do any telephoning?" I asked.

"That's where we slipped up," Wharton said. "There was a kiosk in the place where he stayed."

I had wondered why he had spoken so gently, at least till I knew he had made that slip-up. George's own mistakes were always those that might happen to any man; other people's were those that could never have happened to George.

"What do you think of that damn fellow O'Clauty?" he was saying, and his tone now was one of tremendous indignation. Something had happened, I gathered, and it was not George who had slipped up.

"What's he done?" I asked.

"He's bolted!"

"Bolted?"

"Dammit, don't you understand the King's English? Bolted—skedaddled—hopped it back to Ireland!"

I was just going to ask why not, when George went splutteringly on. "You know as well as I do that he'd agreed to stay and help all he could. Gave me his London address and everything. Now he's probably back in Dublin."

He rang off then and I couldn't help chuckling. O'Clauty had never, to my knowledge, promised to stay on in town, and if he had, then it was refreshing to find someone sufficiently acute to have worked a fast one on George. In any case, it looked as if he was back in Dublin, and in spite of that bluff about the will, the devil of a job George would have to get him to England again.

I thought George was looking quite pleased with himself when I went into his room.

"Get anything out of Carpenter?" I asked.

"No," he said bluntly. "He's gone back to his old diggings, and he'll be watched."

"A pity," I said. "I'd hoped he'd have come clean about that dope."

He grunted. "Yes, and give himself a certain three years. We shan't be able to get at him through his customers. There isn't one of them who'd ever squeal." He shook his head. "No. What they may do is want more dope. That's why he's being watched."

I went into that pawnbroker business with him, and he seemed quite satisfied. No trace of that private car had been found at Richmond, and how Markovitch was to be picked up he didn't know. I said I'd arranged with the pawnbroker that if Markovitch turned up with anything else to pawn, he was to be held at all costs and the Yard or local police informed. George was good enough to tell me that I couldn't have done more.

"I've seen most of those people again we saw at the club," he said. "That Molde's a queer cove, isn't he?"

"I'd call him unhealthy rather than queer," I said.

"One of the Nobs, isn't he?" George was a bit of a snob in his way, even if he would allude with a simulated scorn to the Big Bugs, and the Nobs, and the Powers-that-Be. "And that Scylla Payton. He's keeping her?"

"I rather gathered so," I said. "What'd you think of her?"

"Seemed all right to me," George said. "Not that I'm much at home with that Society gang."

A hell of a lot of Society about Scylla, I thought to myself. Then he was mentioning Hamson.

"There's a man who didn't strike me as telling the whole truth, and nothing but," he said. "I felt as if I was fencing with somebody, if you know what I mean."

I knew all right, though I didn't say so.

"Now there's something I'd like you to do," George was going on, and his tone had the old familiar unction. "I doubt if there'll be any other job for you in the next day or two, so what about cultivating the acquaintance of that chap Hamson? I feel it's going to be worth it."

"I'll do my best," I said. "I know him well enough already, so he shouldn't find me too obvious."

"Good," he said. "Then I think I'll be pushing along. Richmond first. Then I've got one or two more to see."

"Slow work," I said.

"What else do you expect?" he fired at me. "A penny in the slot and things come out?"

"Maybe," I told him amiably. "Nothing new from the Worrack angle?"

He shot me a look and I knew he was keeping something back. "What more do you want? Haven't I told you already?"

"The last you told me was that duropine had a variable action," I said. "I didn't see anything in that. All poisons have, according to the dose."

He threw up his hands. "And you call yourself a detective!"

"I don't," I said.

He ignored that. His tone took on a long-suffering patience.

"Haven't I enough to do without having to show you how two and two make four? You heard what I told Carpenter about that duropine stuff. Well, use your sense. If you can't do that, then listen to me. I had a special analysis of the stomach contents."

I could have said that he hadn't told me that. But he was referring to his notebook.

"Now then, listen to this. He had a very scratch meal at somewhere round half-past seven. Just sandwiches and a coffee, and he got those at his flat. A fairly strong dose of the poison was found in the lower part of the partially digested meal. The next thing he apparently had was that long brandy and soda, but there wasn't a trace of poison in that."

"Good Lord!" I said, and my fingers went to my glasses.

"You see it now, do you?"

"Yes," I said. "He was given the poison before half-past seven, and the strength was worked out so that he'd die some two or three hours later, and at the club. But there wasn't any additional poison in the brandy. Someone dropped that in from a capsule after Hamson had carried him away."

"Excellent!" he told me ironically. "And why was it worked like that?"

"So that it'd be thought that poison in the brandy had killed him. That gave colour to the suicide motive, especially when the capsule was dropped by his chair." I remember something else. "That was why Worrack felt so seedy that night. The poison was working on him."

"That's it," he said. "Now you see why I'd like you to get acquainted with Hamson. He could have dropped that poison in the brandy before Worrack collapsed. At any time after that blasted mouse appeared." He nodded grimly. "I'd like to know just who was responsible for that. Conroy hinted at a naval officer, and then said he'd gone back to sea again."

"I believe there was one there," I said, as if by no means sure. "But what about callers at Worrack's flat that early evening? Found anything out?"

He pursed his lips, and I knew he was wondering whether to spill the information or not.

"As a matter of fact we know of only one caller. That Lulu Mawne. Conroy let on in confidence that she went regularly about that time."

I remembered well enough, and that quarrel between the two, and how they'd previously been drinking sherry, even if all that was the night before.

"What motive could she have had for poisoning him?" I asked, with a look of bewilderment.

"There's a motive all right," he said. "That Georgina Morbent cut her out with Worrack. A jealous woman'll do anything."

Then he was making for his overcoat and demanding why I was keeping him hanging about when he ought to be at Richmond. I walked downstairs with him to his car, and the last thing he said to me was that I was God's gift to the Yard, so to speak, in the matter of worming things out of Hamson.

I walked on to Charing Cross and took a train to Piccadilly Circus and then strolled along to my club, and I wasn't doing too much thinking about what George had told me, especially in the case of Lulu Mawne. I knew what Wharton didn't know, perhaps, that Worrack was accessible to any members of his club, and that anybody might have called there besides Lulu. Frankly, her motive, whatever I'd thought in the past, didn't strike me as sufficiently strong.

On the other hand, there was the fact that poison was always woman's weapon.

I wasn't in any hurry to ring up Hamson. No need to let him think I was being at all anxious to lunch with him, so I looked through the dailies and the illustrated weeklies, and then saw that it was just turned noon. I rang up his hotel, but there was no reply, and when I checked up through the hotel I was told he had gone out. I left no message, and then was trying to decide where I should lunch myself. To tell the truth I was rather relieved that I had not got Hamson. Wharton had suggested that worming things out of him would be easy, but I knew far better. And I hadn't thought of any plan of campaign.

I remembered a good place to lunch, and as I made my way there I was thinking about Hamson again, and all the queer things I had against him. Worrack's thrusting him on me, for instance, and the way he'd found out who I was. How he'd probably tried to get himself off the list of suspects by swearing he'd never marry Barbara Grays if she came into Georgina's money, and how he'd wanted it kept dark about his supposed connection with the Indian Police. How he'd told me that Barbara wasn't herself that day at the lunch, and how Worrack had said he'd been lying. How he was mixed up with the unspeakable Carpenter, and quite a few more things. But how could I question him about any of them? That was the point, and it had me flummoxed.

I had a fair lunch at rather too stiff a price, and then strolled along Regent Street. Something caught my eye in a shop window, and while I was looking at it I noticed something else—the clear reflection of Hamson as he went by towards Piccadilly Circus. Who should be with him but Scylla! In the brief glimpse I'd had of them I'd seen that they were on very good terms with themselves. In fact, they'd eyes for nobody else, otherwise Hamson must have spotted me.

I followed them at a discreet distance, though I needn't have worried about that, for neither of them looked back. At the traffic block he took her arm and they crossed the street, his head bent down close by hers. I crossed, too, and I followed them down to the Underground Station at Swan and Edgar's Corner. They went straight through and came out on the Lower Regent Street side, and I was twenty yards behind.

They turned right, and then in a few yards halted before cinema. I halted too; in fact I turned down a convenient side-street, and from there took a cautious peep, for I was now not ten yards from where they stood. Then almost at once another girl came up, and she was hailing the pair. Hamson she could not have met before, for Scylla was introducing him. A good-looking girl she was—in the early twenties, I guessed—and very well dressed, and then, before I could get another good view of her, the three were entering the doors of the cinema, like three old friends.

I glanced at my watch and the time was a quarter-past two. So I took a short stroll along the side-street and then entered the cinema vestibule myself, and consulted the time-table of events. The big picture—a well-reviewed one —was timed for two-twenty, and as I came out to the pavement again I was busy on a reconstruction. The second girl, a friend of Scylla's most likely, had not been able to join the two for lunch, but had made a rendezvous for the cinema. All I had to do was to wait for the end of the show and pick them up as they came out.

Then I changed my mind. There were more exits than one, and the three might not stay till the end of the show, but leave when the big picture was over. In that case it would mean my hanging around for most of the afternoon and dodging from one exit to another, and that wasn't good enough. Yet I abandoned the idea with reluctance. I'd have liked to know just why Hamson was being so affectionate with Scylla, about the last one I'd have thought he'd have fallen for. And I'd have liked to know some more about her friend Goldilocks, as I'd christened her. Lovely hair she'd had. Scylla's was the latest thing in platinums, as you've heard before, but the other girl's was two good classes above it.

Then I thought of a compromise and turned back and bought myself a seat. It was a good picture, and when it was on I didn't do much looking round, but when the lights went up I took a careful look or two. But the place was so huge and so packed that looking for those three was a waste of time or an expectation of incredible luck, so I sat the programme out. When I emerged with the crowd there was never a sign of Hamson, so I pushed on to Moroni's for tea in case the three should come on there. But they didn't, and that was that. Then, as I came out again I thought of something else. Whoever READY was, I had about a hundred pounds of his money, and waiting to be used for the purposes of discovering who had killed Worrack. Why not invest some of it in having Hamson watched? That would make the job someone else's headache, and if there were any discoveries I could report to Wharton. But there seemed something just a bit too flamboyant in that idea, and I told myself the original idea was far better—to wait till the Monday and then, if READY had no communication for me, to begin the process of winkling him out into the open.

Sunday morning dawned, and I didn't know it was to be a decisive day for me. All I thought when I woke was that there would be another twenty-four hours to wait before I should know if READY had made a communication. As Wharton would probably be busy with routine enquiries and in no need of me, I did contemplate a restful day. I would take a stroll in the Park, I thought, and then read the papers and do the crosswords and in the evening I'd write to my wife. Then I thought of something rather strange. Bernice was probably too busy to have much time for reading newspapers, but surely she must have heard some talk about the severed head affair. If so, and if she had known Georgina Morbent at all well, then why hadn't she mentioned the affair to me? Particularly, as I remembered, after my asking her about Barbara Grays.

But that wasn't anything to stay in my mind. After breakfast I took my stroll, and it was about half-past eleven when I got back. I glanced at the headlines of the two papers and then wondered if there was anything worth listening to on the wireless. The Home Service mentioned an orchestra, but didn't specify what kind, and the Forces Programme a variety show for workers, so I switched on to see what. As soon as the sound came on I realised that the last time I'd listened it had been to the Forces Programme, though heaven knew why, and I was just going to change over to the Home Programme when I heard something that made me wince. Who should I be hearing but my old comic friend and his gag about the hens!

". . . and what do you think the hens were singing? 'Hold tight, hold tight.'"

I didn't switch off, but cynically awaited the next part of the same old gag. The applause subsided, and it came.

"And the price of eggs! Have you noticed how they've gone down? Only tuppence each now. That's right, and one of my hens was saying to another, 'Lay more eggs, eh? I should say so. Spoil my figure for two bob a dozen!'"

I switched off then and went back to my newspapers. Did you see it? Not the joke, but something that lay behind? I didn't—at least, not at that moment. Afterwards I knew how lucky I'd been to have had that cynical mood still on me, for if I hadn't, then that train of thought would never have returned.

This, then, is what happened. I picked up the *Observer* and saw that the crossword was one of the less interesting kind to me. But the *Sunday Times* one was a good stand-by for an odd half-hour, so I felt for my special pencil which had a rubber at one end. It was not in my pocket, so I looked casually around, and my eyes fell on the wireless set again.

Then came the train of thought. Those dreadful programmes that masqueraded under the name of humour, and, as a contrast, the slickness and originality of the same sort of thing relayed from America. My old friend and his gag about the hens. Well, it was not a bad gag once. "I should spoil my figure for two bob a dozen!" Quite an economic sermon could be preached from that text, with its human bearing on the size of families.

Then all at once I was lying back in my chair, fingers at my glasses. Something had come back. Something that Worrack had said, and I was frowning as I tried to remember it. Then came something else, and all at once.

I was on my feet and moving restlessly about the room. A couple of minutes and I was letting out a breath. Then I think I smiled feebly to myself, and the smile was a modest pat on the back.

Another minute and I was sure of everything. By sheer luck I had stumbled on the perfect theory. Perfect wasn't the word; it was unique! In all my years of theorising I had never known a theory so fool-proof, so comprehensive, and so satisfying. Then as I stood where I was, fingers idly polishing my glasses, new pieces fitted themselves into the puzzle, and each settled snugly into place. A dozen of them, there were, and only one that didn't quite fit. An important one, too, so it seemed then, and yet I didn't know. Maybe I had put it in a bit cock-eyed, for it just *had* to fit. And maybe when I'd had another good look at everything it'd be just as good a fit as the others.

You've guessed by now what that brave new theory was, and so you'll be thinking just how much of a fool I was not to have hit on it before. But if you haven't guessed it, then I won't keep you long in suspense. The things I did next should make everything clear.

First of all I looked up that copy of Georgina Morbent's accounts which her bank manager had given me, and which I'd noted in my book. Then I went down to the telephone kiosk in the vestibule and had a look at the directory. The name I was looking for was W. M. Chataway, and I found it.

CHATAWAY, W. M., M. D., 163, Comport St.
Consulting Physician.

What did I do then? I think I just smiled a bit foolishly and as a kind of mental relief. The main test had been made, and the theory was all that I had claimed for it.

As I walked slowly up to my room again I was thinking of my own hospital. I call it that because I was—still am in a more honorary capacity—one of the Governors. Old Vaughan, the Librarian. He wouldn't be at the hospital on a Sunday. He'd be at his flat. Or would he be out taking the air? Where could I find his number?

I looked it up in my private book and there it was. There was a tremendous relief when I at last heard his voice at the other end of the line.

"Hallo, Henry," I said. "This is Travers. Ludovic Travers."

"My dear chap," he said. "This is a surprise."

"I'm on leave," I said. "Next week I'll pop in and see you all if I may."

"Delighted," he told me. "But why not have some lunch with us to-day?"

"I'd have loved to," I said, "but I just happened to be engaged. Next week—yes. Oh, and Henry. There's a little confidential matter I'd like you to do for me now, if you can. It's like this. A friend of mine is consulting a specialist, and I'd rather like the highly confidential low-down on the man. His name's Chataway. W. M. Chataway."

"Chataway," he said. "I think I can help you. Hang on a moment, will you, and I'll look something up."

It didn't take him more than a moment.

"Oh, yes," he said. "Your friend can go to him with every confidence. He's an excellent fellow. I knew him at University, and later he went on to Paris."

"I thought he must be pretty good," I said. "I often think, between ourselves, that those fellows just off Harley Street are every bit as good as those in it."

"And cheaper," he said, and chuckled. "But you can tell your friend that everything's in order. I won't say Chataway's the world's best gynaecologist, but he's a remarkably good man."

"Most grateful to you, Henry," I said. "Next week we must have that lunch."

He asked after Bernice and then we rang off. Everything had gone so well that I couldn't quite realise the full extent of my luck. Then I began planning the next move, and all the while I was cursing the fact that it was Sunday. But I was now too restless to settle to anything, and at all costs I had to get busy on ends that were still a bit loose. Perhaps by evening I might have advanced so far as to be in a position to pay a call on Barbara Grays.

I changed into uniform, which seemed the best available disguise, and outside the flats was lucky enough to catch a bus at once. It was as lovely a morning as I'd ever known in February, and I was on top of the world. The quiet streets had never looked so good and my heart overflowed with feelings of kindliness for my fellow passengers. And as a reward I promised myself lunch at a certain restaurant, and I even began imagining what I'd have. But that was just a bit precipitate, for it was a lunch I was never going to eat.

CHAPTER XIV
THICK AND FAST

I TOLD YOU I'd been lucky. Well, I was to be more so, and only because of the hour it happened to be. As I came to the far end of Comport Street it was exactly a quarter-past twelve, which shows that I'd lost no time. Had I been two minutes earlier, or later, I should never have had the astounding piece of good fortune that befell me. But in justice to myself I should say that things might have followed the same course, if in a different way and after a loss of at least a day. What I was making up my mind to do, in fact, was to call on Dr. Chataway, give him a dud name and the address of my camp, and say I'd come to consult him on a highly personal matter. I had that matter all ready, and by the Monday, when I would make an appointment, I would have it word perfect.

But I wanted to run my eye over his place, just to get from it, if I could, some rough idea of the lay-out and what the man himself was likely to be. Far-fetched, you may think, and you may be right, but at any rate it was something to do.

Then things happened. I was getting very close to No. 163, when a girl came out of a door just ahead. She passed without a look at me, not that I expected one, but I had a quick look at her, and who should she be but the girl who had met Hamson and Scylla outside that cinema! She looked as if she was going places. Smartly dressed and made up, and carrying a dainty bag beneath her arm, and the sauciest little hat perched above her unmistakable hair.

I looked back after her and then was moving quickly forward. I was right. It was Chataway's door out of which she had come. There was his plate, and—and then I was whipping round, and just in time to see her turning into Martindale Street. If Goldilocks was going places, then I'd go along too. But I'd keep my distance. If it was Hamson she was meeting, and I was pretty sure it was, then I had to play a mightily wary game.

At the bottom of Martindale Street she crossed over to a bus stop. It was five minutes before a bus came up and it appeared to be the one she was waiting for. I was on her heels as she entered, and giving a quick look at the few passengers. Hamson wasn't there. If he had been I'd have bolted upstairs, so I went right down the bus. Goldilocks took a seat so I moved back just behind her, and she didn't even take one look at me.

When the conductress came along I was fumbling for change, so she took Goldilock's threepence first. Then I shifted nearer the door and also took three-pennyworth, which would deposit me in Chelsea High Street. Then a man alongside me got out and was good enough to hand me his newspaper. He must have been a good fellow, for though I've seen enough solicitude for the troops, this was my first experience of thoughtfulness for a major. But maybe I look older than I flatter myself, or else it was some subtlety on his part, for on the front page there was a lot about a court-martial on a colonel. But I was well hidden behind that paper when Goldilocks got out.

She knew where she was going. Forty yards past the stop she turned into Wilford Lane. Then she took a short cut to Cheyne Walk, and in a couple of minutes was entering a small restaurant which was new to me, and which called itself the Brown Squirrel. Someone who knew squirrels quite well had painted the attractive sign, and I had a good look at it till I thought Goldilocks had found a pew. Then I took a quick look inside.

She was there, and a man with her, and that man wasn't Hamson. I whipped off my glasses as an additional disguise, then went rapidly to the table I'd reconnoitred. There were then two tables between Goldilocks and me, and each was occupied, but it was the best I could do. She had her back to me and there seemed to be no mirror in which I could be seen, so I put on my glasses again and studied the menu. Prices were half a crown or three shillings and the latter included coffee. I ordered the three shilling lunch, and in a couple of minutes was tackling some not bad soup.

Then I tried to squint round the back of the man in front of me to have a look at Goldilocks' male friend. When I did so I had a shock that made me go hot and cold. At first I thought I must be wrong, and then I knew I was right. Tall he certainly was, and there was that beard, and the definitely foreign look. His voice I couldn't catch, for the heads of the two were together and they were talking confidentially across the narrow table. At that moment I'd have given a couple of READY's fivers for a seat two tables up, for I knew that the man I'd just seen could only be Markovitch.

The meal went on slowly but nothing happened. Now and again I caught a glimpse of the two, and that was all. Then I began wondering who had chosen the rendezvous, for that might give me a clue to what Markovitch was like. But either might have chosen it, for it wasn't by any means cheap and nasty. The food was plain but definitely good, and the surroundings, though faintly arty, were far from the Olde Tea Shoppe kind of place that flourished there before the war.

I lingered over my coffee and then got behind my newspaper, in case the two should make the first move, and I'd taken the precaution to pay my bill. As it was, the two had passed my table almost before I knew it, so I waited a few seconds and then made my own way out. There they were ahead of me, and making for the High Street. When I got there they were nearing the bus stop on the other side of the road, and I wondered just what I should do next. A bus came up and I saw that only Goldilocks was taking it, so I turned back again. A wave of her hand to Markovitch and she was out of sight. Markovitch smiled to himself, and nodded, and then without hesitating crossed the road.

Two buses came up and he took neither. The third—and again it was very much of a shock—was for Richmond, and that was the one he took. He went on top and so did I, and I sat at the back where I could keep an eye on him. I did see him take out a notebook it might have been, or a piece of paper, and jot down something, but then more passengers were getting on and the glimpses I had of him were only occasional.

Well, we went over Putney Bridge and then turned right, by Putney Common, and finally stopped at Richmond just over the bridge, and there Markovitch got out. As he passed me I had a real good look at him, and he fitted that pawnbroker's description to his very eyelids. When he moved on along the road I was twenty yards behind him, and that went on for a good quarter of a mile. Then he turned into a garage and I went slowly by.

What I guessed was that he had parked his car there, so I had an old envelope ready. But it was five minutes before a car came out, and I had gone all hot and cold again, thinking that something unexpected had happened. A garage hand ahead of it gave the driver the road. I got the car number as it drew slowly round and as it passed me I saw the driver. Then I made for the man.

"Pardon me," I said, "but that car that's just gone out. I think the driver's someone I know."

"Perhaps you do, sir," he said. "Who'd you think it was?"

"Brown," I said. "Percival Brown, the big contractor." He shook his head. "That wasn't him, sir. That was Dr. Halberg."

"Damn silly of me," I said. "But Halberg. Wait a minute, though. I do know a Halberg."

"This one lives at Malcroft," he told me, and I said he wouldn't be the one. Then I said I was sorry I'd troubled him, and he said it hadn't been any trouble at all.

What to do next I didn't quite know. Where Malcroft was I hadn't much idea, except that it was well out in the long grass beyond Twickenham, and somewhere north of Staines. So I went back to the bus stop and had a word with a driver waiting to go on duty. He told me there were buses every hour and the next was due in twenty minutes. When he said it was a good hour's trip I made rather a face, for it would mean getting back to town in the black-out.

"You needn't worry about that," he told me. "There's quite a fair train service. Every half-hour or so."

Well, I waited for the bus and took it. If I hadn't been so anxious to get to the other end I'd have enjoyed that journey on top of that bus, for we weren't long in leaving bricks and mortar behind, and but for a few eruptions of pink tile and asbestos, one might have been far from town. As for Malcroft, it was a sleepy little place. Before the war its main street would have been jammed with cars; now there was hardly a car in sight.

But that street boasted one road junction and I went up to the policeman on duty and asked him where I could find Dr. Halberg's house. He told me to keep straight on; it was a large red-brick place standing back from the road. I couldn't miss it, he said, because it was really two houses with a connecting way built between.

It took me just five minutes to reach it, and as I passed I slowed down my steps. It was as the policeman had described it, and there was the covered way on the ground floor that connected the two largish houses. A short drive led to each, and on the gateway of one a brass plate said:

MALCROFT NURSING HOME

On the brass plate on the gate of the farther one was:

J. Harbin-Lewis, M.B., F.R.C.S.
V. Halberg, M.D.

I did not want to make myself noticed so I walked on for a bit and came back on the other side of the road. What I thought was that here was a nursing home to which Chataway possibly sent his patients, though there would be far more in it than that. But I kept straight on to the little town and then made my way to the railway station. There was a train that should leave in half an hour, so I went to the police station.

A sergeant was on duty, and taking things easy, for a tea-tray stood on his desk and he was reading a Sunday paper. By chance I had my Yard papers on me and I handed them to him. Maybe I wasn't being too wise in questioning him, I thought. Local men have their pull, and the job I was on was a tricky one. Still, I decided to risk it.

"Yes, Mr. Travers," he said, and cast a quick look at the crowns on my shoulders, "what can I do for you?"

I mentioned Wharton's name, and he knew that well enough.

"He'll be down here in all probability before long," I said. "I'm making the preliminary enquiries, and they're highly confidential. There's a Doctor V. Halberg living here, isn't there?"

He said there was, and a very clever doctor too, so they said, though his own doctor was a someone whose name I didn't catch. An Austrian, this Halberg was, and he hated the Nazis like hell. He was well vouched for, and had come as assistant to Dr. Lewis soon after the war. But about eighteen months ago, he said, Dr. Lewis had been called up and since then Dr. Halberg had carried on alone.

"A private practice, is it?" I asked.

The question was badly worded but I got the answers I wanted. Dr. Halberg had very little practice in the actual town and the main affair was the nursing home. There were three nurses there usually, though he believed there were only two now.

"Halberg married?"

"No, he's not married," the sergeant said. "There's a housekeeper there, and some staff. A gardener, and a boy as well, I believe."

I thought that was enough for the moment, so I thanked him and told him again he'd be hearing from Wharton. Then I began making my way slowly towards the station, and it was a good thing that I had plenty of time, for if I'd been hurrying bat-eyed along, the whole course of things might have changed. As it was, I saw the man ahead of me and his back and gait seemed vaguely familiar. With him was a smaller man, and as the two turned into the station yard I knew the taller of the two was Hamson!

Something made me slow up and it was a good thing I did, for when I came to the corner, there was Hamson saying good-bye to the other man, who turned at once and came by where I was standing. I was lighting my pipe and I took a quick look at him. An indeterminate sort of cove, he looked; something like an elderly clerk, and what Hamson should have been doing with a man like that was more than I could guess. Or what Hamson was doing in Malcroft either. But something was telling me to chance my arm and follow the man, and then, again, something was reminding me that it was getting on towards dusk. That last something assured me that if I did follow the man he would only take me to Halberg's house.

But all the same I was scared stiff that Hamson should see me. Luckily I had bought my ticket when I made the enquiries about trains, so I watched the platform from the vantage-point of the bridge crossing. Hamson had gone well along the plat-form, so as soon as the train drew in I nipped down and took a seat at the near end, and a pretty filthy third-class compartment it was. But I had it to myself for a few stations and by then I'd lost all anxiety about Hamson's looking through the train. There was no reason why he should, so I told myself, but I sat behind that same old newspaper for all that.

When we drew in to town I delayed my exit and when I got out to the barrier Hamson must have been well on his way. It was almost dark, but I found a telephone kiosk and rang up Mrs. Grays. I didn't expect her to be in, but she was.

"How are you?" I said. "Still feeling better?"

"Very much better," she said.

"Can you put up with me for a few minutes if I come round at once?"

She didn't reply and I thought the line was dead. Then she merely said she'd love to see me, and that again was that.

I couldn't find a taxi but I did get a bus, though the short journey took the best part of half an hour. Barbara Grays was waiting for me, and so was an excellent glass of sherry. She was certainly looking very much better, and I told her so. We also talked about the perfectly magnificent weather we were having, and the talk was so artificial that you could have cut it with a knife. She was trying not to appear anxious, and I was thinking how to slide easily into the exceedingly awkward news which I had come specially to give.

"I haven't seen much of Hamson these days," I remarked. "Have you run across him at all?"

"Not a great deal," she said, and it seemed to me that her voice had a studied indifference.

"I wonder if I might be highly personal," I went on. "You may even think it rude."

"Why not?" she said. "Surely these days it's the fashion to be rude."

"But some of us remain old-fashioned," I said. "What I was going to say was, that I had an idea—I don't know who put it in my head—that you and Hamson were practically engaged."

She smiled, and with the same indifference. "My dear Major Travers! You of all people listening to gossip!"

"Don't be hypocritical," I told her archly. "I love it, and so do you. La Rochefoucauld was eternally right. There's always something in the misfortunes of our friends which is not wholly displeasing to us."

"It would have been a misfortune if I had been engaged to Tommy Hamson?"

I smiled. "You know too many answers. But to go on being rude, are you thinking of marrying him when all this dreadful business is over?"

"But why should I marry Tommy Hamson?"

I shrugged my shoulders. "Why *do* people get married?"

Then she was asking me if I would have another sherry. I said I wouldn't, and it was when I was taking her glass and my own to the side-table that she put her question.

"You didn't come here to-night to talk about Tommy Hamson?"

"I didn't," I said. "I came here to redeem a promise. That if I discovered anything about your sister I'd reveal it to you before going to the police."

"What have you discovered?" Her eyes were fixed on me with a disconcerting intensity, and I took my time about going back to my chair.

"I think you know most of it yourself," I said.

"What do you mean?"

"Just what I say. Perhaps that's why I'm being so abrupt. If I'd thought you knew nothing, then I think I'd have been afraid to tell you."

That frightened her, and that was the last thing I'd intended. But it did tell me that there were things about which she knew even less than I.

"Will you let me tell you about it in my own way?" I went on.

She nodded, and I caught the nervous movements of her hands.

"This is what happened," I said. "I may be wrong in little details but the main outline I know is right. The story begins for both of us on that morning when your sister came here to see you. She gave you a piece of news. I imagine she gave it perfectly calmly, but to you it was something like the end of the world—as things turned out. What she told you was that she was pregnant."

She didn't nod or even move her head, and her eyes were so intensely on mine that mine turned away.

"The gist of the talk that followed was something like this," I went on, "and your voice was certainly raised, because you were angry at her obstinacy and the matter-of-fact way she was taking things. Perhaps you took it for granted that she'd be marrying Worrack at once, and that she had no intention of doing. Then you thought she'd go away for a long holiday and have her child, but she had no intention of doing that. Then came the biggest shock of all, when you realised what that operation really was."

It was no prudery on my part but I couldn't look at her as I told her that. But she made never a sign and I knew that so far I was right.

"It was you, probably, who described the man as he really was," I said. "She preferred to call him a doctor, or surgeon. In any case you couldn't budge her. Her mind was made up. Perhaps both your voices were raised then—that I can't say. I do know that she fainted. She was sick perhaps, as women are in early pregnancy, and when you rushed out for sal volatile, you caught your maid by the door. What she had heard, if anything, you didn't know, but though you came to the final conclusion that she'd heard nothing incriminating, you dismissed her. To keep in her good books, in case she might have heard anything, you paid her well."

I looked up at her then, and it was her eyes that turned away.

"When you asked your sister who the doctor was, and where his surgery was, I think she told you he lived in Dublin, and that she was giving out that she was going to see O'Clauty and her horses as an excuse for the crossing. After the operation, of course, she would have gone to see O'Clauty. And one other thing. I think she made you swear by all that was holy that you'd never say a word to Worrack. That's all—at least so far."

"All," she said, and I scarcely heard the word, for she had spoken it to herself. Then she was shaking her head. Another moment and her question came so fiercely that it startled me.

"Who else knows it besides you?"

"No one," I told her quietly. "Didn't I promise I'd come to you first?"

"I'm sorry," she said. "I oughtn't to have doubted you."

Her lips quivered and I thought for a moment she was going to cry. That was why I went so hastily on.

"If you'd asked me how I discovered it, then I couldn't have told you, because it involves all sorts of people and things. I will say I only discovered it a few hours ago—and—"

"Those other people. They will talk?"

"Oh, no," I told her, and smiled reassuringly. "There'll be no talk. I think I can safely promise you that. But what I would like to do, and believe me when I say I'm sincere, is to say how I sympathise with you in the dreadful predicament in which you found yourself when you discovered she'd never been to Ireland at all. And, of course, when you didn't hear a word from her. You simply couldn't go to the police. You might have mentioned the pregnancy—and yet I don't know. Even that would have been too dangerous."

I had to shake my head when I thought of something else.

"You must have gone through hell, even that day at Moroni's—when you were trying to make yourself out indifferent. Then there was I, blundering in with that ring and asking you to identify it."

"It was good of you," she told me quietly. "I'll never forget it."

"No, no," I said quickly. "Thanks are the last thing I want. But just one thing more, and then I've finished. There's something else you did, and I'm certainly not going to upbraid you for it. I think you broke your word to your sister. Perhaps you had to. You just had to confide in someone or you'd have gone mad. That was why you confided in Worrack. That was why he in turn confided in me. You both hoped I'd discover something, and the whole business could be cleared up without the intervention of the police."

She made no reply. It was a moment or two before she spoke. "What are you going to do?"

"Well, I've redeemed my promise and I can't do more unless you can give me overwhelming reasons to the contrary, I've simply got to go to the police."

"But you mustn't!"

"Listen," I said gently. "Why be afraid of the police? Do you think they haven't any hearts? Do you think they want to drag your sister's name in the mud? I tell you that's the last thing they want to do. There'll be no scandal—that I can assure you. But justice has got to be done. Whoever was responsible for your sister's death not going to be allowed to get away with it. There's something else. What about Worrack? Do you think he committed suicide? I don't, and—between ourselves—the police don't. There's something else that has to be paid for."

"The police will come here again?"

"No," I said. "I think I can promise you even that."

I got to my feet, for there seemed no more to say. Then her hand went out and I thought she was motioning me to sit down again, so I sat down.

"That ring. You still have it?"

"Yes," I said ruefully. "There'll have to be some very curious explaining done to show how I got it."

"It didn't upset me when I saw that ring," she said. "I knew about it all the time."

My eyes fairly bulged.

"There's something I ought to say in fairness to you," she was going on. "I thought I'd never have to say it, but now I must. It wasn't Peter Worrack who got you to come to his flat. It was myself."

"Good Lord!" I said, and then a light began to dawn. "But it wasn't you who sent me a certain letter?"

"Yes," she said. "It was I who sent that too."

"Then you're READY!"

She smiled wanly. Perhaps it did sound a bit foolish. "Yes," she said. "And afterwards I was afraid it was something you would guess."

CHAPTER XV
READY FOR ACTION

"Good Lord!" I said again. "Then it was you behind that door!"

She stared at that.

"I saw your gloved hand on it," I said. "But I never guessed it was you!"

Talk was easy now and there were no hesitations.

"But why did you think of confiding in me?" I asked.

"Your wife had told me about you long ago," she said. "Then I remembered it, so I got her address from the hospital and wrote to her. In very strict confidence, I made it, and perhaps I didn't tell her the truth. She said she knew you'd be glad to help, and she told me you would be at the flat on leave. She promised she'd never say a word. Then I was afraid to take advantage of her kindness, so I went to Peter Worrack."

"I see. And that was why he hinted that you were up to the neck in the business, so that I'd never dream you were behind him."

"Yes," she said. "I knew I had nothing really to fear. I'd been foolish perhaps, but that was all. Then, when Peter was dead, I was in despair again. Then I forced myself to write that letter. As soon as I'd sent it I wished I hadn't. I thought you'd discover me from the name."

"The name?" I said, and then saw it. "Your hair, of course. But thank heaven you did write it. Which reminds me. How did you come into possession of that pawn-ticket?"

"I can't tell you," she said, and shook her head. "That's something you must never ask me."

"But, listen," I said. "The only basis on which you and I can work together is absolute confidence. You've got to tell me!"

She shook her head again, and once more I had the idea that she was near to tears.

"Well, let's hope you're right," I said, and shrugged my shoulders resignedly.

"But you've got to trust me," she said, and the hell of a lot of logic, as I thought, was in that. Then she was wanting to know what else I had found out.

"The man responsible for your sister's death," I told her. "If not that, then the man who pawned her jewellery. That's why I've got to go to the police. It's a matter of honour. It's a matter of two honours. They're employing me and so are you. That's why I'll do my damnedest to protect your interests."

"It's good of you," she said. "Too good of you."

"Don't you believe it," I told her. "But there's something you *can* tell me. Have you any idea who killed Worrack?" She turned her head away and her tongue was nervously moistening her lips.

"I know who killed him." she said calmly.

"Who?"

She shook her head again. "I can't tell you. It's something you must never ask me."

But she'd given me the answer all the same.

"Well," I said, and stirred in my seat as if to go. "That's something we'll be bound to find out. And, unless I'm mistaken, within the next forty-eight hours."

As I got to my feet I remembered something.

"That ring. I ought to have given it back to you."

"Keep it," she said. "I'd like it to go to your wife."

"Far too generous of you," I said. "She'd never accept it. But you and she must talk that over later. And there's the money. Best part of a hundred pounds."

"Keep that too," she said. "Perhaps you may have to use it."

"Some time I'll send you an account," I said. "And my word still stands. You can rely on me to make your interests my own."

As soon as I'd said that I knew how pompous it must have sounded, and then I thought of something else.

"Will you answer me a plain question? I've asked it before. It's about Hamson. Did you ever entertain any idea of marrying him?"

She turned away again. "And if I did?"

"Nothing," I said. Then I was going to hint that I had her interests to consider, and leave it at that, but she spoke first.

"Have you anything against him?"

"Maybe no. Maybe yes," I said. "But that's something that I can't tell."

"I'm not going to marry him," she told me calmly, and she was giving a challenging look as if she expected some comment. But then the door bell rang.

"Who can it be?" she said, and suddenly looked frightened.

"I'll have a look," I said. "I'm going now in any case."

When I opened the door, there stood Hamson.

We each tried not to look surprised. Then I said I was just going, but he made me come back with him. He wasn't staying a minute, he said, and his taxi was waiting. If I was going home we might share it.

"How are you, Barbara?" he asked her solicitously. "Much better, Tommy. And you?"

"Oh, I'm all right," he told her amusedly. "Nothing's ever wrong with me."

"I happened to be near," he went on, "so I thought I'd pop in for a word."

"You'll have a sherry?"

"Thanks, no," he said. "Got a taxi outside ticking up the shillings. But what about lunch with me to-morrow? Feel equal to it? Somewhere nice and quiet?"

"Sorry, Tommy," she said, "but I just don't feel like lunching out."

"What do you think?" he asked me. "Oughtn't she to get out? What's the sense of sitting here and moping?"

"I'm not moping," she told him unruffledly. "It's just that I don't feel like going out."

"Wish to God I knew what had come over you these days!"

The brief explosion passed and he was shrugging his shoulders. Then he smiled, and a most attractive smile he had, I'll say that much for him.

"Well, some time later then?"

"Some time later," she said, and nodded. Then her hand went diplomatically out to me.

"Good-bye, Major Travers. So good of you to call. And do give my love to Bernice. Good-bye, Tommy. Thanks for calling, too."

Down we went to the taxi. It was dark as blazes but he had a pencil torch, and it rather looked to me as if he'd gone home after getting off that train, and had come to the flat specially provided. As soon as the taxi moved off he began to talk. His tone was a drawling quality as if he was mildly bored, or else cocksure.

"What are you up to these days?"

"I?" I said. "Oh, like Satan, walking to and fro."

"Good. But you're helping the police, aren't you?"

"In a limited way," I said. "Something to do, and it passes the time."

"Got any suspects yet?" There seemed to me some sort of mockery in his tone, and he was beginning to get my goat. I'm a pugnacious individual at times, though you mayn't have thought so.

"Yes," I said, as if suddenly interested. "Rather funny that you should ask it."

"Oh?" he said, ears pricked suddenly up. Then the irony came in again. "I suppose I'm not on the list by any chance?"

"Why not?"

"As you say, why not?" I heard his little chuckling sneer. "Any questions you'd like to put to me?"

Ever ridden in a taxi in the black-out? With someone in one corner and you in another, and a voice coming eerily from the pitch dark? Then you know how unnatural everything was. I've told you that his damned superiority had been getting my goat. That's why I lost my temper, even if I didn't show it, and said the damn silly thing I did.

"Questions?" I said. "Well, perhaps there are."

"Such as?"

"Well, such as why did you have to kill Worrack?"

As soon as that slipped out I could have bitten off my tongue. But he was saying nothing, and I didn't feel like making worst out of worse. Perhaps he was taking it for a joke, I thought, and then I knew he wasn't.

"So you guessed that, did you?" he suddenly said, and his voice was so low that I hardly heard him.

"Maybe," I told him laconically.

I heard him let out a breath. "Remember how you ate my bread and salt that day?"

"I do," I said. "But what about it?"

"Is this in confidence between you and me?"

"Why not?"

"Damn you, Travers! Can't you ever be explicit?"

"When it suits me," I said. "But if you want to make any confidence, you can. I shan't blab, if that's what's worrying you."

There was a silence again, and the taxi was moving on through the dark, deserted streets. Another minute or two and we'd be at his hotel. Then he spoke.

"I did kill him. But it wasn't my fault."

I wondered if he had a gun on him, and if I should do more than hear the crack of it. Why should he let me go on living, once he'd told me that? Or did he trust me after all? Had he known all along that I knew?

"Well, what about it?" he was saying.

"Nothing about it," I said, and was waiting for the crack of that gun. "But that other one. Did you kill her too?"

"Blast you! What do you mean?"

The brakes were grinding as the taxi slewed, and then was coming to a halt.

"Here you are, sir," came a hearty voice. "Warfield's Hotel."

My side was by the pavement and I got out.

"Thanks, Hamson," I said. "Sure you won't let me pay?"

He growled a something which I didn't catch, and in another second I was moving off in the dark. Across the road I stopped and looked back. The taxi was driving off and I seemed to hear Hamson's steps as they turned towards the hotel. And then I was letting out a breath as I moved on again. What had prompted Hamson to make that confession I don't know, but it appalled me, and scared me, and though the night was chilly, my forehead was damp with sweat.

By the time I was in my room I had made up my mind. Hamson didn't matter. Maybe he had had no hand in the death of Georgina Morbent, and as for keeping his confidence about Worrack, that I would certainly do, for Wharton would discover it in his own way. Especially after what I was going to tell him. And at once, for I had changed my mind about waiting for the morning. I was lucky enough to find him at the Yard.

"Sorry to be a nuisance, George," I said, "but could you slip round and see me? It's very urgent."

"Why can't you come here?"

"To tell the truth I'm too damn tired," I said. "It'll be worth it. I assure you that."

"On to something?"

"Yes," I said. "What about a meal? Had anything yet?"

"Meal!" he told me, and snorted. "A hell of a lot of time I get for meals."

"Expect you straightaway," I said, and hung up before he should change his mind.

Then I began thinking about Hamson, and my bet was that before morning he'd be dead. He'd do himself in, for after what he'd told me he'd know there was no other way out. Then I was wondering what it was that Worrack had known about him that had made his elimination a grim necessity. I could see why Worrack had forced Hamson on me as a colleague. What he had thought was that with the flair for detection with which he credited me I should spot something in Hamson for myself.

But I didn't want to do too much thinking, so I ordered a couple of service suppers and pottered about to pass the time. Then I did realise that as soon as I opened my mouth to Wharton I'd be likely to let out a considerable deal which would take some extraordinary explaining. That worried me and I had only managed to hit on a scheme when he arrived.

"All togged out, are you?" he said when he saw me in uniform.

"Purposes of disguise," I told him, and took his hat and coat. "How are things with you?"

"Damn slow," he said. "Got a trace of that car at last and followed it as far as Twickenham, and that's the lot. Nobody's called on Carpenter and he's done nothing suspicious." Then he was cocking an eye at me. "You're looking a bit tired."

"I am," I said. "That's why I'm going to have a pretty stiff drink. What about you?"

Beer was his tipple, so I passed him a bottle and then we got down to the meal. No sooner had I swallowed the first mouthful than I set my scheme in motion. From my fob pocket I produced that ring and gave it to him across the table.

"You'd better keep this, George. No necessity for a receipt."

"Good God!" he said. "Where'd you get it?"

"That's a long story," I said. "Put that ring away and then I'll tell you. And don't forget you'll have two hundred and fifty quid in your pocket."

He gave a sideways nod to indicate he was far too fly to have his pocket picked, and then before he could speak I was away on a new tack.

"Tell me something about—about shady women's doctors, George, will you? I've become rather interested since this morning."

He stared, and then his expression changed and I knew he was putting two and two together.

"That's right," I said. "You must have run across plenty of them in your time."

"Why all the humbug? Why don't you say what you mean? You aren't talking about doctors, you're talking about abortionists," he said. "But you don't want me to tell you about them. You ought to know enough yourself. Dirty, furtive little swine, that's what I call 'em. Living up back streets usually."

"But not all of them, surely. What about that recent case of a doctor with a first-class practice and reputation who'd been making a packet out of doing the job, and for years."

"Of course there are all sorts," he said, beginning a glare and thinking better of it. "The man you instanced simply moved among a better class, that's all."

"What's the actual process—without going into details —and how long does it take?"

"A matter of a minute or two, that's all. Then the patient simply pays up and walks out. But what the fellow has advised her is then to go to her own or some other doctor. It is impossible to detect what has really been done, and he treats her according to whatever symptoms she describes."

"A lot of it, these days, is there?"

"Is there not!" he said.

"Just one other thing," I said. "These fellows seem to me to get into the hands of the police because of a patient's death, at least in most cases. Why should a patient die?"

"Several reasons," he said. "Simple shock, though that's rare. The peritoneal cavity may have been pierced and there may be shock from that. In most cases it's septic poisoning owing to dirty conditions or instruments."

"That explains things," I said. "And now I'll tell you what I found out."

I began with Hamson and seeing him with Scylla Payton, and he was interrupting at once.

"What did I tell you? Scylla Payton, eh?" He gave himself a nod of approval. "Didn't I tell you it'd pay hand over fist to keep an eye on Hamson?"

"That's right, George," I said, for it suited my book to let him think I'd accepted his advice. "You certainly do get some brainy ideas."

Then I told him about Goldilocks. George interrupted with a joke. If one was Scylla, then I ought to have christened the other Charybdis.

"She was Goldilocks to me," I said, after a suitable chuckle, and then I began telling him about that wireless comic and his gag about the hens spoiling their figure for two bob a dozen.

"You see, George, I remembered that Worrack had told me once that Georgina Morbent was extraordinarily proud of her figure. He'd also told me she wasn't the marrying sort. Didn't want children and so on."

"Yes. Get on with it," he told me impatiently.

Well, I told him about the statement from the bank and how I'd checked up on Chataway, and had then decided to run an eye over the Comport Street lay-out. When I came to Goldilocks his eyes bulged, and he didn't interrupt. And so on through the rest of the afternoon and evening, though with no mention of either Hamson or Barbara Grays.

"My God, we're on to something!" he said, and was waving his napkin about. "It's plain as the nose on your face. Funny, wasn't it, that I should have that intuition about keeping an eye on Hamson?"

"Well, there we are, George," I said. "We know what Georgina and her sister talked about that morning, and why Georgina was sick, and why Barbara sacked the maid, and we know why Barbara wouldn't go to the police. But there's something that's been worrying me. We believe Georgina went from Richmond in Halberg's car to Halberg's house—it wouldn't have been the nursing home—and underwent the operation. You've told me that it would be over in a matter of minutes and then she could have been driven back to the hotel. Why then did Georgina not keep her room at the hotel? Why did she assume that the operation was going to be a matter of some days?"

"Perfectly simple," he told me with a snort. "She drew out three hundred pounds, two-fifty in pound notes. Those were to pay Halberg. A hell of a price, you'll say, for a few minutes' work, but you bet he kidded her on. After all, he had to have some justification for that exorbitant fee. I'll bet he told her she'd have to have a few days' rest and he'd keep an eye on possible complications. And I'll bet something else. What he intended to do was to move her the following day to the nursing home part of the show. He'd tell the nurse in charge that she was being treated for after-effects of the operation, or whatever the jargon is."

"You're right," I said. "But she died on his hands from some sort of shock and all he could do was embalm the body till he could dispose of it. Since he'd pawned more than one lot of things I'd say it had happened to him once before, so he knew just what to do."

"I'll bet he was making a young fortune out of the game," Wharton said. "Two-fifty for one operation and then another hundred and fifty or so from the jewellery."

I thought he was going to mention the ring, so I cut hastily in.

"Something else is explained, too, and that's where Hamson comes in. Barbara couldn't inherit till Georgina was known to be dead. When Barbara got the money and Hamson married her, then there'd have been still more shared out among the gang. But about that severed head. You bet your life the head was cut off because the rest of the body would have shown the real cause of death. The perforation you mentioned, for instance."

"Oh, yes, it all fits in," he said. "The problem is, just how do we get to work."

"Well, for what it's worth this is my idea," I said. "If I hadn't had that uncanny luck to see Goldilocks come out of Chataway's door, this is what I was going to do in the morning. Goldilocks is either Chataway's secretary or secretary-receptionist, and I should have rung up and made an appointment under an assumed name, and I'd have gone there in uniform, saying I was on embarkation leave. When I got to Chataway's place I'd have made the acquaintance of Goldilocks. Then I'd have told the doctor that my wife was much younger than I and we'd been married two years and were very disturbed because we had no children. All that would have given me the chance of summing him up. When I came out, I expect I'd have seen Goldilocks again and I ought to have had her summed up too."

"I've a damn good mind to try it," Wharton said, and then chuckled. "There'd be blue merry hell if my wife ever found it out."

"You're the ideal one to carry it off," I said. "There isn't a man at the Yard could come near you by streets."

That landed him and he said he'd try it. Then he was finishing off his beer and wiping his moustache with voluminous sweeps of his table-cloth of a handkerchief.

"You think Chataway and your pal Goldilocks are both in it?" he asked me.

"You never can tell," I told him. "But Halberg-Markovitch is in it. There's no shadow of doubt of that."

"I know," he said, and then was chuckling delightedly. "Tell you what. I'll bet you a new hat that everything's over inside two days."

"I won't bet," I said, "but I may stand you a lunch if it is. But what about me, from now on? Anything in mind for me to do?"

He pursed his lips. The brow furrowed and beneath it I knew the crafty old brain was working something out—or trying to keep something back.

"I've got it worked out to the last move," he announced. "As Montgomery says, it's in the bag. Let me see."

The brow furrowed again and the lips pushed out the huge moustache.

"Yes, that's it," he said. "All you do is sit tight and make no move at all."

Then he was making notes in his book and scowling at them.

"That's it," he told me again. "You be in here at midday to-morrow and I'll report progress. Perhaps I'll be ringing you up again towards night, but that we'll see about. Then, on Tuesday morning we ought to be ready to run down to that Malcroft place." He gave me one of his most unctuous smiles. "I've got a first-class job for you there. Suit you to a T."

"Thanks very much," I told him dryly, but to his back, for he was already making for his hat and coat. At the head of the stairs he thanked me for the meal and said how lucky it had been that I'd taken his advice about keeping an eye on Hamson. He also added roguishly that one day he might make a real detective out of me.

"Where are you off to now?" I asked him, as he was moving off.

"To Malcroft," he said, "and the hell of a journey that'll be in the black-out."

"Good luck!" I called after him and then had a little chuckle of my own. That little scheme had come off. So engrossed had he been in my disclosures, and then in plans of his own, that he'd forgotten to ask me how I'd come into possession of that emerald ring.

CHAPTER XVI
THE TRAP IS SPRUNG

I SLEPT like a top and it was almost nine o'clock when I finally awoke. When I'd dressed I went downstairs through force of habit, though I knew there could be nothing for me in the Personal Column of the *Telegraph*. Monday meant only four pages in the paper so I looked them hastily through and there was nothing about Hamson and suicide.

When I'd finished breakfast I had an idea, and a damn silly idea it was. I'd ring up Hamson and give him the tip that the police were on to him. After his confession, I thought I owed him that much at least.

Only about ten rooms in that hotel had direct communication, as you may have gathered, and it was lucky that his was one of them and I could call him direct. But he wasn't in, and when I called the hotel they told me he'd left a good hour before.

There was no comment on that, but the girl did tell me that he'd said he mightn't be in till very late.

I hung up and then was rather relieved he hadn't been in. Then naturally I began thinking about his part in things, and dramatically enough they fitted together. Though Barbara Grays hadn't been openly engaged to him, had she been his mistress? I thought that maybe she had, or else how could she have come into possession of that pawn-ticket? He had dropped it, I thought, or she had been jealous and had found it in a pocket. The shock of the discovery must have been terrific, for it told her that he was mixed up in Georgina's disappearance, and probable death, and that whoever pawned the ring, he had obtained the ticket, and probably the cash to redeem it, as his share in the affair. There was still further proof that Worrack had forced him on me so that my supposed perspicuity should discover what his part in things had been. Then, when Worrack had been murdered, Barbara had gone much further and had sent me the actual ticket. No wonder, I thought, that things had cooled off between her and Hamson.

And what about the method used by the gang? Somehow I couldn't help thinking that Chataway knew nothing. Vaughan was a shrewd man and a knowledgeable one, and when he vouched for Chataway, then he had been sure of what he said. So the scheme, as I saw it, was worked like this. A pregnant woman consults Chataway through Goldilocks, who perhaps insists on knowing beforehand what the consultation is about. After the consultation, Goldilocks may have to type for Chataway a condensed report, and that would tell her all she would need to know. Later, the approach to the woman is made, but so warily that if she doesn't bite, then no harm is done. Chataway's clientele would be wealthy people, I thought, so that one catch would pay amply for a score of disappointments. As for Hamson, he would be the liaison between Goldilocks and Halberg.

But as the strain of waiting for George Wharton was rather too much for me, I went along to my club for an hour and then walked back. It was a quarter to twelve when I got in and it was not till a quarter-past that George actually rang up.

"Everything went off swimmingly," he said and I knew he was bursting with satisfaction at having pulled off that visit to Chataway.

"What about C. himself?" I asked.

"I think he's all right," he told me. "But the little pal of yours. You had a good look at her, didn't you?"

"I did," I said.

"Notice anything peculiar?"

"No," I said. "What should I have noticed?"

"Oh, it was nothing important," he told me quickly. "Ring you up again at about nine to-night? It won't be before, so you needn't stay in."

Then he rang off and I was puzzling my wits to find out what I'd missed about Goldilocks. But I hadn't any luck, and that afternoon, to keep my mind off things, I went to a cinema. Then I took a stroll in the park till close on dusk and after that treated myself out to dinner. Well, before nine o'clock I was back in my room and listening for the telephone bell. It was nearer ten than nine when it at last came.

Wharton's voice was pregnant with events.

"That you, Travers? It is? Thought I'd let you know that everything's set."

"Good," I cut in.

"I want you at the Yard at half-past eight sharp," he was going on, "and in uniform. Don't be late, or everything'll be thrown out of gear."

"I'll be there," I said. "Nothing else you'd like to tell me?"

"Not now," he said. "Too dangerous. But if you play your own part all right, you'll be standing me that lunch."

Then he rang off. For a moment I was furious with him, and then as usual I had to chuckle. Everything would be all right if

I played my part—whatever that was to be. George was leaving himself a bolt-hole. If anything slipped up on us, it was a million to one on my getting the blame.

You bet your life I was there on time; in fact Wharton wasn't ready and I had to wait. Then we set off in his car. He and I sat in the back, and with the driver in front was the pawnbroker's manager. I guessed he'd be wanted to identify Markovitch.

Wharton didn't tell me a thing about what had been happening. He was far too busy rehearsing me in the part I had to play. Everything had been fixed up. Halberg was being told that a certain Major Smith—myself—had brought a charge against him, but if he could slip along to the police-station, everything might be settled amicably and out of court, as it were.

This was the ingenious charge, that on the late evening of the fourteenth of January I'd had my car at the side of the road, not too far from that nursing home of his, when he'd come by in his car and had nearly killed me. He'd also broken my front bumper. I'd just had time to take his number but I hadn't been able to follow things up because I'd been away on duty, and had just come back to Twickenham, where I lived. A fictitious address had been provided for me.

There was a bit more to it than that, but George kept fussing as if I'd never played a part before. The fact was, that he was visualising himself in that same part, and we were well through Twickenham before I was asking him for the love of heaven to leave me alone and credit me with at least a minimum of *savoir-faire*.

We'd moved deceptively fast and it was not much after ten o'clock when we drew into the station yard. An Army car was there with a broken front bumper, and I knew George had done things in style, even if he had fitted the damage to the kind of car he'd been able to get. Halberg was due at half-past ten, so we had plenty of time. My pawnbroker friend was to be outside to make the identification, and if Halberg wasn't Markovitch, then there'd have to be some modification of plans, and the fact would be signalled through by the buzzer to the room where I was to go. Otherwise everything would be as arranged.

In the local Inspector's room there was an air of expectation. Wharton introduced me, and then was fussing about and arranging where I ought to sit, and where Halberg should sit. The Inspector pronounced himself as word perfect, and George was telling him not to be anxious or that'd spoil everything. I nearly told him to get to hell out of the room himself and leave us to it. On the table, by the way, which was under the very nose of Halberg, were the usual trays of papers, and an official-looking paper to which the Inspector would refer. There was also a newspaper artistically placed, but what that was for I didn't know.

Well, the time slipped by and at last the buzzer went. The Inspector picked up the receiver, nodded, said O.K. and then replaced it.

"He's just coming, sir," he told Wharton, and out George slipped to get the report of the pawnbroker. My heart was beginning to race but that Inspector looked cooler than a cucumber.

Three minutes or so we waited, and then steps were heard. The buzzer hadn't gone again, so we knew our man. Then there was a tap at the door.

"Dr. Halberg to see you, sir."

"Ask the Doctor to come in," the Inspector said cheerfully, and in Halberg came. He had an overcoat buttoned up to his chin, and a dark felt hat in his hand. I should warn you that he had very little accent, and even that little I shall not attempt to reproduce. What I did know was that he'd put on much more of it when he'd posed in the pawnshop as Markovitch, the Russian exile.

"Ah! come in, Doctor," the Inspector said. "We shan't keep you very long. At least I hope not. This is Major Smith. You may have noticed his car outside. Well, not his car, a Government one. The one he claims he was driving."

Halberg shot a look at me and I nodded curtly.

"Sit down here, Doctor, will you?" the Inspector told him amiably. "This little business isn't going to take us long. We're all men of good-will—at least I hope so. Perhaps you'd like to hear Major Smith's story."

I told my story, and mightily indignant I was. I'd thought I had a puncture and had got out to have a look. When I was standing in the pitch dark—about seven o'clock it'd be—and by the rear off-wheel, a car suddenly whizzed by me. It caught my coat as I leapt back and then it just hit the front off-bumper. Luckily I'd managed to get the car's number and I'd seen it was a dark saloon. I'd had the number traced but hadn't been able to follow the matter up till the previous night.

"But that is impossible," Halberg told me with an ingratiating smile. "My car was not out on that night. That I can prove." He turned to the Inspector. "How is it that Major Smith is so sure about the date?"

"I was sure and still am," I cut in belligerently. "I was thinking at the time that it was the fourteenth because my wife's birthday was the following morning and I hadn't bought her anything."

The Inspector allowed himself to smile. "I think that's good enough proof, don't you, Doctor?"

Halberg shrugged his shoulders. "What can I do? In a court of law it would be his word, perhaps, against mine. As a civilian I should be at a disadvantage."

"I resent that," I said.

"Now, now, Major," the Inspector said placatingly. "We've got to be reasonable. The Doctor doesn't know, perhaps, what English law is like."

"Reasonable," Halberg said, picking him up. "I would wish to be reasonable, as you call it. I can claim—and I can prove—that it was not my car that did the damage. Nevertheless I wish to be reasonable."

"Just how reasonable?" I said, and far more pacifically.

"For whatever damage was done I will pay. Get the Government or the Department to send me the bill and I will settle it at once. If the Major has any personal claims, I will settle them too."

The Inspector gave me a look of reprimand. "Well, I call that more than reasonable. If the Major isn't prepared to settle on those terms, then I don't think much of his case."

"Seems fair enough to me," I said. "If the Doctor agrees, I'll have everything worked out and send him the bill. It won't be much. It was the principle of the thing, not the money."

"Very fair on both sides, very fair indeed. I'll just make a formal note to the effect that everything's agreed on."

He picked up his pen, stuck it in the ink and then was consulting that fake document.

"What's the date?" he said, and before either of us could answer was picking up the newspaper.

"Oh, yes," he said, and laid the paper down in another place. "Now just a formal note."

He began writing something, but it was Halberg in whom I was interested. And no wonder. When that newspaper was removed, there, under his very eyes, were a platinum watch, a platinum wrist-watch and that emerald ring. He had started, then shot a look at me, but my eyes had dropped in time and I had been fiddling with the buckle of my Sam Browne. Then he had looked at the table again, and then had pushed back his chair.

"Hallo, Doctor, aren't you going to wait?" the Inspector asked him, but as if not too interested.

"I have just remembered," Halberg said, and was fidgeting nervously with his hat. "There is a patient whom it is necessary that I should see. I had forgotten. But you will understand."

"Quite, quite," He got to his feet, and his eyes didn't even fall on those pieces of jewellery. "I'll get the Major to send everything on."

"Thank you. Thank you." He had been backing towards the door and bowing to us both. Before the Inspector could open the door, he was out. I got to my feet, but the Inspector motioned me back again and put a finger warningly to his lips. In the room was extraordinary quiet, and then we heard the sound of an electric starter and the whine of gears as a car moved rapidly off.

A door to my left opened and in came Wharton. His ear, I guessed, had been at the keyhole, but I was wrong. There was a glass partition above that door and his eye had been behind a periscope.

"Capital!" he said, and clapped me exasperatingly on the back. "Couldn't have done it better myself. You too, Inspector."

"What now," I asked.

"Now he'll be telephoning his pals in town," he said. "Giving them the high-sign that the game's up." Then he was nodding down at those pieces of jewellery. "Artistic. That's what I'd call it. Just that little artistic touch that always pays. What do the advertisements say? Not too much and not too little. Well, we'd better get going," he went on piously. "Everything ready, Inspector?"

Everything was ready, but in another room. Wharton took a chair and clamped on some earphones and I gathered that he was about to listen in to Halberg's telephone, or keep in touch with those already listening-in outside.

The Inspector was leaving us to it, and when he'd gone I asked George what was being done about Halberg escaping.

"Escape my foot!" he told me. "Four men are watching his place at this very minute. Two of them have motor-bikes that can do an easy seventy."

"How long before anything will come through?"

"Look here," he said, and gave me a look of exasperation in which he tried none too well to put a touch of humour. "Nothing's going to happen yet. Even if he rings somebody up, that's only half the game. We've got to see what happens to the one at the other end. You slip along down the town and have a look round. Come back in an hour. Get yourself some lunch."

"If that's so, I think I will have a stroll outside," I said, though I was none too pleased about his wanting to get rid of me. Not that it would have been much fun sitting there doing nothing, and watching him with those earphones and his face like a mixture of walrus and Buddha.

"See you in a couple of hours or so," he said, and was hauling out his pipe.

I strolled along to the little town. Tuesday seemed some sort of market day and there were several people about, and in that perfectly wonderful February sun it looked a cheerful place. I noticed a tiny cinema I'd missed on the Sunday, and then I came across an antique shop. Antique dealers are friendly people who never press you to buy, and I went inside for a look round. There wasn't much there and what furniture there was was a wicked price, and that, I was told, was due to the war. Then, among the oddments of china, I found a rather attractive Liverpool cup and saucer, and saw it packed ready for despatch to my wife. Then the dealer and I had a yarn about this and that, and before I knew it the best part of an hour had gone.

Well, I couldn't stand the waiting any longer so I made my way back to the police-station.

"I don't think I'd go in there, sir," the Inspector told me as I was making for Wharton's room, and the grimace told me he'd probably been kicked out himself.

"Nothing happened then?" I asked.

"Yes. Halberg's telephoned," he said. "Did it almost as soon as he got in."

"Know who it was?"

He grimaced again. "I don't, sir. I know it was to a woman."

"A woman," I said, and shrugged my shoulders. Then I nodded towards Wharton's room. "What's he up to now?"

"I reckon he's got all them watched that Halberg was likely to telephone to," he said. "His men'll report here if anything suspicious is happening."

"What about Halberg?"

"We hope he'll bolt," he told me. "Probably he's now disposing of the rest of that body. At least, that's what the Super thinks."

"If he told you that, then it's probably the last thing he thinks," I said, and he gave a knowing grin.

"Well, I'll push off and get some lunch," I said. "If he does happen to mention me at any time between now and Christmas, tell him I'm at the Royal George."

I made my way to that hotel and ordered the lunch. There was some time to wait, so I had a beer and watched some dart players. At one o'clock I heard the news, and very little there was, and by that time I'd almost finished my meal. At half-past I was back at the station. The Inspector wasn't about, and the officer on duty said he'd gone to dinner. I pushed on to Wharton's room, and I could hear him talking. But I couldn't make out the words so I gently turned the knob. Then the words came clear.

"Fine! Fine!" he was saying. "Got the pair of them, did you? . . . What'd they say? . . . The Free State, eh? Well, that's not a bad spot. . . . Put up a bit of a fight! You don't tell me. . . . I see. I see. . . . Yes. I'll be along some time this late afternoon. Got a job to do here first."

"Put up a fight," I said to myself. Well, I pitied the chap who had tackled Hamson, with that neck of his and shoulders like the end of a barn. Probably a couple of Wharton's men had tackled him at once, and even then they wouldn't have had too easy a time. I was wondering too who the other one had been. Scylla, was she, or Goldilocks?

As I made my way inside that room Wharton was beaming at me.

"What's the news, George?" I said.

"Couldn't be better," he told me. "Your little friend Goldilocks bolted first, and now we've just collared the other two."

I nodded.

"What're you looking miserable about?" he said to me.

"That hotel lunch," I said. "But did I catch something about a fight?"

"It wasn't much," he said. "Just enough to make a nice little charge of resisting arrest."

"Then Hamson must have been out of form," I said. "If he'd really made up his mind to resist arrest, even two of your men wouldn't have collared him."

"You think so?" he said. The earphones were now off and the spectacles on, and he was peering at me over their tops. "That's rather strange in a way. You see, we weren't any too keen on arresting him."

I stared. Then before I could speak he was going on.

CHAPTER XVII
BAT-EYED CUPID

"As a matter of fact," he said, "we didn't arrest him at all."

"But you said—"

"Oh, no," he said, and far too dictatorially I thought. "It was you who said things. We didn't arrest Hamson because we had no reason to. It was Molde we arrested."

"Molde!"

"Good Lord!" he said. "What's coming over you these days. Of course we arrested Molde."

"What for?"

"Dammit!" he exploded, "what should we have arrested him for! Being concerned in the death of Georgina Morbent, of course."

"What about Worrack's death?"

"That'll be easy," he told me with a snort. "That can be cleared up at any time."

I smiled quietly to myself. That was all he knew.

"But Molde," he said. "He was easy. I had my eye on him from the start. Funny you didn't spot him too?"

"I know," I said. "Tell me I'm a dud detective and some time you hope to take me in hand."

He raised expostulating hands to heaven. "What the devil's come over you? You're that damn touchy I can hardly open my mouth."

"Sorry," I said. "But what was that about Molde?"

"A dope-fiend." he said. "Riddled with it. I didn't have to look at him twice. And that Scylla Griffiths—"

"Griffiths?"

"Yes. Payton's her stage name. A pretty tough one she is too. But your pal Goldilocks. You had a good look at her, so you said. Did you see her fingers?"

"I didn't," I told him.

"Well, they're spatulate, like Scylla's. Sisters, that's what they are. Laura Griffiths is her name. Secretary-receptionist to that Doctor Chataway."

"Then I got something right," I said.

He ignored that. In fact his tone became markedly milder.

"A hell of a game, wasn't it? The sister doing the spotting and passing women on to Scylla and Molde. And something else I can tell you. Do you know what that Molde was allowed by his father?"

I said I didn't. What means had I got for finding out things like that?

"Two-fifty a year," Wharton said, and as if it was peanuts to him. "Why, that flat of his and the lady's costs more than that. And what about the way he splashes money about? Going to gambling places and the devil knows what. Where does he get his money? That's what I asked myself, and she's got none either. From being a pal of Halberg's—that's the answer, and from a little spot of blackmail. You don't think that abortion business stops at operations, do you? Finest game in the world for a spot of blackmail afterwards."

"True enough," I said. "That side of it hadn't struck me."

"Another thing," he went on. "Conroy told me a lot. That Molde had owed Worrack at least two hundred and fifty quid, for instance, and he'd paid up. Where did he get the money from?"

I could have told him, but I didn't. Molde got that money from blackmailing Hamson. Both Worrack and Molde had known things about Hamson.

"I'll tell you where he got his money from," he was saying. "Or you can work it out for yourself. Mrs. Morbent paid Halberg two-fifty, didn't she? Well, there's the answer."

"Yes," I said, and tried to make it admiringly. "That's the answer." I could have added that it was the wrong answer but I kept my mouth shut.

"Well, so far so good," he said. "Molde put up a bit of a fight when he was collared. That must have been funny. Scylla did some swearing, so I was told. Laura went quietly. I guess she'd sense enough to know that making a fuss wouldn't get her any-where."

"And what now?" I asked.

"Now I'm going along to collect Halberg," he said. "Then I'm going to search both places. But there shouldn't be much of that. He had a local builder in a day or two ago to do some concrete work in the cellar. Might just as well have put up a notice out-side—'This way to the body.'"

"Well, you certainly do find things out, George," I said.

"The Old Gent's not dead yet," he told me with a sideways nod of approbation. Then the oil fairly oozed out of him. "You haven't done so badly yourself."

"We aim to please," I told him ironically, but it just bounced off his hide.

"Want to come with me to Halberg's place?"

I shook my head. That part of the game never did intrigue me. I hate arrests and scenes, which shows what a bum detec-tive I am.

"I don't blame you," he said. "Tell you what. You go to Rich-mond in my car and I'll take the local one. You can get a train or a bus from Richmond. Then I'll ring you up when I get back myself."

"That's good of you, George," I said. "I think I'll take your offer."

"Only too glad," he told me effusively. "You and I have got to look after each other."

"That's right," I said. "And damn the Government's petrol!"

I thought I'd riled him at last. But the noise he was making was only a chuckle.

It was three-thirty when I got to Richmond and nearly five when I entered the flats. As I did so a man rose from the far cor-ner where there were chairs for people who had any waiting to do. I only saw the man out of the corner of my eye; then I knew it was Hamson, and that he was making straight for me.

"Afternoon, Travers," he said, perfectly calmly. "Can you possibly spare me a minute."

"I think so," I said, rather offhandedly. "Been waiting for me long?"

"Nearly a couple of hours," he said. "I'm an obstinate devil, though. I'd given myself till eight o'clock; if you hadn't turned up, then, I was going."

"Well, come upstairs," I said, and then called to Frank to send up tea for two. After all, I did owe a repayment of that bread and salt.

As soon as we were in my room he was remarking that I looked as if I'd had a tiring day. I said I was a bit tired but I'd be fit as a flea after a cup of tea.

"Been exciting for me, too," he said. "Laura Griffiths has been arrested."

"Good God!" I said. "How did you know that?"

"One of Bill Ellice's men saw the whole thing," he told me. "I'd engaged him to have Laura watched."

"The devil you had!" I said. "Know anything else?"

"Nothing at all. I hoped you might help."

Tea came in then with margarined toast and little cakes. I poured out and as I passed his cup, passed some news with it.

"Molde and Scylla have been arrested too."

His eyes narrowed. "A damn good thing too," he said, and gave a little grunt. I could have said it was a damn good thing for him. Worrack gone and now Molde.

"They've been pulled in for being concerned with the death of Georgina Morbent," was what I did tell him, and rather obtrusively passed the salt for his toast.

He didn't say a word at that. He did say it was good toast and real good tea, and a cup was just what he'd been wanting too.

"Like to hear a story?" he suddenly asked me.

"Who doesn't?" I told him.

"This is a true one," he said. "It virtually begins when Molde tried to touch me for a loan of five hundred quid. He had God's own amount of papers in his pockets to prove his solvency and his prospects. You know what a careless, untidy devil he is. That's why he didn't notice the pawn-ticket when it fell on the floor. He never knew I'd got it. He thought it was Worrack who'd found it and he'd dropped it in that office. Sure this isn't going to bore you?"

"Carry on," I told him. "I'll let you know right enough when I'm bored."

"Well," he went on, "I'd been doing a lot of worrying about Georgina, as I told you once, and I couldn't understand why the devil Barbara wasn't worried too. Yet she *was* worried about something, and that puzzled me still more. And when an old police wallah is worried he tries to do something about it. Still, there was I in possession of the pawn-ticket that Molde had dropped. And I knew about Scylla's sister. I only guessed she was her sister when she brought her to the club one night and I saw her fingers. Also I found out she was working at a doctor's, and he a gynaecologist. That made me think a bit. Even if I didn't see half the things I should have seen."

He gave a slow shake of the head.

"The trouble with me, as you may have noticed, is that somebody must once have told me I had brains and I've been trying to convince myself of it ever since. Too damned clever by half— that's me. So this is what I did about things.

"I threw out hints and I tried to get Barbara to open out. When she didn't lie she just shut up like a clam. Sometimes she drove me nearly crazy, like that day at lunch. So I decided to be clever and to hell with what happened to myself. What I did was to drop that pawn-ticket in her room, so that she'd think it an accident. You know what I mean. If that didn't start anything, then I knew nothing would." He shook his head again. "You see, I thought at the time she was pretty fond of me. I was fond of Georgina too. We all were, and something had to be done about it.

"I didn't give a damn about myself."

Then he was producing a little red book from his breast pocket. It was a bank pass-book and he opened it and marked the spot with a finger as he passed it to me. I read the entry. Five hundred pounds paid to H. Lewton-Molde. And I couldn't see any entry made for repayment.

"Yes," he said as he put the pass-book back. "I lent Molde that five hundred after all." He tapped his pocket. "I have his

IOU on me now. I can see you're thinking it was a hell of a sum to lend a bloke like Molde, and maybe it was. But I'm an obstinate cuss and I was prepared to pay. Also I didn't know then that you were taking a hand in the game on behalf of Worrack."

He passed his cup and waited till I'd filled it.

"Thanks," he said. "Best cup of tea I've had for weeks. But I was mentioning Worrack. I told you I'd killed him, didn't I? So I did. And this is how.

"Remember that morning when I was in your flat and Worrack rang you up to say you were to be at the club that night and that he was going to make a disclosure? He also said I was to come. Then Molde dropped in on us and I've often wondered why. He and I went off together, and then the devil whispered something in my ear. I'd got Molde absolutely under my thumb, and I didn't give a damn what I said to him or how I treated him. So what I made up my mind to do was to scare the daylights out of him and put him off the scent, in case he might have come to suspect he'd dropped that ticket in my room after all. So I told him that Worrack was having special enquiries made about something, and you were working for him, and you'd often worked with the police. I said I'd learned, by just happening to come into your room when you were telephoning, that Worrack was going to make a sensational disclosure at the club that night and that it was something to do with a pawn-ticket. I made it just gossip, mind you. Didn't throw out any hints about himself. Just sort of chatted and let it sink in. Made him swear, of course, that he wouldn't repeat it."

He'd been talking with eyes on nowhere. Then he suddenly looked straight at me.

"That's how I killed Peter Worrack. After that, Molde couldn't possibly afford to let him live. He had to kill him and he had to try to get back that ticket." His lip curled. "I told you I was a brainy sort of cuss."

"I'm beginning to think I've got you all wrong," I said. "But here's something I may tell you some time. What happened to me when I caught Scylla looking for that ticket."

"Well, there we are," he said. "Worrack was dead and you dropped me like a hot potato. You'd given me one little commission about Jean, but I could have told you a whole lot more if I'd have liked. But you didn't want me, so I thought I'd act on my own. I gave a hint by asking your advice about a detective agency, and then I fixed things up with Bill Ellice. A good chap, Ellice. Do you know he actually found out that Georgina had spent her last night at a Richmond hotel!"

"The devil he did!" I said admiringly. Heaven forbid that I should give Bill Ellice away.

"He found out a lot more," he went on. "I reckon that if we'd had another couple of days we'd have had the whole thing worked out."

He absent-mindedly pushed away his plate as if he had finished both tea and tale.

"I guess you would," I said. I knew I was looking very much of a fool and there was no doubt about my feeling one.

"One thing I must say," I went on. "When you castigated yourself just now you showed neither justice nor mercy. I think myself that you tried to do a damn fine job. In fact, I'll go farther and say you have done a fine job. But for what you did, things wouldn't have happened to-day. Sometime I may be able to tell you why."

"That's decent of you, Travers." He nodded to himself. "I'd rather like to say something too. It's a pity you and I didn't work together. I like you, Travers, and I'm damned if I don't tell you so to your face."

I couldn't say a thing. Funny how embarrassed we can sometimes be when someone suddenly makes a forthright statement.

"There's something I'll tell you now," he went on. "I didn't think I'd ever tell it to a soul. It's horrible and it's rather preyed on my mind. Do you think Molde is mad?"

"I don't know," I said, and frowned in thought. "Unbalanced—yes. And a pervert. But in a lot of things only too sane."

"I think he's mad and no one knows it but me," he said. "Let me try and prove it. I told you I let him have that five hundred. He was most grateful. Really and truly grateful. Like a small nephew to whom you give an unexpected bicycle, shall we say, or like a dog when he knows you're going to take him for a walk." He hesitated for a moment as if he hardly liked to go on. "When I gave him that cheque he was like that. Then he gave the most extraordinary smile, as if he'd thought of something that particularly pleased him. Something secret and rather furtive. 'I'll see you don't lose anything over this.' That was the gist of what he told me, and when he said it he looked even more pleased; you know, as if he saw himself doing whatever it was he intended to do."

"And what did he do?" I had to ask.

"Hacked off that head," he said. "Went down to Malcroft and did it himself, or got that doctor to do it."

"Horrible," I said. "Thought you were marrying Mrs. Grays, and didn't want her to have to wait for the money."

"That's what it amounts to," he said, and began getting to his feet.

"I wish I could do something." I don't know why I said that. Perhaps it was a vague expression of all I was feeling. "You've certainly had a raw deal. You're in bad with Mrs. Grays and I don't see quite what you can do about it."

He smiled. "My dear fellow, I've got nothing to grumble at. I went into it with my eyes open. But about that lunch. You can manage it soon?"

"I'd love to," I said, and meant it. "To-morrow, perhaps, but I'll let you know."

He wouldn't let me go down with him, and as we stood for a moment at the head of the stairs I asked him where he was going.

"Home," he said, and smiled wryly. "A slow place these days, but it suits me somehow."

"If anything turns up later to-night I may give you a ring," I told him. Then I held out my hand.

"Good night, Hamson. Sorry I've been such a special kind of idiot."

"Don't you believe it," he said, and as he turned, "It wouldn't worry me if I had a bit more of your special kind of idiocy myself."

* * * * *

I watched him down the stairs and then went back to the room. Somehow it seemed uneasily empty and in less than no time a restlessness was on me. So I had a bath and got into mufti. Then I saw to the black-out, and finally opened a bottle of beer. Then suddenly I had an idea, though less of an idea perhaps than the wish to talk to someone who was not myself.

I thought Barbara Grays might be in, and she was.

"Hallo, Mrs. Grays," I said. "This is Ludovic Travers. I thought I'd let you know that all that business has been cleared up. You may see something in the morning papers but there'll be nothing about yourself."

"Thank you," she told me quietly. "I don't know how I can ever repay you."

"I do," I said quickly. "There's something you can do for me."

"I'd love to," she said. "What is it?"

"You promise you'll do it?"

"Of course I promise."

"Then it's this. There's someone you've very badly misjudged. I've seen him and I've sent him round to see you. He's on his way, and you've got to see him."

There was no answer and I thought the line was dead.

"If you wish it," she told me at last. "Is it . . . Tommy Hamson?"

"Got it in one," I said, and added a quick good-bye.

That was that and then I rang Hamson.

"Glad you're in," I said. "There's an urgent message for you."

"From whom?"

"Mrs. Grays. She most urgently wishes to see you and didn't like to ring you direct. I told her you'd be on your way in five minutes or less."

"Thanks," he told me quietly. "Less is right."

So much for that. I took a pull at my glass and stretched out my long legs in comfort. And I couldn't help smiling sheepishly at myself. A fine bat-eyed old fool I was to be taking the role of Cupid. Yet, I thought, and maybe the smile had in it something of the Rabelaisian, if I were in the raw and on that pedestal in

Piccadilly Circus with a nice little bow and arrow, I'd probably be the year's sensation.

I took another pull at the beer and life seemed rather good, and I was far too comfortable to ring down for my dinner. Another case practically over, I thought. And then I remembered something that had puzzled me. I hate loose ends and this was one.

Molde must have known in advance that Georgina was going to Malcroft, and he as certainly knew that her proposed visit to Ireland was a blind. Why then was he such a fool as to report that he had seen her *leaving* Euston? That was the very thing he should have expected.

As soon as I propounded that question, I got the answer. Molde had the wrong idea. He and Scylla thought they saw Georgina about to make a journey, and to Ireland, which might have meant all sorts of things from their point of view. That's why they hastened to make the report and find out the truth. Then afterwards they twisted their tale to make it appear that they'd always thought she was coming *from* a journey instead of being about to make one.

Another little point that needed clearing up was what particular brand of blackmail Lulu had threatened Worrack with. But it was *Worrack* whom I had heard mention the word blackmail. Probably all Lulu had done was to lose her temper—after making advances to him perhaps—and threaten to inform the police about the club. Still, that wasn't much of a loose end, however important it had looked at the time.

One other little thing I thought of then. I had told Wharton that the dope in the brandy gave a suicide motive. That's what Molde may have intended when he gave Worrack the poison earlier in the evening. But Molde had been even more cunning than that. If it hadn't been discovered that there was no poison in the brandy *actually*, then it should have been the perfect evidence of his cast-iron alibi, for he had stuck close to me all night, and I must have sworn that he had never been near that brandy.

I finished the beer and wondered if I should order a dinner. Then the telephone bell rang.

"That you, Travers?" came Wharton's voice.

"Yes," I said. "What's the news?"

"Everything's fine," he said. "Our Malcroft friend has spilt all the beans."

"What about Molde? What's he said?"

Wharton grunted. "They tell me he's doing nothing but going into hysterics. Maybe he needs a shot of dope. But about yourself. Can you be round here about ten in the morning?"

"It'll suit me," I said. "And congratulations, George. Afraid I've been a bit disgruntled all day."

"We all get fits like that," he told me with ample forgiveness. "But what I wanted to mention was that we're running Molde on the double charge after all. We think there's an easy case."

"Good," I said. "Congratulations again. You've done fine."

"What about you," he said. "I was just telling one of the Big Bugs that if it hadn't been for you, the case might have taken us months."

"Thanks, George," I said. "Unless you're pulling my leg."

"Leg, my food" he said. "What about that lunch you owe me?"

"To-morrow, if you like," I told him, and didn't mention that I'd probably be bringing Hamson.

Funny, wasn't it? Times when I could have murdered George and murdered him good and proper, yet when I was ringing through for a dinner, my tail was wagging like one o'clock and I was feeling pleased as Punch. Another case over, and perhaps I hadn't been such an utter and comprehensive fool as I'd thought.

Then, as I dropped into my chair again, I heard a queer scratching noise from somewhere; it went as soon as it had come. A mouse, I thought, and then frowned. There was another loose end that hadn't been cleared up. Who the devil was it that had let loose that mouse at the club?

Tubby, for a certainty, I thought. Then the wind outside caught my ear, and I saw Tubby somewhere on the high seas, and on convoy duty perhaps. Good old Tubby, I said to myself, and included him in the kind of universal benevolence that had been flooding me. Whatever Wharton asked me, Tubby should not be betrayed by me. Sooner or later Wharton would be asking me if I had any ideas, for he hated loose ends. What should I say? That I didn't know?

Then I had a brainwave. I'd say brazenly that it was I who had brought that mouse! I'd wanted to kick up my heels and be for once the life and soul of the party. That was what I'd say, I thought, and it would be worth it to see the look of pious horror that would come to his face.

THE END

THE BIRDS AND THE BEES AND THE CASE OF THE RUNNING MOUSE (1944)

THE FACTS OF LIFE (AND DEATH) IN CHRISTOPHER BUSH'S FORTIES DETECTIVE FICTION

Note: Discussion of a major plot spoiler to Christopher Bush's The Case of the Running Mouse *begins in the fourth paragraph of this afterword, so if you have not read the novel already, take heed. The reader is warned.*

GOLDEN AGE detective fiction remains to this day, nearly a century after its first dawning, routinely dismissed by detractors as frothy, cozy concoctions whose authors have carefully removed any bitter taint of real world unpleasantries, particularly those which pertain to the illicit sexuality and violence that more than occasionally takes place within it. During the Second World War, however, crime fiction (like the real world itself) was undergoing tremendous upheaval, with the fast-rising popularity of hard-boiled mysteries by such writers as Raymond Chandler, Peter Cheyney and James Hadley Chase. In tandem with American noir cinema, this tough and tantalizing mystery sub-genre impacted even traditionally staid British mystery, where headlong excitement tended to take a back seat to the dallying delights of detection. In the case of Christopher Bush, who published his first tale of the investigative adventures of gentleman amateur sleuth Ludovic "Ludo" Travers in 1926, sexuality becomes more of a felt presence in his mysteries during these wartime years, as we learn that Ludo Travers and men and women of similarly good social standing have been, at times, no better than they should have been. To riff on songwriter Cole Porter, certainly no shrinking violet when it came to sexual intimations, in Forties Ludo Travers mysteries like *The Case of the*

Running Mouse (1944) "the birds do it, the bees do it/even educated Brits do it"—sometimes rather naughtily indeed and with quite nasty results.

In his essay "Raffles and Miss Blandish," which appeared in print the same year as Bush's *The Case of the Running Mouse*, George Orwell, an admirer of the decorous Edwardian detective fiction of Arthur Conan Doyle and Doyle's contemporaries R. Austin Freeman and Ernest Bramah as well as the rogue stories of E.W. Hornung and Maurice Leblanc, was famously critical of the wartime influence of American crime fiction and its British imitators on British crime fiction and society. Orwell graphically likened the act of reading Englishman James Hadley Chase's "sordid and brutal" crime novel *No Orchids for Miss Blandish* (1939), which enjoyed tremendous popularity in the UK during the war, to taking a "header into the cesspool." In books like *Miss Blandish*, Orwell complained, "one is not, as in the old-fashioned crime story, simply escaping from dull reality into an imaginary world of action. One's escape is essentially into cruelty and sexual perversion." Orwell speculated that the rise in popularity of such fiction owed something to the "mingled boredom and brutality of war." In another essay from this period, "The Decline of the English Murder" (1946), Orwell contrasted classic genteel English true crime cases like those which concerned, respectively, the notorious Mrs. Maybrick and Dr. Crippen with a merely tawdry recent affair, the Cleft Chin Murder, where an American army deserter and wannabe gangster, Karl Hulten, accompanied by his vacuous, thrill-seeking English pick-up, an 18-year-old named Elizabeth Jones, murdered a taxi driver with a cleft chin, taking the dead man's paltry eight pounds to bet at dog races. Of this singularly and sickeningly pointless and stupid crime Orwell observed: "Perhaps it is significant that the most talked-of English murder of recent years should have been committed by an American and an English girl who had become partly Americanized."

Like his male contemporaries in Britain's august Detection Club, a convivial social organization of the finest writers of detective fiction in the UK, Christopher Bush though of humble birth publicly adhered to the standards of an English gentleman. Although he appears certainly to have been a reader of American hard-boiled crime fiction, Bush in his crime writing maintained a sense of decorum which was entirely absent from the salacious books that so disgusted George Orwell. Yet Bush had lapses from his own standards in his life where women were concerned. Like his Detection Club colleague Cecil John Charles Street, Bush left his wife and cohabited contentedly with another woman for decades. Moreover, an earlier affair of his resulted in the birth of an illegitimate son (the distinguished British composer Geoffrey Bush). The author seems to draw on these experiences in his portrayals, throughout the Ludo Travers mystery series, of designing, sexually aggressive women, which gives his books something of the flavor of hard-boiled mysteries, with their constant depictions of predatory *femmes fatales*. This aspect of Bush's crime fiction reaches its apotheosis in *The Case of the Magic Mirror* (1943), which pits Travers against a dangerously alluring old flame, Charlotte Craigne, and directly quotes Raymond Chandler's *The High Window*, published the previous year. (Chandler is known for his gorgeous rapacious women, who are always trying to destroy Philip Marlowe, Chandler's provokingly fastidious, if slightly shop-soiled, PI hero.) Intriguingly a major plot point in Bush's novel is Charlotte's attempt to blackmail Ludo into doing her bidding by showing him a photo of a boy who purportedly is her and Ludo's illegitimate son.

The next year Bush published *The Case of the Running Mouse,* wherein not one of the female characters, including the "nice girls," to use the language of the era, appears to be a virgin. The most striking case in this regard is that of the vanished Georgia Morbent, whose lover, Peter Worrack, under the impression that Travers is a private detective (on a lark Ludo plays along with this), hires Ludo to trace. Ludo makes comparatively little progress toward finding Georgia until her severed head shockingly pops up in London. Gradually Ludo discovers that Georgia, having been impregnated by Peter Worrack (unknown to him), had departed not to meet an employee in Ireland as she had claimed she was doing but to keep an appointment with an abortionist—one which tragically turned fatal, with Georgia dying as a result of the operation.

Georgia's pregnancy is a secret which the author keeps well, though *Mouse* being a fair play mystery we are told of Georgia, through the words of Peter Worrack, (1) ". . . she said she wasn't marrying a second time. Kids and a home and all that sort of thing weren't her line." (2) ". . . she had a superb figure. One of the things she was most proud of." Although Georgia runs a private gambling club in London, a fact which would have filled Bush's puritanical Detection Club colleague Freeman Wills Crofts with righteous horror (see Crofts's pious crime novel concerning what he terms "gambling hells," *Fatal Venture*, 1939), Travers summarizes the missing woman as "a damn good sort. One you could trust to the last inch." In stark contrast with Freeman Crofts and his sententiously moralizing series detective, Inspector Joseph French, Ludo Travers declines to judge erring humanity:

> Who was I . . . to adopt a superior or puritanical attitude because [Worrack] chose to get a living in his own way and meet, in what he considered a square way, a definite demand? . . . And wasn't I also fond of an occasional gamble? . . . And who was I, in any case, to make myself a custodian of war-time or any other morals? . . . just because I had chosen to masquerade as a private detective, what right did that give me to be hypocritical about my patron?

Bush treats Georgia Morbent's death as a genuine tragedy, not as deserved retribution against a woman who behaved badly. Earlier in the Travers series Bush had dealt with abortion (in *The Case of the Tudor Queen*, 1938, where the actress murder victim had become pregnant out-of-wedlock by her murderer and in *The Case of the Climbing Rat*, 1940, where one of the murder victims is a disgraced Harley Street doctor who was prosecuted for performing an abortion), but only in *The Case of the Running Mouse* does the author focus so squarely on a matter, which, though little acknowledged in crime fiction of the day, was a major social problem increasingly aired in public in the 1930s and 1940s. Unquestionably *Mouse* is a unique mystery novel for its time.

In her guidebook *Mystery Fiction: Theory and Technique*, published just a year before *The Case of the Running Mouse*, author, editor and literary agent Marie F. Rodell gives us an outline of the strictures regarding sexuality under which crime writers of the time still worked, despite the rise in popularity of hard-boiled and noir fiction. Concerning abortion specifically, Rodell advised that the subject "is considered legitimate mystery material if it is handled carefully and, of course, condemned. Apparently it is regarded by the fans as closer to murder than to sex."

When Ludo Travers in *The Case of the Running Mouse* delicately asks his friend Superintendent George Wharton of Scotland Yard to tell him "something about—about shady women's doctors," the "Old General" makes sufficiently clear where he stands: "Why all the humbug? Why don't you say what you mean? You aren't talking about doctors, you're talking about abortionists. . . . You ought to know enough about them. Dirty, furtive little swine, that's what I call 'em. Living up back streets usually."

But then Travers makes clear that what he is wondering about are reputable physicians, leading to this interesting exchange:

> "What about the recent case of a doctor with a first-class practice and reputation who'd been making a packet out of doing the job, and for years?"
>
> "Of course there are all sorts. . . . The man you instanced simply moved among a better class, that's all."
>
> [. . .]
>
> "A lot of it, these days, is there?"
>
> "Is there not!"
>
> "Just one other thing. . . . These fellows seem to me to get into the hands of the police because of a patient's death, at least in most cases. Why should a patient die?"

"Several reasons. . . . Simple shock, though that's rare. The peritoneal cavity may have been pierced and there may be shock from that. In most cases it's septic poisoning owing to dirty conditions of instruments."

In the novel Georgia's abortionist, who operates in collusion with a gynecologist's receptionist, is an anti-Hitler Austrian refugee physician by the name of Halberg. Doctors who came to trial for procuring abortions in the UK after the war were disproportionately foreigners, notes Barbara Brooks in *Abortion in England, 1900-1967*, perhaps because they tended to be unshielded by the "professional solidarity which protected English doctors." (Brooks cites the cases of a Dr. Sutorowski and a Dr. Bieberstein.) Bush may have partly had in mind a real life case of a purported doctor and charming villain who two years before the publication of *The Case of the Running Mouse* was convicted of manslaughter in the horrid demise of Helen Mary Pickwoad (1914-1942), a 28 year-old woman from Liverpool who was found dead, notes Amy Helen Bell in *Murder Capital: Suspicious Deaths in London, 1933-1953*, in the City "in a Marble Arch motel room littered with used bandages, medical supplies and a cigarette box with temperature readings on the back of it." At trial the eminent pathologist Bernard Spilsbury, countering the defense's calm that Pickwoad had had the abortion done in Liverpool, testified that the unfortunate woman's death had resulted from "sepsis from a perforated uterus," contracted by her within the last few days, when she unquestionably had been in London. Tasked with finding those responsible for the tragedy, police arrested Pickwoad's married London lover, a 27-year-old army captain by the name of Edward Tickell who had procured the services of an abortionist, in addition to the abortionist himself: a man with the tony handle of George Frederic Montague de Fossard (or, as he also styled himself, the Comte de la Vatine).

The grandson of handsome and dapper Latvian immigrant Charles Fredrick Von Fossard and a nephew of the elocutionist and classical tenor Alfred Von Fossard, George Fossard

(1898-1967) bears resemblance to the native French abortionist Gustave Rionne in Christopher Bush's *The Case of the Climbing Rat* (1940), who married an aunt of Ludo's wife and practiced plastic surgery, performing abortions covertly—though Georges Fossard's ancestry seems to have been French by way of Germany. Fossard served a three-year prison term in connection with his abortion trade in 1931-34 and upon his release began styling himself a plastic surgeon and performing face lifts, though he had only nine months' training at King's College, London, having left the school without taking exams. A corporal in the Somerset Light Infantry during the First World War, Fossard while on leave in 1919 from active service in Cologne, Germany (which British troops has occupied, as part of the Allied maintenance of the German Rhineland as a buffer zone between France and Germany under the Treaty of Versailles), wed solicitor's daughter Dorothy Louisa Curtis, seven years his elder and the first of his several wives; the marriage lasted only a few years.

Oddly Fossard's immigrant grandfather had married a woman whose grandfather Henry Baker, rector of the stunning classical All Saints Church in Nuneham Courtenay, Oxfordshire, had dismissed a maid for getting pregnant by his groom. Although she delivered the child she remained despondent over the state of her personal affairs, her groom lover being either unwilling or unable to marry her, and in 1829 she fatally poisoned herself with arsenic (which in classic fashion she claimed she needed in order to poison rats), thus illustrating, over a century before Helen Pickwoad's sad death, the grave dangers an unwanted pregnancy could pose for a women.

Like the fictional Georgia Morbent, Fossard's victim, Helen Pickwoad, came of a good family, making the affair even more shocking to the British public in 1942. Her father, Howell Pickwoad, was a colonial civil servant who served at various posts in Africa, including Nairobi, who retired with his family to The Old Vicarage at the village of Wangford in Suffolk, forty miles east of Great Hockham, Christopher Bush's adolescent home. There he and his wife brought up their adolescent daughter Helen and son William Mervyn, two years Helen's elder, with whom Helen was living in Liverpool in 1939, keeping house for her brother, now an actor, and making trips to London to keep up her love affair with Edward Tickell. At the trial Tickell wore his army uniform every day and conducted himself with dignified reserve, impressing the jury and securing an acquittal for himself, but Fossard was found guilty and sentenced to five years' imprisonment for the botched May 20 abortion.

Helen's father died just five months later at the age of 62, but her brother William Mervyn Pickwoad lived on and prospered, after the war attaining fame on stage and the large and small screen as the actor William Mervyn. His film roles included parts in *A Touch of Larceny* with James Mason, *Operation Crossbow* with Sophia Loren, *Murder Ahoy* with Margaret Rutherford, *Hot Millions* with Peter Ustinov, *The Railway Children* with Jenny Agutter and *The Ruling Class* with Peter O'Toole, while on television he was known for playing a variety of very British authority figures in the Sixties and Seventies, such as the popular Chief Inspector Charles Rose in several crime series, Bishop Cuthbert Heyer in *All Gas and Gaiters*, the Duke of Tottering in *Tottering Towers* and Mr. Justice Campbell in *Crown Court*. One of his films, the shocker *Circus of Horrors* (1960), details the murderous activities of a mad plastic surgeon (played by German actor Anton Diffring).

Upon his release from prison George Fossard departed for Australia, as a representative of the Big Brothers Movement, a non-profit youth migration program. (One fears the worst.) By 1950, however, Fossard, now grandly calling himself Count George Frederick de Fossard de la Vatine and claiming to be an artist, was back in London, however, and back on trial, this time for obtaining £900 (about £29,000 or 40,000 USD today) under false pretenses. Nine years later he made the news pages yet again, in a story picked up internationally by the AP, when 25-year-old brunette striptease artist Louisa Worsley announced that she and the 65-year-old "count" (actually 61) were planning to wed, as soon as Fossard obtained a divorce from his third wife, (the mother of his son Nicholas), from whom he had been separated since 1933. The count, the news story divulged to ingenuous readers, was an "aristocrat whose title stretches back into history" and an "artist who specializes in portraits of ballet dancers and church bishops." Recalling Raymond Chandler, we might idly wonder whether Fossard's new *inamorata* Louise Worsley was a brunette "to make a bishop kick a hole in a stained-glass window."

To be sure, there were other cases in the UK in the 1940s of doctors—real doctors with actual degrees—being arrested and convicted for performing abortions, like Crichton Alison, son of a Scottish minister and a prestigious Harley Street practitioner who in 1940 was "found guilty of conspiring with a male medical student and a woman to perform illegal abortions" and was sentenced, along with the other man, to a five-year term of penal servitude. After his release, Alison remained on the cutting edge of sexual controversy, in 1950 editing a 36-page pamphlet, *Men in Women's Clothes*, a collection of "case histories of transvestism." And then there was Canadian native Alva Delbert Evans, a posh Piccadilly surgeon who for two decades had run "two private nursing homes in the West End" where he performed abortions at considerable profit to himself until the police finally caught up with him in 1944 (though court records reveal he had skated on a patch of very thin ice in 1932). In a system very much resembling that described in *The Case of the Running Mouse*, Evans charged his abortion patients fees which ranged from 100 to 350 pounds, in addition to nursing home fees. The women paid Evans these large sums in cash, the only entry made in his books being a three-guinea consultation fee. Convicted of performing illegal abortions, Evans, like Georges Frossard and Crichton Alison, was sentenced to a five-year prison term. (On the trials of Crichton and Evans see Brooks, *Abortion in England*.)

Intriguingly Evans had served in the General Hospital Army of the Rhine at Cologne, in charge of the Venereal Disease Center in 1920, at the time a young Georges Fossard was posted in the city. In Cologne the collision of British troops and German civilian women, many of them prostitutes, had produced a 350%

increase in cases of VD, much to the mortification of British authorities. "We are doing all we can to combat it," wrote a British general of the problem, "but it is difficult in a large town of this nature where there are 30,000 women of loose character." (See Keith Jeffery, "'Hut ab,' 'Promenade with Kamerade for Schokolade,' and the *Flying Dutchman*: British Soldiers in the Rhineland, 1918-1929," in Conan Fischer and Alan Sharp, eds., *After the Versailles Treaty: Enforcement, Compliance, Contested Identities*.) In short, during his service in the Great War Dr. Evans had seen at first hand the dire problems resulting from unprotected sexual activity.

In the Thirties and Forties British abortion advocates and opponents alike deplored illegal medical procedures which placed women's lives in unnecessary jeopardy, but they offered very different solutions to the problem, one side more restriction by tightening the enforcement of anti-abortion laws, the other greater liberty by making abortion "safe, legal and rare." Where Christopher Bush stood on the matter is not clear from the text of *The Case of the Running Mouse*, but my own guess, given Bush's personal history and his sympathetic presentation in the novel of the plight of Georgina Morbent, is that he thought British women like Helen Pickwoad deserved better options for securing their health and well-being than those which British law then sanctioned.

Curtis Evans

www.ingramcontent.com/pod-product-compliance
Lightning Source LLC
Chambersburg PA
CBHW062309200726
48292CB00004BA/1228